"I can never be sorry that the first years of Charles's life were happy," Jennifer declared.

"And they shall continue to be so," Julian assured her. "Our son's welfare is my prime concern, and that is precisely why I offered you the opportunity of returning here."

"What will you expect of me in return for this altruistic gesture of yours?" Jennifer inquired.

"Quite naturally you shall resume your role as mistress of this house."

"Very well, Wroxam, I shall manage your house and run it as you would wish. But that is all. The door between our connecting chambers is now locked…and shall remain so for as long as I reside under this roof."

In three giant strides Julian covered the distance between them and imprisoned her in his arms. His determined mouth clamped over hers, parting her lips and winning the response she seemed incapable of denying.

He raised his head. "I do not think that you are as indifferent to me as you would have me believe.…"

THE RELUCTANT MARCHIONESS

ANNE ASHLEY

HARLEQUIN®

TORONTO • NEW YORK • LONDON
AMSTERDAM • PARIS • SYDNEY • HAMBURG
STOCKHOLM • ATHENS • TOKYO • MILAN • MADRID
PRAGUE • WARSAW • BUDAPEST • AUCKLAND

ISBN 0-373-30474-9

THE RELUCTANT MARCHIONESS

First North American Publication 2005

www.eHarlequin.com

Printed in U.S.A.

ANNE ASHLEY

was born and educated in Leicester. She lived for a time in Scotland, but now resides in the West Country with two cats, her two sons and a husband who has a wonderful and very necessary sense of humor. When not pounding away at the keys on her computer she likes to relax in her garden, which she has opened to the public on more than one occasion in aid of the village church funds.

Chapter One

Idly glancing out of the parlour window, Lady Carstairs noticed a fine carriage, pulled by a team of gleaming black horses, draw to a halt before a certain house in the Square. Her interest was immediately captured, not so much by the sight of the fine equipage, but by the lady who, a moment or two later, alighted from it, and stood statue-like on the pavement, staring fixedly up at that certain superior dwelling.

'Good heavens!' she exclaimed. 'I wonder if there has been a death in the Stapleford family, Serena? I cannot recall having heard of any such recent event.'

Her daughter, raising her head from between the covers of the book obtained that morning from the lending library, transferred her short-sighted gaze to the relevant spot across the Square. 'Just because the lady happens to be dressed from head to toe in black, Mama, does not necessarily mean that she is in mourning,' she pointed out. 'A great many females display a marked partiality for decking themselves out in that particular colour.'

Lady Carstairs frequently found her elder daughter's sound common sense most irritating. On this occasion, however, she was prepared to overlook it. 'You are right, of course. And the veil may have been donned merely to conceal her identity.' A distinctly malicious glint added a sparkle to her eyes. 'And I for one could not blame her for taking such a precaution if she intends to call upon that odiously unfeeling Marquis of Wroxam!'

Serena could not forbear a smile. Her mother never missed an opportunity of passing some disparaging remark about the haughty aristocrat who continued to ignore her very existence. 'I've heard you utter a great deal to Lord Wroxam's discredit over the years, Mama, and perhaps you have good reason, for he has undoubtedly earned himself the reputation of being excessively high in the instep, but I am forced to own that on the few occasions I have seen him at some ball or rout, his conduct has always been exemplary.'

'Ha!' Lady Carstairs scoffed. 'And with good reason! He'd not wish to bring more disgrace to the proud name he bears than he already has done. There was enough gossip and scandal surrounding him years ago over the mysterious disappearance of his young bride.'

'Yes, so I understand.' Beneath the crop of tightly crimped brown hair, Serena's brows drew together in a thoughtful frown. 'However, I have never for one moment believed that silly rumour that he'd killed her.'

Lady Carstairs allowed irritation to surface this time. 'And why not, pray? Are you so well acquainted with the Marquis that you can be sure that he had nothing whatsoever to do with her disappearance?'

'No, Mama,' Serena responded in her quiet way. 'I

cannot recall that I've ever spoken to him in my life.
I doubt he's even aware of my existence. Nevertheless, I've heard enough about him over the years to
be sure that he's a highly intelligent man, not given
to foolish starts, or prone to wildly eccentric behaviour. Therefore, I cannot help wondering why he married Lady Jennifer Audley in the first place if he had
not truly wished to do so. After all, he's very wealthy,
possibly one of the richest men in the country. I doubt
very much that money was ever a consideration when
he chose to marry the late Earl of Chard's daughter.'

'I suppose there is something in what you say,' her
ladyship was forced to concede.

'Furthermore, if he had arranged her death, he must
have had a very good reason for doing so. If it had
been because he had suddenly desired to marry someone else, surely he would have wanted his wife's
body to be found so that her demise was beyond question. And the Marchioness never was found, you
know,' she reminded her mother.

Her ladyship merely nodded her head in agreement
this time.

'I know that his name has been linked with numerous beautiful women over the years, but I never
heard tell that he betrayed the least desire to marry
any one of them. Also, he is a stickler for the proprieties. Common report would have us believe that
he never permits any of his paramours to stay at
Wroxam Park, nor does he encourage them to visit
his town residence either. Unchaperoned ladies are
never welcome at his home. Which makes me wonder,' she added, once again gazing across the Square,

'whether the female now mounting the steps will succeed in gaining admission.'

It was precisely this very problem which was to tax the young footman, Thomas, when he opened the door a moment later. He knew his master's views on admitting unchaperoned females, no matter what age, into the house. None the less, this caller was undoubtedly a lady, and one of some means if the carriage which had conveyed her here and her attire were anything to go by. Furthermore, she only wished to enter in order to leave his lordship a letter. What possible harm could there be in that?

'What seems to be the trouble?' a voice from directly behind him suddenly demanded to know, and Thomas, hurriedly moving to one side, was more than happy to leave the decision of whether or not to admit the caller in the hands of his strict mentor.

One swift, assessing glance was sufficient to convince the highly discerning and experienced butler that the visitor was certainly respectable. He did not, however, permit this consideration to weigh with him. 'Lord Wroxam is not at home, madam,' he confirmed, polite but resolute. 'I would therefore suggest that you call again tomorrow, when we expect his lordship to return, if that is convenient.'

'No, Slocombe, it most certainly is not convenient,' the caller astonished him by responding in a quiet, well-spoken voice. 'You barred my entry to this house once before, as I remember... You shall never do so again. Now stand aside!'

It was not so much the cool, authoritative tone which had the butler automatically obeying the command as the sudden awakening of a long-dormant memory which sent an icy-cold shiver of apprehension scudding its way down the length of his slightly arthritic spine.

Closing the door quietly, he turned to stare at the slender figure now standing in the hall, the unshakeable sense of foreboding growing ever stronger as he tried ineffectually to glimpse the features behind the veil. 'If you would kindly state your name and business,' he said in a voice which distinctly lacked its customary aplomb, 'I could perhaps be of some assistance to you in his lordship's absence.'

There was a moment's silence before the lady slowly turned and raised one shapely hand to her veil. 'I believe you already know precisely who I am, Slocombe.'

Thomas, an interested bystander, could hardly believe the evidence of his own eyes. It was not so much the first glimpse of the exquisite face, framed in a riot of the deepest auburn curls, which had him almost gaping in astonishment as the sight of his strict mentor's suddenly ashen features.

'M-my lady... So it is you!' Slocombe murmured, quite oblivious to the fact that the young footman was now quietly slinking away, eager to inform his compatriots belowstairs of the astonishing fact that the iron ruler of the household staff had betrayed clear signs of having lost his composure for the very first time.

'As you see,' she responded, her own voice remaining cool and controlled, betraying no hint of emotion. 'As you are very well aware, I am quite unfamiliar with the layout of this house, so you may indeed assist me, Slocombe, by directing me to the library, where I shall undoubtedly obtain all the materials necessary to write your master a brief letter.'

The butler once again found himself automatically obeying the command. Leading the way across the chequered hall, he opened a door to allow the visitor to sweep majestically past him and noticed, as she did so, the faint smile appear as she took swift stock of her surroundings.

'Yes,' she murmured, while moving across to the desk. 'I had imagined the library here would be just like this.'

Without uttering anything further, she calmly seated herself, took out a sheet of paper from the top drawer, and reached for the pen in the standish. Not once did Slocombe see the slender white hand that moved back and forth across the page falter even for a single moment. Evidently she knew precisely what she wished to write, and did so quickly, signing her name with a flourish at the bottom of the page, before sanding the letter and sealing it with a wafer.

'Until this day I have never given you an order, Slocombe,' she reminded him, rising to her feet, 'but I am about to give you yet another now. I entrust this into your safe keeping. You are to hand it to your master, personally, on his return.'

Slocombe found himself automatically accepting the letter held out to him. 'It shall be as you wish, my lady,' he replied, and then watched her walk gracefully back across to the door. 'My lady, I...'

As his voice faltered, she turned again to look at him, her striking green eyes distinctly lacking any semblance of the youthful warmth he well remembered. 'Regrets, like sins, cast very long shadows, Slocombe, do they not? No matter how much we might wish to do so, neither of us can alter what has taken place in the past, so I would advise you not to waste your time or mine in making the attempt. I bid you goodday,' and with that she walked quietly out of the house, leaving Slocombe prey to painful memories and many bitter regrets.

He shook his head sadly, not quite knowing what to make of this totally unexpected turn of events. One thing was very certain, however—her ladyship's return would ensure that nothing in the Stapleford household would ever be quite the same again.

An hour later the lady whose visit had had such an effect on Lord Wroxam's butler was entering a house in another fashionable part of the town. After dispensing with her outdoor garments, she went straight into the sunny front parlour, and had only just made herself comfortable in the chair by the window when the door opened, and a young woman of similar age entered the room.

'Ah, Mary!' She held out her hand. 'Come to see if I'm any the worse for my ordeal?'

Mary grasped the outstretched hand, giving the slender fingers an affectionate squeeze before releasing her hold, and subjecting the lovely face smiling up at her to a swift scrutiny. 'Well, I must say, Miss Jenny, you don't look as if you've suffered any ill effects.'

'No, I found the visit remarkably painless, but perhaps that was because he wasn't there.'

Mary paused in her straightening of the drapes. 'And where had he taken himself off to?'

'I didn't choose to enquire. And Slocombe, unlike you, Mary, is a very correct and conventional servant.

He would never willingly volunteer such information.' A hint of a smile played around perfectly formed lips. 'And my unexpected appearance had discomposed the poor man quite sufficiently without my adding to his discomfiture by demanding to know his master's whereabouts.'

'Bah! I'll discompose him right enough, if ever I get my hands on the heathen man!'

The smile grew more pronounced. 'Your devotion to me, Mary, is always most touching, but you do poor Slocombe a grave injustice by thinking him unfeeling. He was merely following his master's instructions to the letter when he barred my entry to the town house all those years ago. I do not doubt for a moment that he honestly believed my uncle would offer me asylum. And talking of my oh, *so loving* relative...'

Rising to her feet, Jennifer went across to the escritoire to collect the list she had made that morning, and glanced briefly at the single sheet. 'It is the Chard ball this evening. I think—yes—I rather think it is time that Lady Jennifer Audley Stapleford, Marchioness of Wroxam, announced her return to the polite world. My uncle found himself quite unable to offer me sanctuary years ago. It will be amusing to see his reaction tonight when I turn up, uninvited, to his ball.'

Mary looked gravely across the room at her young mistress, thinking as she did so that there was little resemblance now to that lost and frightened girl she had discovered wandering the streets of the capital.

'Miss Jenny, are you certain sure you're doing the right thing? I cannot help but feel myself you'd have been better to have remained in Ireland. You were safe there.'

'And I shall be safe here,' Jennifer responded, once again touched by her loyal friend's evident concern. 'As I've mentioned before, my uncle is an immensely weak and ineffectual man. He'll cause me no problems.'

'Pshaw! I weren't meaning that little squint! It's *himself* I'm thinking of. If half the tales I've learned about him are true—'

'Why is it, Mary,' Jennifer interrupted, 'that you always become so very Irish when you're concerned or annoyed?'

'Because I am Irish. And proud of it, I am too!'

'And so you should be.' The glance Jennifer cast her contained more than just a hint of affection. 'But as I've already mentioned, Wroxam's not due home until tomorrow, so there's not the remotest possibility that I shall come face to face with him tonight.'

'But you're bound to do so sooner or later.'

'That, sadly, is inevitable now that I have set the wheels in motion. None the less, I am prepared.'

A moment's silence, then, 'But what if he should find out, Miss Jenny?'

'I have taken great pains to ensure that he does not.' The reassuring smile did not come so easily to her lips this time. 'Come, Mary, stop worrying. Your time would be much better spent in making me look the part for my debut into the polite world of London Society.'

Since her arrival in the capital a month before, Jennifer had deliberately kept her identity secret. She had not, however, remained hidden away in the house she had hired for the duration of her planned stay in town. Apart from that one occasion long ago, when she had travelled to London on the common stage in the hope of seeing her husband, only to find herself barred from entering the town house, she had never visited the capital before nor since, until now. Consequently she had found much to occupy her during her present stay and had visited many places of interest.

She had also taken the opportunity to refurbish her wardrobe, and it had been during one of those several visits which she had made to a certain famous *modiste* in Bond Street that she had discovered that her uncle and his Countess held an annual ball at the beginning of each Season. By all accounts it was a truly splendid occasion, attended by the cream of society, an event not to be missed.

Just when the notion had first occurred to her to attend the ball, Jennifer was not perfectly sure. Her sole reason for returning to England had been to seek an interview with her estranged husband, and request that he take immediate steps to end their fiasco of a marriage. That remained her main objective. At the same time, however, she saw no earthly reason why she should not enjoy herself for the duration of her stay. For several reasons she had been denied the pleasure of a Season in town, and it had occurred to her that this was the golden opportunity to rectify this sad lack of experience.

As she mounted the impressive staircase that night, her ever lively sense of humour came to the fore. The servant who had relieved her of her elegant evening cloak had not attempted to question her lack of invitation card. How different her reception had been this time compared to years ago, when her appearance on the doorstep after being denied entrance to

Wroxam's town house had been met with a certain amount of suspicion, and her uncle's reception had been anything but warm. She doubted very much that he would be precisely overjoyed by her unexpected arrival now. One thing she was determined on—she would never grant her uncle the opportunity of asking her to leave a second time!

As she reached the head of the stairs and moved along the passageway towards the crowded ballroom, she realised she had timed her arrival to perfection. The Earl of Chard and his Countess, no doubt believing that they had greeted the last of the latecomers, had abandoned their positions by the door, but were still close enough to the entrance to hear their servant, his voice clear and carrying, announce her.

The momentary hush which followed was almost too much for Jennifer's self-control, and it was only by exerting a tremendous effort that she stopped herself from bursting into laughter at the astonished glances bent in her direction as she moved gracefully forward, her beautifully made black evening gown clinging to her every curve, its colour enhancing the perfection of her flawless complexion.

'Good evening, Uncle Frederick,' she said, when at last she reached him.

She could not forbear a further smile at his expression of astonished disbelief. She may at one time have harboured less than charitable feelings towards him for not coming to her assistance when she had desperately needed some comfort and support, but that was no longer the case. Her father and his younger brother, she clearly remembered, had never been close, so Jennifer could hardly blame her uncle for not wishing to become involved in the affairs of

a niece he barely knew. Added to which her husband
had earned himself the reputation of being a hard and
ruthless man to those who crossed him, as she had
discovered for herself. Only a fool, or perhaps a very
brave soul, would ever cross swords with the Marquis
of Wroxam.

'I can quite understand your astonishment at seeing
me again after all these years, Uncle, but I am in truth
your niece Jennifer.' Not offering him the opportunity
to respond, even had he felt able to do so, which she
very much doubted, she turned her attention to his
Countess, a female she barely remembered. 'Ma'am,
it has been many years since last we met, not since
my dear mama's demise, if my memory serves me
correctly.'

'Er—that is correct,' her ladyship managed faintly,
momentarily glancing at the beautifully arranged dark
auburn hair, and the glinting green gems adorning the
slender neck and small, perfectly shaped ears.

'I hope you will overlook my impertinence in inviting myself to your party. And please do not blame
your servants for admitting me to the house. I'm
afraid I led them to believe that I had merely mislaid
my invitation card.'

'Do not give it another thought,' the Countess responded promptly, thereby proving that she at least
was beginning to regain her equilibrium, even if her
husband was still a long way from regaining his. 'Of
course you are most welcome.'

Jennifer doubted that this was true, but decided not
to prolong their discomfiture, and took the opportunity presented by the arrival of yet another latecomer
of moving away.

By this time her identity was beginning to spread

through the ballroom like wildfire. She strongly suspected that, before too many more minutes had passed, there wouldn't be a guest present who hadn't been informed of precisely who she was. She was fast becoming the cynosure of all eyes, some of which were openly admiring, while others betrayed varying degrees of curiosity or astonishment. As she moved further into the room, it occurred to her that, when she had made her first and very brief visit to the capital, she would have been overawed by such blatant interest. This, however, was not now the case. She was no longer a diffident child, but a self-assured young woman, quite unafraid to hold her head up proudly, and return bold stares from strangers without so much as a single blink.

Had her upbringing been different, had she not tragically lost her dear mama fifteen years ago, the people now present tonight might not all have been total strangers, she reflected, moving ever further down the long, brightly lit room. Had her mother lived, her father might have continued to take an interest in the estate, instead of spending most of his time in London, foolishly squandering vast sums of money at the gaming tables. His frequent absences from the ancestral pile had meant that few people had ever visited the house, and Jennifer quite clearly recalled the loneliness and seclusion she had been forced to endure during her formative years, having only the servants and her governess to bear her company, and receiving the occasional visit from a considerate neighbour or two.

One might have expected her marriage at the ridiculously young age of sixteen to the Marquis of Wroxam to have improved her lot, and to a certain extent it most certainly had, for she had enjoyed far more freedom, and had made several new friends during her months at Wroxam Park. Her father's demise within a few weeks of the wedding taking place had, quite naturally, curtailed any kind of socialising on a grand scale, and the visit to the capital which her husband had planned had been postponed until the following spring, by which time, of course, Wroxam and his Marchioness had gone their separate ways.

'Who? Who did you say it was, Serena?' The question, spoken in a high-pitched, carrying voice, broke into Jennifer's sombre reflections, and she turned her head to discover an elderly lady, dressed in a purple gown and sporting an ugly turban in the same dark hue, regarding her more keenly than most. 'So, you're Caroline Westbury's gel, are you?'

'Caroline Westbury was my mother, certainly,' Jennifer responded, inclined to be more amused than annoyed by the impertinent enquiry. 'You have the advantage of me, ma'am.'

'May I present my godmother, the Dowager Lady Fairfax, my lady.'

Jennifer transferred her gaze to the young woman who had been sitting beside the Dowager and had now risen to her feet. 'And my name is Serena Carstairs,' she added, in response to Jennifer's finely arched, questioning brow.

'I am pleased to make your acquaintance, Miss Carstairs,' Jennifer responded, bestowing a warm smile upon the tall young woman who appeared decidedly ill at ease.

'I knew your father too,' the Dowager suddenly announced, evidently experiencing none of her goddaughter's embarrassment. 'Charming rogue!' She cast a vague glance in the general direction of their host. 'Not like the present holder of the title. What a devilish dull dog he is!'

'Godmama, please!' Serena said faintly, casting a further apologetic glance, but Jennifer was not in the least offended, for the Dowager had spoken no less than the truth, and yet she found herself, surprisingly, automatically coming to her uncle's defence.

'He is certainly lacking the charm my father at one time was reputed to have in abundance. My uncle is, I understand, a man of sober habits. Which, I might add, I consider no bad thing. At least he would never bring disgrace to the proud name he bears, and he has, so I am led to believe, restored the ancestral home to its former glory.'

'There's no denying your father turned into something of a rakehelly fellow in later years,' the Dowager conceded. 'Changed after your mother died, as I remember,' she added, thereby betraying the fact that she had known the late Earl quite well. She peered frowningly up at his sole offspring. 'Which reminds me…I thought you were supposed to be dead too. Just goes to show you, Serena, that one shouldn't listen to every piece of gossip one hears!'

Appearing as if she wished the floor would open beneath her, Serena turned to Jennifer the instant Lady Fairfax's attention had been claimed by a lady of similar age. 'Please forgive my godmother. She has turned seventy, and doesn't always consider carefully before she speaks.'

'There is absolutely no need for you to apologise, Miss Carstairs,' Jennifer assured her, drawing her a little away from the outspoken lady who was causing such discomfiture. 'I do not object to plain speaking, and to be frank I found Lady Fairfax's remarks most—er—interesting.' An irrepressible glint appeared in her eyes. 'I had no notion that I had been presumed dead all these years. What, may I ask, was supposed to have befallen me?'

Serèna made a despairing gesture with her hand. She hàd no desire to repeat the foolish rumours which had been circulating years before, but she quickly discovered that the lovely Marchioness could be quite persuasive when she chose.

'So, Wroxam was rumoured to have put a period to my existence, was he?'

The sudden gurgle of mirth was as infectious as it was unexpected, and Serena found herself chuckling too. 'But no one of any sense believed it for a moment,' she assured her.

'None the less, even my case-hardened husband must have found it faintly disconcerting to be thought a murderer.'

'That I could not say, my lady. I am not well acquainted with his lordship,' Serena frankly admitted, 'even though when visiting the capital we are privileged to make use of my uncle's residence in Berkeley Square.' She appeared to hesitate for a moment, then went on to ask, 'Was it perhaps you Mama and I saw visiting his lordship's house earlier today?'

Jennifer did not attempt to hide her surprise. 'My, my, what excellent eyesight you must possess, Miss Carstairs, to have been able to penetrate my veil!'

'On the contrary, my lady, my sight is poor. My mother doesn't approve of my wearing spectacles when we go out in the evenings. I do not see very well without them, but I do manage to notice certain things. It was the way you walked into the room. I remembered that the lady who called at Lord Wroxam's house this afternoon had a similar graceful way of walking.'

Jennifer could not help but feel flattered, and smiled warmly at her new acquaintance. 'I did indeed pay a call at my husband's house,' she confirmed. 'Unfortunately he was not at home.'

'No, he has been out of town for several days. At the races, I believe.' Serena laughed a little self-consciously. 'What a dreadful gossip I sound! I'm afraid, though, that the comings and goings of gentlemen of your husband's standing do become common knowledge. I think I'm right in saying, also, that he had entered a filly in one of the races.'

'How disappointed he must feel that he did not win!' Jennifer found herself unable to suppress a smile of smug satisfaction. 'I had an interest in the outcome of a certain race, and made a point of finding out the result.'

Ignoring her companion's glance of mild surprise, Jennifer guided her towards two vacant chairs. 'Tell me, Miss Carstairs,' she continued, once they had made themselves comfortable, 'is this your first visit to London?'

'Good gracious, no! I had a Season several years ago. It was a complete disaster,' she freely admitted. 'I simply did not take, and do not expect that this time will be any different. Dear Papa wished me to have another chance, however, before my sister's come-out next year. I'm certain Louisa will be a success. Unlike me, she's very lovely.'

Jennifer subjected her companion to a prolonged stare. It was true that Serena could never be described as pretty. Her mouth was too wide and her nose was too long for beauty. She was rather tall, too, and built on generous lines, but she had been blessed with a pair of fine grey eyes, and a good complexion. She decided that she rather liked Miss Serena Carstairs.

'This is my first real visit to the capital,' Jennifer disclosed, after a further moment's silence. 'I have been spending some time visiting places of interest. Perhaps, if you are free tomorrow afternoon, you would care to accompany me out somewhere? There are plenty of interesting sights I have yet to see.'

She turned her head to discover her uncle and his wife heading in her direction, and hurriedly rose to her feet. 'Perhaps we shall be granted the opportunity to talk again later, Miss Carstairs.'

Like so many others, Serena followed the Marchioness's progress across the room, thinking once again how very gracefully she moved. She could not in all honesty say that she had ever given any thought at all to what the austere Marquis of Wroxam's wife would turn out to be like. But she couldn't say that it had come as any surprise to discover that the Marchioness was strikingly lovely. However, she would not have expected her to be so charming and unaffected, totally devoid of pride or conceit; the exact opposite, in fact, of her arrogant, unapproachable husband.

Serena glanced about the room at the other guests present, wondering if they too were speculating on where the lovely Marchioness had been hiding herself all these years, and deliberating, perhaps, on what might have caused the break up of her marriage. Serena herself would never dream of prying into such personal concerns, but she couldn't help hoping, as she continued to watch her new acquaintance, now in conversation with their host and hostess, that she would, indeed, be granted the opportunity to become much better acquainted with the delightful Marchioness.

Chapter Two

It was mid-afternoon on the following day when the Marquis of Wroxam arrived back in town. Having to contend with the heavy volume of traffic, he had been silent for some little time, concentrating on negotiating a safe passage through the busy London streets, which had left his companion, Mr Theodore Dent, free to look about him.

As they entered the more fashionable part of the city, Mr Dent became aware of the attention they were receiving from several passers-by. From a young age his friend the Marquis had cut a figure in society, and it was by no means unusual for his presence to be noted wherever he went. The looks cast in his direction this day, however, seemed rather more prolonged than usual.

'I say, Julian, you ain't been getting on your high ropes more than usual of late, have you, and causing offence in certain quarters?'

One of his lordship's famed, haughty dark brows rose. 'Anyone listening to you, my dear Theo, might be forgiven for supposing that I attain some perverse kind of pleasure from offending my fellow man.'

'Well, I wouldn't go so far as to say that. But you don't care a jot when you do.'

Thin lips curled into an appreciative smile. 'There have been occasions, Theo, when I have asked myself why I include you in my small circle of friends. I can only imagine it is because I admire your innate honesty.' He took his eyes off the road to cast his amiable companion an enquiring glance. 'Would it be too much to ask why you might suppose I have offended someone of late?'

'Because I've noticed one or two people casting rather odd looks in our direction during the past few minutes.'

'In that case it is more than likely that you are the one attracting attention,' his lordship responded drily. 'If you will go about looking like an oversized wasp you are bound to startle the populace.'

Not in the least offended, Mr Dent glanced down at his striking yellow-and-brown striped waistcoat that fitted snugly across his large barrel of a chest. 'The trouble with you, Julian, old fellow, is that you're so damned unimaginative when it comes to dress. Can't think why you've been considered a leader of fashion all these years!' He saw the ghost of a smile hovering around the Marquis's mouth once more. 'People never take much notice of me no matter how I'm rigged out,' he went on. 'It's much more likely that certain folk have got wind already of your narrow defeat at the races yesterday.'

'You may possibly be right,' his lordship responded, not noticeably depressed by the fact that his prized entrant had been pipped at the post by an Irish-bred filly. 'Did you manage in the end to discover the owner's name?'

'Yes, it's young Lord Fanshaw. The trainer was a bit tight-lipped about it, but I managed to discover the horse originally came from the O'Connell Stables. I was assured the present owner wouldn't be interested in selling the animal, though.'

'Pity,' his lordship responded, expertly turning into the Square. 'I might possibly have made an offer for that filly.'

No sooner had he drawn his fine bays to a halt before his house than the door opened and his footman came tripping lightly down the steps. If his lordship noticed the odd glance his servant cast him before taking charge of the equipage, he certainly gave no sign of it, as he led the way into the house and across the hall to his library.

After filling two glasses, and handing one of the delicate vessels to his friend, he carried his own wine over to the desk, leaving Mr Dent to make himself comfortable in one of the chairs by the hearth.

'My secretary is so efficient, Theo. A veritable treasure!' Perching himself on the edge of the desk, his lordship began to browse through the neat pile of papers awaiting his attention. 'He deals with most of my correspondence, only ever leaving me those letters which he thinks might be of interest.'

He eventually came to one which his tactful secretary had not opened, and instantly recognised the childish scrawl. 'Why Deborah must feel the need to continually send me letters, I cannot imagine.'

He held the missive at arm's length, the better to decipher its hurriedly penned lines. 'Ah, she is missing me, and thinks I'm the biggest beast in nature for preferring to visit the races than spending time in her company, and she is utterly pining for me.'

He tossed the letter into the wastepaper-basket. 'Of course, what she's really pining for is a brooch, or earrings, or possibly even a necklace, to match the ruby bracelet I gave her the other week. She really has become quite tiresome of late—clinging and avaricious. It's high time I found myself a replacement. What say you, Theo?'

'I've been your friend for a good many years, Julian,' Mr Dent responded, after fortifying himself from the contents of his glass, 'but even I would never dream of offering advice on such personal concerns. And certainly never in matters of the heart.'

'My dear Theo, you delude yourself. My—er—heart is never involved, believe me.'

'Cool fish, ain't you, Wroxam?' Mr Dent subjected his lordship's rather harsh-featured face to a prolonged stare. 'You've had half a dozen mistresses and more during these past years, but not one of 'em has meant a groat to you.'

'I wouldn't go as far as to say that,' his lordship countered, after giving the matter brief consideration. 'I became mildly fond of two or three. But I cannot in all honesty say that it caused me even a moment's disquiet to terminate any one of my—er—several pleasurable liaisons.'

He raised his eyes from their contemplation of the patterned carpet to see his butler enter the room. 'Yes, Slocombe. What is it?'

'Forgive the intrusion, my lord, but I gave my word that I would hand this over to you personally on your return.'

Not even by the slight raising of one of those haughty dark brows did the Marquis betray the least emotion as he took the letter from Slocombe, broke the seal and ran his eyes over the few lines written in a beautifully flowing hand.

'One moment, Slocombe,' he said, arresting his butler's progress across to the door. 'When was this delivered?'

'It was not sent, my lord. Her ladyship called here herself yesterday, in the late afternoon.' He stared solemnly across at the desk. 'She penned the letter in this very room, sir.'

There was just a faint hardening about the Marquis's square, powerful jaw, but his voice when he spoke was as cool and controlled as ever, devoid of the faintest hint of emotion. 'Are you quite certain that it was she?'

The butler raised grave eyes to his master's. 'Oh, yes, my lord. Very certain. Her ladyship has... changed somewhat, but not so much that I did not recognise her at once.'

His lordship dismissed the butler with the faintest nod of his head, before easing his tall frame off the desk and moving across to the window to stare sightlessly across the Square.

'Not bad news, I trust?' Mr Dent ventured.

'I'm not quite sure whether it is or not,' the Marquis responded, after a further moment's thoughtful silence. 'It would seem my wife has taken it into her head to reappear in the world.'

'Eh?' Mr Dent wasn't perfectly certain that he could have heard correctly, and found himself saying, 'Jenny, do you mean?'

'My memory can be a little hazy on occasions, but I believe I've only ever had one wife.' His lordship gestured towards the desk where he had left the short missive. 'Read it for yourself.'

Theodore hesitated, but only for a moment, and reached the desk remarkably quickly for a man of his size. 'Dear God in heaven!' he muttered, not quite able to believe the evidence of his own eyes. 'Can it ·be true, do you suppose? Poor little soul…and after all this time.'

'So, you too assumed that she was dead?' There was an unmistakably sardonic note in the Marquis's attractive deep voice now, one which his friend had detected far more frequently in recent years.

'Well, yes…I suppose I did,' he reluctantly admitted. 'After all, Julian, you were never able to find any trace of her. But I never supposed for a moment that you had had anything whatsoever to do with her disappearance.'

'Some most certainly did.'

'Not any of your friends, Wroxam, not those who know you well,' Theodore assured him, before glancing down once more at the letter still clasped in his large hand, and frowning as a thought suddenly occurred to him. 'Can you be sure that this was in fact penned by Jenny? Do you recognise the handwriting?'

'No, I cannot say that I do. I never read but one of the letters she wrote to me shortly before her disappearance.'

Theodore wasn't perfectly certain, but he suspected that there had been just an element of regret in his lordship's voice. 'So, it might all be a hoax?'

'No, I do not think so. You heard yourself what Slocombe said. He had no difficulty in recognising her.' His lordship returned to the desk and relieved Theodore of the missive. 'I cannot recall that she possessed such a stylish hand. Vastly superior to darling Deborah's childish scrawl, I must admit.'

'Well, what do you expect? Jennifer's certainly no—' Mr Dent caught himself up abruptly when he detected the mocking glint in his lordship's grey eyes. He shook his head, his own expression suddenly grave. 'Do you know, Julian, I still find it hard to believe that Jennifer would ever do what you said she did. I've never been able to understand it... She worshipped the ground you walked on.'

'Do you imagine I lied to you?'

There was no trace of mockery now in his lordship's eyes, and Mr Dent found himself lowering his own. 'Of course not, Wroxam.' He shook his head sadly. 'You'll go and see her, though, won't you?'

'Perhaps.'

Mr Dent was quite unable to contain his bewilderment at this seeming lack of interest on the Marquis's part. 'But surely you're just a little curious to discover where she has been hiding herself all this time, interested to see just how much she has changed?'

'I've always considered curiosity faintly vulgar, my dear Theo. Thankfully I've never suffered from a surfeit of it.' His lordship moved languidly across the room to the decanters to replenish his glass. 'I have survived all these years without seeing my wife...I'm certain I can continue to do so.'

Mr Dent might have experienced only mild surprise at his friend's attitude, but the vast majority of polite society swiftly became astounded by the Marquis of Wroxam's display of seeming indifference to his beautiful young wife's return.

He continued to behave just as though nothing untoward had occurred: visiting his club, his friends, and attending one or two very select parties in the evenings. The Marchioness, too, was seen about town a good deal, her husband's return, seemingly, not inducing her to curtail her own pleasurable activities. Since the night of the Chard ball she had attended several parties. However, by accident or design, the Marquis and his lovely wife, frustratingly, never appeared at the same function.

If certain people knew what had induced the Marchioness to disappear all those years ago, they were certainly not divulging their knowledge, and Society could only continue to speculate on what might have caused the break up of the marriage, and wait for events to unfold. Quite naturally, the Marquis of Wroxam's movements continued to be monitored with immense interest by the majority of the polite world, but it was not until the end of the following week that he was spotted turning his fine bays into Curzon Street, and drawing his curricle to a halt outside a certain house which had been hired for the Season.

The footman who admitted him left him kicking his heels in the hall for a short time only, before showing him into a comfortable room which overlooked the street. The morning sun's bright rays, streaming through the window, seemed directed on the room's sole occupant. The bright aureole of light which surrounded the slender figure seated at the desk, busily engaged in writing a letter, enhanced the fiery tones in the beautiful crown of deep auburn curls which had so captured his lordship's attention all those years ago, when he had caught his first glimpse of her happily frolicking in a field of wild flowers.

Even his closest friends would have been hard pressed to guess precisely what was passing through his lordship's mind as he came to stand in the centre of the room, for his expression remained as inscrutable as ever. Only the pulsating throb at his temple, and the faint hardening of his firm jaw betrayed the fact that he was not as indifferent as he might wish to appear at this, his first sight of the lady he had not set eyes on for almost nine long years.

'You may sit down, Wroxam,' she invited softly, without bothering to raise her head, or pausing in the task of writing her letter.

He chose to remain standing, watching the finely boned white hand moving back and forth across the page. It wasn't until she had completed her task, and had sanded down the missive, that she finally raised her head, offering him the first clear view of the delicately featured face.

During the past days more than one person had had the effrontery to remark upon his wife's loveliness. Now he could see for himself that their admiration had been wholly justified. She had been undeniably a very pretty girl, and he was forced silently to concede that the passage of time had been generous to her, enhancing the delicate cheekbones, and the sensual curve of perfectly moulded lips. Only those striking green eyes, clear and sparkling, remained unchanged.

'Evidently you prefer to remain standing.' Her pleasantly mellow voice was perfectly controlled and, like her expression, gave no hint of any emotions which she might be experiencing at this their first encounter in a very long time.

His own self-control had always afforded him a deal of gratification. He admired restraint in others too, and yet for some perverse reason he found this peerless display of self-mastery on his wife's part faintly irritating. Surely she must be experiencing some small sensation at their coming face to face again?

'No doubt your time is precious,' she continued, in the same level tone, 'and mine too is limited, as I plan to leave the capital for a few days.'

There was just a faint hint of amusement playing round her mouth as she rose to her feet, and moved gracefully over to the window, offering him a perfect view of her lovely figure, which remained just as slender as he remembered, but which had developed more feminine curves.

'I suppose I ought to consider myself honoured that you took the trouble to visit me at all.'

The hint of sarcasm was not wasted on him, and he frowned slightly. 'In the letter you left for me, you chose not to disclose the reason why you wished for this meeting,' he reminded her, wondering fleetingly why she was dressed in sombre black.

'I would have thought, Wroxam, that the reason would have been blatantly obvious to a man of your keen intelligence.' She turned to look at him again, her eyes assessing as they looked him over slowly from head to foot, before finally holding his faintly sardonic gaze without so much as a single blink. 'I think it is high time that we legally terminated this farcical union of ours. I can appreciate that divorce is not easy, and it might take some time to attain, but I am sure that a man of your standing should not find it impossible to achieve.'

'Perhaps not,' he agreed. Reaching into the pocket of his impeccably tailored jacket, he drew out his snuffbox and made use of its contents before closing the delicately painted lid with a flick of one practised finger. 'Without wishing to appear vulgarly curious, however, might I be permitted to know why, after all these years, you should suddenly wish to end our marriage.'

'If, by that, you are asking whether I wish to attain my freedom in order to marry someone else…the answer, Wroxam, is no, I do not.' The sardonic glint in her eyes was no less pronounced than that in his own. 'My one experience of—er—wedded bliss was more than enough, I assure you.'

His expression darkened, making it abundantly obvious that he was not even faintly amused by this display of flippancy. 'Might I remind you, madam, that I was the injured party in our union, and not you.'

Although there remained a suspicion of a smile about her mouth, her voice was sombre enough as she said, 'That is something I am never likely to forget. Nor do I imagine for a moment that you are ever likely to forgive me for making a cuckold of you. Therefore a divorce would be beneficial to us both.'

It would, of course. Yet for some reason he was quite unwilling to commit himself, and found himself asking, 'Why in all these years did you never once make the least attempt to contact me? Was it, perhaps, to extract some petty form of revenge for my leaving you at Wroxam Park, not responding to your letters and refusing to see you?'

'Strangely enough, no, it was not.' Her sigh was clearly audible. 'If I am honest I would be forced to admit that for many months I did feel bitterly resentful towards you. But you must remember I was very young at the time, more child than woman. As the years passed, however, I began eventually to view things differently. After finding your faithless wife in bed with another man, your behaviour was very understandable. Had our roles been reversed, I most certainly wouldn't have wished to have had any contact with you.

'I'll not bore you with details of how it came about that I was able to make a new life for myself. Suffice it to say that Fate chose to look kindly upon me, and I have been immensely happy during our years apart. I was urged on many occasions to contact you, but I chose not to do so for—for several reasons which I will not go into.' Again she sighed, and this time it sounded decidedly heartfelt. 'During recent months, however, something occurred which forced me to reassess my situation. My options were clear—either I could remain the lost and forgotten wife, or enter into the world that I had left so long ago, for a short time at least.'

She turned once more to stare out of the window. 'You would eventually, I do not doubt, have considered seriously the possibility of remarrying in order to beget an heir. My reappearance at a time when you were endeavouring to take steps to have me legally pronounced dead would, to put it mildly, have been most unwelcome.' Her chin rose as she turned to look across the room at him again. 'Well, unfaithful I might have been; vindictive I am not. For both our sakes a divorce is the only option.'

For the second time that morning his lordship discovered himself experiencing sensations he had not felt for a very long time. Anger and bitter resentment over her adulterous behaviour remained, but along-

side these lingering emotions tender feelings were beginning to establish themselves.

He was both annoyed and amazed by these unexpected sensations, and for the first time in his life
found himself at a loss to know how to proceed.
Before he had been granted even a few moments to
consider carefully how to respond, the door behind
him opened, and he turned to see a young woman,
also dressed in sombre black, enter the room.

Registering his presence almost at once, the intruder stopped dead in her tracks. 'Holy Mary, Mother
of God!' she exclaimed. 'So it's yourself come at last,
is it?'

The Marquis, unaccustomed to being addressed in
such a fashion, instinctively felt for his quizzing-
glass, and peered through it at the intruder as though
she were a creature from another world. More than
one member of Society had withered beneath his lordship's haughtily raised dark brows, but his contemptuous gaze appeared to have little effect on this brazen
creature. She stared back at him for several moments,
her dark eyes bold and assessing, before turning to
his wife.

He found himself quite unable to understand one
single word of the ensuing conversation. By the several dark-eyed glances he received, and his wife's frequently suppressed smiles, it wasn't too difficult to
guess the subject under discussion. What quite
amazed him, however, was the fact that his young
wife not only appeared to understand Gaelic perfectly,
but that she had evidently mastered the barbarous
tongue and was able to respond fluently!

'Well, if you're certain sure you wouldn't prefer
me to stay, Miss Jenny,' the intruder remarked, re-

turning to a language that they could all understand, 'I'll away and finishing the packing.'

His lordship waited only for the young woman to depart before addressing his wife once more. 'Might I enquire who that bold-faced creature was?'

'Her name is Mary Harper. You, sir, would consider her a servant; I look upon her as a friend.'

She had responded swiftly enough, but there had been just a hint of reserve in her manner, as though she resented his prying. He had by this time, of course, detected several changes in her. Only physically did she bear any great resemblance to the female he had married nine years ago. There was little evidence now of that diffident, biddable girl. Undeniably during their years apart she had developed into a young woman who knew her own mind and was more than capable of making her own decisions.

'At least now I do not need to enquire precisely where you have been hiding yourself,' he remarked sardonically. 'Your—er—servant has cleared up that little mystery.'

'Yes, Wroxam, I have been residing across the sea in Ireland.' She moved over to the desk, and began to gather together the papers she had left there. 'And now, if you would excuse me, time is pressing. Perhaps you will be good enough to let me know when you have spoken to your lawyers. I shall be more than happy to agree to your terms and conditions. I require nothing from you except my freedom.'

Anger welled again, though whether this stemmed from pique at being so summarily dismissed, or the fact that she had made it plain that she required no financial assistance from him now or in the future, and he was therefore of no further use to her, he could not say.

'There is no need to ring for your servant,' he assured her curtly, when she reached for the bell-pull. 'I am quite capable of seeing myself out,' and then did so, without uttering anything further, not even a word of farewell.

His lordship had informed no one, not even his loyal butler, where he had intended going that morning, but Slocombe had a fairly shrewd idea of precisely whom his lordship had visited that day when the Marquis, grim-faced, his manner more curt than usual, returned to the house late in the afternoon. After issuing instructions that he was not to be disturbed in any circumstances, he took himself into the library, locking the door firmly behind him against any possible intrusion.

Compared to most members of his class, his lordship had always been a man of moderate habits, especially where the consumption of strong liquor was concerned, but this first encounter with his young wife after so long had disturbed him more than he cared to admit, even to himself, and he sought refuge in the contents of a certain crystal vessel.

After collecting both glass and decanter, he lowered his tall frame into his favourite chair by the hearth, his mind's eye having little difficulty in conjuring up a clear image of the female he had married: slender, graceful, and self-assured, as she had stood by the window, conducting their first meeting with praiseworthy control. Seeing her today, every inch the gracious, impeccably behaved lady, it was difficult to imagine that she had been that unfaithful little strumpet who had dealt such a severe blow to his pride by committing adultery with the young brother of his nearest neighbour. Yes, he mused, finding it impossible to thrust Jennifer's image from his mind, his good friend Theodore Dent had been so right; it was hard to believe that she was capable of such base behaviour, and if he hadn't witnessed her infidelity with his own eyes, he for one would never have thought her capable of disgracing herself, or him, in such a fashion.

Reaching for the decanter, which he had placed within easy reach, Julian poured himself a second glass, before leaning back in his chair, clearly recalling the incident which he had tried his best to forget during the past years.

It had been on a day in early September when he had returned from London to discover his young bride had gone out riding with Geoffrey Wilburn. He had thought nothing of it at the time. He had been pleased that Jennifer had been able to make friends so quickly with their closest neighbours. It wasn't until Geoffrey's widowed sister, Melissa Royston, had called at the house that he had become a little uneasy over his wife's safety, for Jennifer and Geoffrey, by all accounts, had ridden out together several hours earlier.

He had not needed to think twice about accompanying Melissa to search for the young truants. It had rained earlier in the afternoon, and Melissa had suggested that her brother and Jennifer might have sought shelter in the small cottage by the wood, which Geoffrey had frequently used when out enjoying a day's shooting. Their horses had been tethered outside: clear evidence that they were within. When he had entered, Melissa close on his heels, he had discovered the young couple naked in bed together: clear evidence of his wife's infidelity. Geoffrey had looked terrified; Jennifer merely dazed, as though she had been sleeping soundly and hadn't woken fully.

Even now, after all this time, Julian could still remember the all-consuming anger which had followed those first moments of stunned disbelief. If he had remained, he might well have ended by releasing his emotions in a physical attack on either Geoffrey or Jennifer, or possibly even both of them. So he had merely departed without uttering a single word. By the time Jennifer, looking more than ever the bewildered child, had followed him back to the house, he had regained that ice-cool control for which he was famed.

At least, he reflected, she had not nauseated him further by dissolving into floods of tears while begging his forgiveness. She had merely stood there, head bent, when he had informed her coolly that he would be returning to London immediately, that she would remain at Wroxam Park, receiving no visitors, nor venturing out of the grounds, and that when he had decided what action he intended taking about their future, he would then return and inform her of his decision.

He was forced to concede that it did not redound to his credit that he had not attempted to reply to any one of the several letters she had written to him during the ensuing weeks. He had been more annoyed than concerned when he had discovered that she had disobeyed his strict instructions and had visited his London home. It had been on the following day, when he had called at the Earl of Chard's town residence, expecting to find her there, that he had first begun to fear for her safety.

A swift return to Wroxam Park had disclosed the fact that she had surprisingly not returned. The services of a Bow Street Runner had proved ineffectual in uncovering her whereabouts. As the years had passed he too had begun to believe that some misfortune must have befallen Jennifer, and yet not once had it ever crossed his mind to take steps to have her legally proclaimed dead... And all this time she had been living quite contentedly in Ireland!

His eyes narrowed as he reached for the decanter yet again. He couldn't help wondering how she had managed to survive all this time. She had no relatives, not even distant ones, residing across the sea, he felt sure. Furthermore, she had taken nothing with her— nothing except the few clothes which she had managed to carry in a cloak-bag. With the exception of her wedding band, every item of jewellery had been accounted for. Only the pin money he had given her during their few short months together had been missing from the drawer.

So who had taken care of her? Who had clothed and housed and fed her? Who had supplied her with sufficient funds to return to England, to hire that fashionable residence and to live in comparative luxury? Who was her protector now? An emotion, every bit as virulent as anger, welled up inside him; an emotion he had never experienced before and one he chose not to define.

After tossing the contents of his glass down his throat, he rose to his feet and went out into the hall to discover his butler hovering there. Slocombe, who had worked for the Stapleford family all his life, would not have supposed for a moment that his master had consumed most of the contents of a brandy decanter. There was not even a suspicion of a slur in the Marquis's voice when he announced his intention of dining at his club that evening, nor was there even a suggestion of a stagger as he mounted the stairs to his room.

If he appeared slightly unsociable whilst he remained at his club, no one thought too much about it. His lordship was never a garrulous companion, not even when in the company of his particular friends. His mistress also found nothing amiss in his manner when he paid her a visit later that night. His love-making was as peerless and passionate as ever, and totally satisfying, at least for her. His lordship, however, felt singularly unfulfilled and slept fitfully.

He awoke to see the dawn of a new day and, without disturbing the woman sleeping soundly beside him, rose from the bed and began to scramble into his clothes. Never before could he remember feeling so lethargic, so completely dissatisfied with life. He gazed down at his sleeping mistress, lying amongst the crumpled sheets, her ample breasts exposed, inviting further intimacy, and experienced not the smallest desire to remain. He raised his eyes to study the pretty face, with its full, sensual lips slightly parted, and the riot of golden curls stretching out across the pillow. Then, unbidden, a more delicately featured face, framed in a riot of fiery curls, appeared before him. He closed his eyes in a vain attempt to obliterate the image. If Deborah with all her sensual expertise had failed to thrust his wife from his thoughts, then it was high time he found a female who could!

Chapter Three

Within half an hour of Jennifer's return to town she had received the first caller to the house. No sooner had that visitor departed than another arrived, and from then the door-knocker was never still.

'Saints' preserve us!' Mary exclaimed, entering the front parlour midway through the afternoon to discover her young mistress quite alone for once. 'Haven't these heathen people anything better to do with their time than pay calls and sit about gossiping all the day?'

Well aware that her faithful confidante staunchly disapproved of time-wasting, Jennifer could not forbear a smile. 'One would not suppose so on the evidence of this day. You must remember, though, Mary, that only the favoured few are blessed to live such comfortable lives. For the vast majority it is quite otherwise, as we both are only too well aware.'

She turned away from the window as a thought suddenly occurred to her. 'And speaking of which… have you managed to discover anything further about your sister?'

Mary shook her head. 'And I'm not so certain sure

that it isn't a blessing in disguise, Miss Jenny. We both know what she was. Thank the good Lord my sainted mother never discovered what Kate had become!'

'You mustn't think ill of your sister, Mary,' Jennifer said softly. 'She was forced into that kind of life in order to survive…whereas I…'

'You're no whore, Miss Jenny! And you never were!'

'I know of at least one person who would disagree with you,' Jennifer responded, resuming the seat she had occupied for most of the afternoon.

'His high-and-mightiness can think what he likes!' Mary snapped, betraying quite clearly that she did not hold the Marquis of Wroxam in the highest esteem. 'Why, I don't suppose for a moment that he's deprived himself of his pleasures, whereas—'

'Whereas I have lived the life of a nun,' Jennifer put in, momentarily wondering why she had chosen to deprive herself of the company of younger men, when she had been given numerous opportunities to do quite otherwise during the past years. 'And you're quite right about Wroxam, Mary. Lady Carstairs took great delight in informing me only last week that he's had a string of beautiful mistresses living under his protection.'

Mary expressed her opinion of Serena's mother by giving vent to a derisive snort, before subjecting her young mistress to a prolonged and thoughtful look.

She possibly knew Jennifer better than anyone else did. They had been through so much together, especially in the early stages of their friendship. She had witnessed moods of almost black despair, displays of fiery temper and, increasingly over the years, she had observed the joy and contentment which had come into Jennifer's life. Yet, she would be the first to admit that there were occasions when even she was hard pressed to know what her young mistress was thinking and feeling, most especially where the Marquis was concerned.

'I must say, Miss Jenny, his lordship didn't turn out to be quite as I had been expecting,' she admitted at length.

'No?' Jennifer responded, betraying a mild interest. 'As I recall, you had no difficulty whatsoever in recognising precisely who he was when you discovered him in this very room, even though you'd never set eyes on him before.'

Mary shrugged. 'Intuition, I suppose. Although you've never spoken of him often, you have done so on the odd occasion, and I suppose I built up a picture in my mind. I knew he'd be proud and haughty. And he most definitely is! But I also imagined he'd be tall, dark, and handsome.'

Jennifer took a moment to consider this. 'Well, you were at least two parts correct. He's tall and he's dark. He's certainly striking, but I do not recall that I ever considered him particularly handsome.'

Leaning back in her chair, she allowed her mind to wander back over the years. 'I remember vividly the very first time I ever saw him. He was staying with his friend, Theodore Dent, whose parents were my father's nearest neighbours. I was in a field, as I recall, gathering wild flowers, and I looked up to discover the Marquis there, looking so striking, so very distinguished, astride a handsome bay. I rather think I fell in love with him at first sight.' There was a distinctly self-deprecating ring to her sudden shout of laughter. 'Dear me! What a naïve, gullible little fool I used to be! I actually believed that he loved me in return. What was worse, I imagined we'd live happily ever after!'

Unlike her young mistress, Mary found nothing amusing in this totally sincere confession. If the truth were known she had been startled when she had entered this very room five days before to discover his lordship standing there. After his treatment of her friend and mistress, Mary had made up her mind that she wasn't going to like him in the least, and the haughty attitude he had adopted towards her had given her no reason to question her preconceived notions about him. Yet, she had detected something in those cool grey eyes of his that had convinced her that he wasn't so indifferent to his lovely Marchioness as he might wish to appear.

'Are you so certain sure that he never loved you, Miss Jenny?'

'Very sure, Mary,' was the swift response. 'I'm no longer a romantic child. I do not try to delude myself. Wroxam married me because I was a complete innocent, uncomplicated, biddable and chaste, someone of good birth who would bear him the heir he required, and who would not attempt to interfere in his lifestyle.' She laughed this time in genuine amusement. 'My, my, how I have changed! Unless I much mistake the matter, I'm interfering in his life at the moment to a very great extent. I do not doubt that Society is watching his movements as avidly as it's watching mine. How irritating he must find it all! Like myself, he is essentially a very private person who values his periods of solitude.'

'And you, Miss Jenny? Are you finding all the attention slightly wearisome?'

'I might well come to do so in time. At the moment, though, the experience still retains the charm of novelty. You must remember, Mary, that this is my first real visit to the capital, and I'm enjoying it very much.' She shrugged what one languishing dolt had been overheard to call the most perfect shoulders in London. 'Besides, I doubt we'll need to remain for very much longer. Once Wroxam has seen his lawyers, and has taken steps to end our disastrous marriage, we'll be able to return to Ireland.'

'Are you certain sure he'll see his lawyers?'

'I should imagine he has done so already. He wouldn't wish to be tied for life to a faithless wife.' Jennifer regarded her loyal companion in silence for a moment, easily detecting the flicker of uncertainty in dark eyes. 'What makes you doubt that he will?'

Mary shook her head. 'I don't know. It was just something I thought I saw in his eyes when he paid his visit that made me wonder whether—' She broke off, as she clearly detected the sound of the door-knocker. 'Oh, now who's that, do you suppose? I'll leave you in peace to receive your caller, Miss Jenny. Just tell me which dress you'd like me to lay out for tonight.'

'I'll wear the gown I wore for my uncle's ball, I think, and the emeralds.'

Mary tutted. 'Black again! You know very well that Master James wouldn't have wanted you to do that. He knew well enough how much you loved him.'

Jennifer made no attempt to respond. She merely glanced rather sadly down at the empty grate, but looked up again, the sadness swiftly fading from her eyes, when the door opened directly after Mary's departure and a tall man appeared on the threshold, his large frame almost filling the aperture.

'Why, Theo!' Without the slightest hesitation she stretched out both hands in welcome. 'How lovely to see you after all these years!'

He came forward to capture those slender fingers in his own massive hands, and held them with surprising gentleness. 'Jenny, you're a sight to take the most hardened man's breath away! What a relief it is to see you looking so well, so radiant!'

A hint of mischief added a sparkle to those wonderful green eyes that he remembered so well. 'My dear Theo, never tell me that you numbered amongst those who thought Wroxam had done me a mischief?'

'Certainly not!' he answered, looking as indignant as it was possible for a man of his amiable disposition to appear. 'Wroxam may have his faults, but he ain't no murderer.'

'I sincerely hope you're right, dear Theo,' she responded, the teasing glint more pronounced than ever. 'When he paid me a visit last week, he certainly looked as though he could quite cheerfully have strangled me.'

Theodore found himself chuckling at this artless disclosure. The Marquis had said very little about the visit he had made, save that he had found his wife somewhat different than he remembered. An understatement, if ever there was one! Theodore mused. It wasn't so much the physical changes as the differences in her demeanour which had struck him most forcibly the instant he had entered the room. She simply oozed self-confidence now, and had developed into a young woman who, he too suspected, was no longer afraid to speak her mind. Little wonder poor Wroxam had been quite unlike himself since his visit! The lovely Marchioness, unless Theodore much mistook the matter, was no longer in awe of her proud, aristocratic husband!

'I called to see you a couple of days ago, but your manservant informed me that you'd gone out of town,' he remarked, gratefully accepting the wine she had poured for him, while lowering his large frame into the one chair which looked as if it could support his weight.

'He isn't my servant, Theo. He came with the house, together with a very skilful cook and efficient housekeeper. The owner was happy to leave his staff here in London whilst he and his family travelled abroad, for which I have been extremely grateful,' she admitted. 'Good servants are difficult to obtain at the best of times, and almost impossible to find during the Season, so I'm reliably informed.'

Jennifer seated herself in the chair opposite, feeling totally relaxed in this big man's company. But then, she reminded herself, she had always felt comfortable with him. She may once have felt a little diffident in Wroxam's company, but never in Theo's. She had always liked him immensely, even when she had been that shy little girl, almost afraid of her own shadow.

'And why is it, my dear Theo, that I still find you a bachelor?' she enquired, betraying a hint of disapproval. 'Surely at least one pretty girl has managed to capture your interest during these past years?'

'Several have, m'dear,' he admitted, after sampling the excellent wine. 'Trouble is, pretty fillies aren't interested in big, blundering oafs like me.'

Jennifer's smile was gentle. Sadly what he had said was possibly true. He was, indeed, a large man, big boned and certainly not handsome. He had put on a deal of weight during her years away too, which had done nothing to improve his looks. His lack of physical attributes, coupled with a slight awkwardness when in female company, would very likely deter most members of her sex from attempting to try to know him a little better. Which was a great pity, because it was only when one became well acquainted with the Honourable Mr Theodore Dent that one realised what a truly charming and kindly gentleman he was.

She shook her head. 'I wonder at my own sex sometimes. You would make any lady a truly wonderful husband.'

His big barrel chest swelled, straining the silk material of his waistcoat. 'Well, m'dear, I'd do my very best, if I could find a young lady brave enough to take me on.'

He sampled the contents of his glass once again, wondering as he did so if it came from the young Marchioness's own cellar. If so, she could certainly pick a wine. 'But that's enough about me. What have you been doing with yourself all this time?' He saw the decidedly wary expression flit over her delicate features and cursed himself for every kind of a fool. 'Sorry, m'dear. Shouldn't have asked you that. Don't mean to pry.'

'There's no need to apologise, my dear Theo,' Jennifer responded, instantly dropping her guard. 'I felt sure Wroxam would have told you I've been living in Ireland.'

She could tell by his expression of surprise that he

had not known, even before he said, 'No, Wroxam
didn't tell me that. He only mentioned that he'd seen
you.'

Jennifer regarded him in silence for several moments, and Theodore found her gaze disconcertingly
direct, a trait she had never displayed years before.
'But he told you precisely what led to the break up
of our marriage, did he not?'

'Yes, Jenny,' he admitted gently.

She nodded, not unduly distressed to have her suspicions confirmed. 'I thought if he were to tell anyone
then it would be you, Theo.'

'I don't believe he would have confided even in me
if he hadn't been so very concerned over your disappearance.'

She appeared merely sceptical now, and he didn't
hesitate to assure her that this was true. 'He's not a
man to wear his heart on his sleeve, Jenny. You above
anyone should know that.'

She chose not to respond to this. Theodore was
Wroxam's friend, perhaps his closest, and therefore it
would be grossly unfair of her to cast aspersions on
her husband's character by blithely suggesting that
she doubted very much whether his lordship possessed such a delicate organ as a heart. None the less,
she could not resist saying, 'I became aware very
swiftly, after I had entered the polite world, that
Society seemed surprisingly ignorant about our marriage, and I certainly felt grateful to Wroxam for not
making my fall from grace common knowledge.' A
wry little smile tugged at the corners of her mouth. 'I
cannot help wondering, though, what has held him
mute all these years. Was it an attempt to protect my

fair name, or a determination to preserve his massive pride?'

She could see at once that she had placed Theo in an embarrassing position. He was far too honest a person to rush to his friend's defence, unless he was perfectly certain of Wroxam's true motives, and it was quite obvious that he wasn't sure.

'But no more talk about Wroxam and me,' she went on in an attempt to lessen his discomfiture. 'What have you been doing with yourself? I seem to remember that you were not at all fond of taking part in the social whirl, and yet I find you here in London at the height of the Season.'

This brought the cheery smile back to his homely face. 'I very much enjoy the companionship of my friends in the relaxing atmosphere of my club, Jenny. It's the ladies I'm not too comfortable with. Too big and too clumsy, that's my trouble.' He released his breath in a sigh which sounded distinctly mournful. 'I'll need to make the effort tonight. Promised I'd put in an appearance at my aunt's ball. She'd be upset if I didn't show my face.'

'In that case, Theo, and providing you have made no prior arrangements, would you care to be my escort tonight? Your aunt, Lady Morland, very kindly sent me an invitation last week.'

His response was too spontaneous not to be totally sincere. 'Jenny, my dear girl, nothing would give me greater pleasure!'

No one would have supposed for a moment that Mr Dent was in the least happy to be escorting Lady Wroxam when he arrived at Lady Morland's house that night, for his face, as he entered the ballroom to greet his aunt, wore a very troubled frown.

The same could not be said of his lovely companion. If she was experiencing any slight misgivings over coming face to face with her husband in public for the very first time, she certainly betrayed no sign of it. In fact, she appeared quite remarkably composed when Mr Dent escorted her down the length of the ballroom to sit beside the young lady who had become a particular favourite of hers in recent weeks.

Formality having been dispensed with shortly after their first meeting, Serena did not hesitate, the instant Mr Dent had moved away, to apprise her charming new friend of the Marquis's arrival a short time earlier. 'I saw him entering the room about half an hour ago, Jenny. I believe he's still in the room set out for cards.'

'Yes, I was informed by both Lady Morland and her nephew that it was more than likely that he would be putting in an appearance tonight.' She shrugged one slender shoulder, clearly revealing her complete indifference. 'It was only to be expected that we should come into contact with each other on occasions whilst I remain in town, so I saw little reason in trying to avoid any encounter.'

Jennifer looked about her with interest to see who else was present that evening. She had by this time grown quite accustomed to attracting a deal of attention wherever she went, and was not even faintly discomposed by the glances bent in her direction. A great number of those present were now known to her, but one man, whose leering gaze was more direct than most, she felt certain she had never seen before; felt certain too, after a second glance in his direction, that it was her friend who was the object of his interest.

'Tell me, Serena, who is that unprepossessing, middle-aged individual in conversation with Lady Thessinger?'

Miss Carstairs raised her short-sighted eyes to peer across the ballroom. 'Lord Sloane. He has only recently arrived in town. Mama, I believe, knew him quite well years ago. He paid a visit to our house the other day, but I do not think Mama was pleased to see him. She seemed quite unlike herself after he had left.'

'Cannot say that I'm unduly surprised. He looks to be a most unpleasant individual,' Jennifer responded, smiling wickedly as her attention was swiftly captured by quite a different person. 'And speaking of rather unpleasant fellows…'

Serena, following the direction of her companion's gaze, only just managed to suppress a gurgle of mirth, when her eyes eventually managed to focus on the gentleman heading in their direction. As Jennifer had never once spoken of her private affairs, Serena remained quite ignorant of precisely why the Wroxams' marriage had failed. One thing she had become firmly convinced about, however, was that the charming Marchioness, unlike a great number of people, was not in the least in awe of her somewhat austere husband, as she proved by the quizzical raising of one finely arched brow when at last he stood before her.

'Good evening, my lord,' she greeted him politely, if with precious little warmth. 'I had been informed that you were amongst the guests this evening.' She glanced briefly in Serena's direction. 'I assume you are already acquainted with Miss Carstairs, as she too resides in Berkeley Square?'

If his lordship had indeed been oblivious to Serena's existence until that very moment, he at least possessed the innate good manners to disguise the fact, as he acknowledged her for the first time in her life with a slight bow and a semblance of a smile. 'I hope you will forgive this intrusion, Miss Carstairs, and permit me to deprive you of your companion for a short while. I was hoping,' he added, turning once again to Jennifer, with a flicker of a challenging gleam in his eyes, 'to persuade her ladyship to partner me in the next dance.'

Whether or not it was because those sitting and standing nearby were betraying a vulgar interest in the Marquis's surprising display of attention, or the fact that she was determined to show one and all, including her husband, that she was not so faint-hearted as to turn her back on a challenge which prompted her graciously to accept the invitation, Jennifer was not perfectly sure. It was only when she permitted Wroxam to lead her on to the dance floor, and they took up their positions for the commence-ment of the waltz, that she began to experience seri-ous doubts over the wisdom of her actions.

The shapely masculine hand resting lightly on her waist evoked bittersweet memories, almost forgotten, of a time when she had welcomed that gentle touch, reminding her that the man she had married, although cold and unapproachable during the day, had been the most tender, considerate lover at night. Throughout their years apart she had never once sought masculine company above that of mere friendship; had never once even considered embarking on a more intimate relationship…until now. Although her mind might advocate the continuation of a chaste, uncomplicated lifestyle, her body, surprisingly reacting to that masculine touch, was urging behaviour of a totally different kind.

Raising her eyes from the intricate folds of an expertly tied neck-cloth, she discovered her husband staring intently down at her, an expression on his face which might easily be taken for intense satisfaction. It was almost as if he sensed that she was appalled to discover that he still retained the power to arouse her traitorous body. Her resolve, however, remained unchanged. She was no longer a weak-willed girl, and had no intention of dropping her guard where this man was concerned. To do that could only lead to disaster.

'I think, Wroxam, that it might be wise if we did not perform the entire dance in stony silence,' she suggested, gratified to discover that her voice at least remained perfectly controlled, 'otherwise people might assume that you are already regretting your impulsiveness in asking me to stand up with you.'

'I never behave impulsively, madam wife.' His tone was clipped, as though he found the mere suggestion that he ever acted without due consideration insulting. He regarded her in silence for a moment, his expression quite unreadable. 'Did you suppose that I intended to spend the whole evening ignoring you completely?'

'Certainly not! You are far too well bred… Or perhaps far too discerning. You would not go out of your way to add to the gossip already surrounding us.' She could not resist a smile of wry amusement. 'Although

I must confess that I didn't expect quite such a marked show of attention.'

Although he never attempted to respond, he didn't appear wholly displeased by this display of candour on her part. 'Do you realise, Wroxam, that this is the very first time we have ever danced together?'

After expertly avoiding a collision with an energetic young couple, he shrugged one broad shoulder. 'If you recall, madam, your father's demise shortly after our marriage had taken place restricted our social activities. Besides which, I rarely dance.'

'Really?' She didn't attempt to hide her surprise. 'Why, then, have I been singularly honoured?'

'Because I wished to speak with you, that is why, madam wife.' He cast a faintly impatient glance about him. 'I fear, however, that I miscalculated. There are far too many couples here for any degree of privacy.'

Although he might be experiencing some slight irritation, Jennifer sensed that he was not totally regretting his request for her to stand up with him. For a tall and powerfully built man he danced with surprising grace. Reluctantly she was forced silently to concede that they danced well together, easily matching each other's steps, moving in perfect harmony. How many of those avidly watching their every movement, she wondered, would believe that they had never danced together before?

She raised her eyes to discover those dark brows once again meeting above the bridge of that long, aristocratic nose. Only this time his disapproving gaze was most definitely fixed in her direction. 'I fear something about my person displeases you, my lord,' she ventured.

His frown grew slightly more pronounced. 'I'm not

displeased,' he assured her, 'merely curious. On the two occasions I have seen you thus far, you have been dressed in black. I cannot recall that there has been a recent death in your immediate family, so I can only assume that during our years apart you have acquired a penchant for decking yourself out in that particular colour.'

'Widows are wont to dress in black, are they not?' A definite glint, which in a child would have been taken for devilment, sprang into her eyes. 'And you, my dear Wroxam, have been dead to me for years.'

He found to his surprise that he felt more amused than annoyed by this deliberately provocative remark. 'Baggage!' he muttered, totally without rancour. 'Nine years ago, madam wife, you would never have dreamt of uttering such a sally.'

There was just a hint of wistfulness in the smile she cast up at him. 'No, perhaps I would not,' she agreed.

The dance came to an end and she made to return to her seat, but Julian forestalled her by the simple expedient of placing a gently restraining hand on her arm. 'If there is no urgency for you to return to Miss Carstairs, perhaps you would be kind enough to grant me a little more of your time?'

Without waiting for a response, he guided her across the crowded ballroom and into the room set out for cards, where he quickly located a small table in one corner which suited his purposes admirably. 'At least we may be granted a little privacy here,' he remarked, after requesting a waiter to bring them wine.

One finely arched brow rose. 'Privacy, my dear

Wroxam, is a luxury that both of us must be prepared to forgo whilst we remain in the capital.'

'I very much fear you are correct, my dear.' He reached for one of the glasses the waiter had just placed on the table, and stared at his undeniably lovely wife above its rim for a moment before sampling the contents. 'So I shall not waste the precious time granted to us now, but will come straight to the point. Why did you feel the need to discompose poor Theo? I noticed he was quite unlike himself when he arrived.'

For a moment she looked utterly bewildered, then suddenly gurgled with laughter, drawing the attention of the occupants of the tables nearby. 'So he told you, did he?'

'He told me nothing, except that you'd given him quite a turn during the carriage ride here.' He reached for the pack of cards placed on the table. 'Shall we play picquet for…say, a shilling a point?'

Jennifer automatically picked up the cards he had dealt her. 'I assure you, Wroxam, I would never deliberately upset Theo. However, when one is at a loss to know how to proceed in a matter of importance, one usually seeks advice. I now realise, of course, that I asked the wrong person entirely. It would have been wiser to have approached you.' The impish glint was back in her eyes. 'You, I suspect, are far more knowledgeable about such things, and are not so easily shocked.'

He was swiftly coming to realise that his Marchioness had acquired a decidedly mischievous streak during their years apart. He felt certain that he was being extremely imprudent, but could not resist asking, 'On what subject can I possibly advise you?'

The devilish glint returned with a vengeance. 'On how one should go about discovering the whereabouts of a whore.'

His lordship paused in the act of raising his glass to his lips. 'Well, I have only myself to blame, I suppose,' he murmured. 'I knew I was being singularly foolish to have enquired in the first place.' He regarded the lovely smiling countenance in silence for a moment. 'You are jesting, of course.'

Having comprehensively won the first game, Jennifer reached for the pack and dealt two fresh hands. 'On the contrary, I'm in deadly earnest. I wish to locate a particular female's whereabouts in order to repay a debt of gratitude. She offered me sanctuary when I had nowhere else to go. Unfortunately she moved out of her rented accommodation some years ago, and those people living in the area do not seem to know what became of her, or simply aren't saying.' She took a moment to study the cards in her hand. 'Would it be of any use, do you suppose, calling in the Bow Street Runners?'

'I very much doubt it.' Leaning back in his chair, he studied her once again, his lips faintly curled. 'So, when your uncle refused to offer you help, you sought refuge with a whore.'

The scathing note in his voice was not lost on her. 'Highly appropriate in the circumstances, do you not think, a trollop offering sanctuary to another of her kind?'

Although there was a noticeable tensing in the muscles about the square, powerful jaw, he made no attempt to respond, and after a moment she added, 'In fact, it was the whore's sister, Mary Harper, who came to my aid, Wroxam.'

It took several moments before he realised to whom she was referring. 'Your personal maid?'

She nodded. 'Mary, believing that her sister had been successful in finding herself a position as a domestic, came over from Ireland to try her luck. Of course she realised at once what her sister had become…had been forced to become in order to survive. With no references, poor Mary had no more luck in trying to attain a position than her sister had had the year before. It was while she was about the city, in a last vain attempt to find some respectable employment, and I was aimlessly wandering about, feeling lost, alone and utterly wretched, that our paths crossed.'

'So why didn't you simply ask your new-found friend to accompany you back to Somerset, if you were feeling so alone and afraid? I dare say she would have jumped at the chance. It may well have led to her acquiring a position in my household.'

'You are jesting, of course!' He found himself on the receiving end of an astonished glance. 'You don't imagine, surely, that I had the least intention of ever returning to Somerset to the house which had become a prison, where I had been forbidden to leave the grounds, forbidden to receive visitors, where I had been expected tamely to await for the husband who despised me to return when it suited his purposes?'

Her shout of laughter contained a reckless quality. 'My dear Wroxam, naïve I may have been, but I was not completely stupid. Our marriage was at an end. You had made that perfectly clear by refusing to answer my letters, and refusing to see me. What choice had I but to make a new life for myself?'

As had occurred increasingly of late, his conscience

began to trouble him. The original blame for the break up of their marriage might rest squarely upon her beautiful shoulders, but he was forced to own that his subsequent actions could not withstand too close a scrutiny. She had been so very young at the time. Had he, perhaps, acted a little too harshly?

No sooner had the thought entered his mind than he cursed himself silently for this momentary weakness. 'So, you chose to sample the delights of a doxy's abode in preference to the comfort and luxury to be enjoyed at Wroxam Park,' he remarked, derision oozing from his every word. 'How very singular!'

Their eyes met and held above the table. 'Your opinion of me, understandably, is not high, sir.' Her voice, unlike his own, remained perfectly controlled, betraying not the smallest hint of emotion. 'Nevertheless I do not suppose that your contempt is such that you truly imagine that I had any inclination, at the time, of precisely what profession Katherine Harper was engaged in. Had it not come on to rain that day, I doubt very much whether Mary would have invited me to accompany her back to her sister's one-room hovel. When Katherine went out that night to walk the noisome streets in that area of the city, it never crossed my mind to suppose that she would be selling herself.'

To his intense amazement he found himself believing her every word, though why this should be he had no notion. Was he just a gullible fool? he wondered. After all, she had deceived him in the most debased manner years before. In that first letter he had received from her, the only one he had ever troubled to read, she had sworn that she loved only him, and had been unfaithful only once. Understandably enough, he had chosen not to believe her. Besides which, he had considered what she was capable of doing once, she was more than capable of doing again. She simply couldn't be trusted, then or now, and yet… She began speaking again, and he forced himself to listen.

'No doubt, it would eventually have dawned on me that poor Katherine was engaged in the oldest profession in the world had I remained under her roof for any length of time, but Mary and I left the following morning and journeyed to Bristol.' She shook her head, drawing his attention to the sparkling green stones dangling from her ears. 'Looking back, I can only marvel at my own simplicity. During that fateful night, I had decided to travel back to Ireland with Mary, and to support myself by seeking a position as a governess in Dublin. Unutterable madness! Who in his right mind would ever employ a girl of sixteen as a governess, no matter how well educated she may have been?'

'Very few, I should imagine.' He found himself smiling too as she chuckled at her own folly. Her actions had, undeniably, been far from sensible, but they proved one thing—she had never lacked courage, then or now. 'I assume that your attempts at attaining a post in Dublin were not successful?'

'I never reached Dublin, at least not then,' she disclosed. 'In fact, the only vessel bound for Ireland on the day we arrived in Bristol was one destined for Cork. We had little choice but to seek passage. Neither of us possessed the funds to put up at an inn for any length of time.'

'So you reached Cork… What happened to you then?' he prompted, when she fell silent, and knew by the suddenly guarded expression that he was destined to discover nothing further, even before she said,

'I survived, Wroxam…I survived.'

Yes, and how! He regarded her in silence, while mentally assessing the value of the glinting green gems adorning her neck and ears. How had she come by them? His eyes narrowed. Who had been her protector all these years? There must have been someone, surely? So why was she so unwilling to disclose the fact? Or was there something else she was determined he would not discover?

'So, you believe that it is a complete waste of time trying to discover the whereabouts of my companion's sister?' she announced unexpectedly, returning his thoughts to the matter taxing her at the present time.

'I didn't say that,' he corrected. 'I merely advised you not to seek the help of the Runners. Unless this woman has committed some offence, I doubt they'd bestir themselves unduly.'

She frowned at this. 'But I understood that you had brought in the Runners when you wished to discover my whereabouts?'

'That was a different matter entirely. You are someone, my dear. And I possess money and influence.'

She looked faintly subdued and he found himself experiencing a keen desire to help her, though why this should be he simply couldn't imagine. 'If you furnish me with the woman's particulars, I'll see what I can do. There is someone I know who might be able to help.'

Surprise swiftly replaced dejection. 'That is most kind of you, sir! I shall make a list of all the details

I know about Katherine Harper, and send a servant round to Berkeley Square with it in the morning.'

She rose to her feet, which forced Julian to do likewise. 'And now I think it might be prudent if we part company,' she suggested, the hint of mischief returning to her eyes. 'Otherwise some foolish people will begin to imagine that we are about to embark on a reconciliation. And that will never do, now will it, sir?'

Most assuredly not! he was about to retort, but somehow the concurrence lacked the conviction to pass his lips.

Chapter Four

'I'm sorry I cannot oblige you on this occasion, Serena, but, as I've already mentioned, I have made arrangements to spend several days in the country again, so I'll be unable to attend your mother's alfresco breakfast on Friday.'

Jennifer regarded her new friend in some concern, at a loss to understand what could be troubling her. Since the night of Lady Morland's ball, Serena had been quite unlike herself. Frequently subdued, she often appeared as if she were living in a world of her own.

'I do not perfectly understand why you feel the need for my support,' she continued, echoing her thoughts. 'You're certainly not averse to socialising, and I'm sure you must be already acquainted with most of the guests attending your mother's picnic.'

'Yes, I am,' Serena responded, looking if possible more subdued than before. 'That is just the trouble. Lord Sloane is to be amongst the company.'

At last Jennifer began to see a chink of light. She had noticed during the past week or so that whenever

Serena happened to be attending a certain party, Lord Sloane was lurking not too far away.

'What I fail to understand, Jenny, is why Mama encourages his attentions towards me, when I'm certain she doesn't like him at all.'

'Yes, it does seem strange, I must admit,' Jennifer agreed.

Reaching for the newspaper on the table by her chair, Jennifer began to scan the printed sheets, just as though she had lost interest in the conversation. Nothing, however, could have been further from the truth. Since her arrival in London she had become acquainted with a great many people, but only towards Miss Carstairs had she developed a fond attachment.

She considered her friend's dilemma for a moment before adding, 'You, of course, do not need to encourage his attentions, Serena, if you do not choose to do so. I realise that your mother would very much like to see you suitably settled before your sister's come-out next spring. What mother would not? But surely neither of your parents would force you into accepting an offer of marriage from a gentleman you have taken in dislike?'

'I sincerely hope not!' Two angry crimson spots added becoming colour to Serena's thin cheeks. 'Nothing could ever persuade me to marry such a disgusting, dissolute rake as Lord Sloane! I would rather be forced to earn my own living as a—as a governess!'

'Really?' One of Jennifer's finely arched brows rose as she turned her attention once again to the printed sheets. 'Well, talking of such persons, how does one go about acquiring the services of one?'

'What on earth do you want with a governess, Jenny?' Serena demanded to know, swiftly forgetting her own concerns.

A moment's silence, then, 'I—er—promised a very close acquaintance that I would enquire for one whilst I was in London. She is intent on engaging an English governess for her son.'

The door-knocker echoed loudly in the hall, heralding, Serena supposed, the arrival of someone else wishing to see the very popular Marchioness, and she rose to her feet. 'I'm afraid I am singularly ignorant about such matters. One could always advertise, I suppose,' she suggested, just as the door opened, and none other than the Marquis himself strolled languidly into the room.

Her eyes instinctively turned towards her friend, but as always Jennifer appeared completely unruffled, only the slight raising of her finely arched brows betraying the fact that she was mildly surprised by her husband's arrival.

During the past week or so, Serena had been present on three or four occasions when Lord Wroxam had graced the same function as his wife. Although he had never once displayed anywhere near the same attention as he had shown on the night of Lady Morland's ball, he had never once failed to acknowledge his Marchioness by exchanging a few words.

'Well, I must be on my way now,' she announced, suddenly feeling like an awkward schoolgirl beneath the Marquis's penetrating grey-eyed scrutiny, and wishing she could acquire a little of her friend's admirable composure.

'Please do not feel that you must leave on my account, Miss Carstairs,' his lordship assured her politely, and Serena almost found herself gaping. Not only had he remembered her name, but the surprising smile which accompanied the assurance had completely softened his austere features. He really was a most attractive man!

'I must be going, sir. I promised to meet my mother in Bond Street, and am already a little late.' She moved towards the door, but turned back to add, 'I shall see you when you return to town, Jenny. You haven't forgotten, I hope, that you promised to make up one of Mama's party at the theatre on Tuesday?'

'No, I hadn't forgotten. I promise I'll be back in good time.' Jennifer assured her, and quite failed to notice the slight narrowing of his lordship's eyes before he turned to open the door for Serena to pass into the hall.

Rising from her chair, she went over to the table on which the decanters stood, wondering what had prompted his visit. Like Serena, she too had noticed that he had never once failed to acknowledge her presence, exchanging a few pleasantries whenever their paths had happened to cross in the evenings. This, however, was only the second occasion he had attempted to see her in private. Which gave her every reason to suppose that he had something of a personal nature to discuss. Most likely their futures, she mused, wondering why suddenly she felt no desire whatsoever to discuss the matter of their impending divorce. It was, after all, the main reason why she had visited London… It was, after all, the only way forward for them both.

That self-control which Serena so admired came to the fore, and her voice betrayed none of the conflicting emotions warring inside her, as she said lightly,

'This is something of an unexpected pleasure, Wroxam.' Out of the corner of her eye she saw him close the door and move further into the room. 'Is it just a passing visit, or can I persuade you to sit down this time and partake of some refreshment?'

'A glass of wine would be most welcome, for the news I bring will not be.'

He certainly appeared none too cheerful now, as he lowered his tall frame into the chair recently vacated by her friend, but she could not read too much into this. He was not a man given to smiling often, and she had always found it difficult to know precisely what he was thinking and feeling; though why he should look quite so cheerless, if it was indeed their divorce he had come here to discuss, she could not imagine. Unless, of course, he had come up against some hitch.

She succeeded in curbing her curiosity until she had handed him a filled glass and had seated herself in the chair opposite, then she came straight to the point by asking outright whether it was the matter of their legal separation which had prompted his visit, and saw the shapely hand raising the glass to his lips check for a moment.

'No, I'm not here to discuss that,' he disclosed, after sampling the contents of his glass, and giving a faint nod of approval. 'You've developed a discerning palate during our years apart, madam.'

'I can certainly pick a wine, Wroxam. Something which, I do not doubt, I inherited from my father.' She sampled her own, before adding, 'So, what brings you here?'

'The commission I agreed to undertake on your behalf.'

It took her a moment only to realise to what he was alluding, and her brows rose in surprise. Although she had been prompt in furnishing him with a letter containing all the relevant details concerning Mary's sister, she had not expected any response quite so soon. It was quite evident, however, that the news he had to impart was not good.

'She's dead, isn't she?' she said softly, and thought she could detect a hint of remorse in his grey eyes.

'I'm afraid so. The person I engaged to locate her whereabouts discovered that she moved away from the area not too many weeks after you had embarked for Ireland. That is perhaps one of the reasons why you had no luck in trying to trace her. Not too many people did remember her, but the one or two who did were sure that she had moved in with a man who had lived near the docks. This turned out to be true. Sadly, though, she contracted typhus a few months later and didn't survive.'

'And was no doubt buried with a number of others in a communal pauper's grave,' Jennifer murmured, before sipping her wine. There was nothing she could do for Katherine Harper now. There were others, however, and one in particular, who might appreciate her help at the present time.

'Are you acquainted with Lord Sloane, by any chance, Wroxam?'

'And what, pray, is your interest in that individual, madam?'

He seemed faintly annoyed, but she couldn't imagine why this should be. Nor could she understand why she hadn't taken exception to his blunt manner. She had not, however, and found herself more than willing to satisfy his curiosity.

'My interest in him is minimal, I assure you. I have spoken to him but once, and was not favourably impressed. I fear he is the epitome of everything I most despise in your sex—a debauched womaniser, feckless, unscrupulous, a person devoid of any finer feelings.'

His frown disappeared, and a crooked but not unattractive smile tugged at one corner of his mouth. 'A discerning palate is not the only thing you've acquired during our time apart, madam wife. It would seem you have developed a propensity for plain speaking. Which is no bad thing if wisely controlled.'

He paused for a moment to finish the excellent wine and placed the empty vessel on the table by his chair. 'Yes, your assessment of Lord Sloane's character is remarkably acute. He is certainly not the kind of person I should wish a female relative of mine to associate with.'

'Precisely what I was thinking myself,' she murmured, hardly aware that she had spoken her thoughts aloud, until she noticed those penetrating grey eyes firmly focused in her direction.

'One other thing that might be of interest to you,' he said, his gaze unwavering. 'Sloane has only recently come into the title and is believed to be heavily in debt. So it is not beyond the realms of possibility that he's on the lookout for a rich wife.'

Now that was most interesting! Jennifer mused, making herself more comfortable in the chair, feeling remarkably at ease in her formidable husband's company. If what she had just learned was true, and she had no reason to suppose that Wroxam would lie, Lord Sloane's pursuit of her friend Miss Carstairs was even more puzzling.

Dear Serena had been the first to admit that she was no beauty. There was certainly much room for improvement, however. Her warm brown locks would look far more becoming if left to wave naturally, and not permanently crimped into a frizz. Many considered her too tall for a woman, but her carriage was graceful and her figure, slim and curvaceous, was excellent, and would show to far better advantage in simply styled gowns in darker colours. Serena looked every one of her five-and-twenty years, and no amount of frills, ribbons and bows, and delicate pastel shades would succeed in making her appear like a pretty young miss embarking on her first London Season. It was a great pity that Lady Carstairs, whose word was law when it came to her daughter's attire, was not sensible enough to appreciate this fact.

Not all men, however, Jennifer reminded herself, were beguiled by a pretty face. Perhaps Lord Sloane, having attained middle age, might consider that a sensible young woman in her mid-twenties, and one of good birth and gentle manners, would suit him better than a simpering miss straight out of the schoolroom. This might well be the case, but it still didn't explain his pursuit of Serena, if money was, indeed, a consideration when selecting a wife. The Carstairs family, though an old and noble one, was not wealthy, and for the daughter of a Baronet, Serena's dowry was woefully small.

'Something appears to be troubling you.'

The softly spoken remark brought an end to her puzzling reflections, and she raised her eyes to the man seated opposite. Had circumstances been different, had theirs been in any way a normal marriage, man and wife in every respect, she wouldn't have needed to think twice about confiding in him, for he was undeniably an intelligent man whose judgement and advice she would have welcomed. But how could she divulge her concerns to a man who was, not to put too fine a point on it, a virtual stranger? No, impossible! she decided without considering the matter further.

'If I do appear slightly worried, then it is because I feel I have imposed upon you too much already, without taking up any more of your time.

Setting aside her half-empty glass, she rose to her feet, a clear indication that she wished to bring the interview to a close. Julian rose also, not knowing whether to feel amused or annoyed at receiving his *congé*. It was certainly a novel experience being so summarily dismissed, especially by one's own wife.

'Be good enough to send me an account of what I owe you in respect of the expenses you've incurred in discovering what became of Mary's sister.'

The smile that curled his lips this time distinctly lacked both humour and warmth. 'You forget, madam, that while you remain my wife, I am responsible for you, and any debts you may incur,' he reminded her in a tone that was deliberately challenging, and for the first time he saw something akin to fear flicker in the depths of those lovely eyes.

Feeling inordinately pleased with himself for having at last managed to pierce that masterly self-control, he moved over to the door. 'By the by,' he turned back to add, as though the thought had only just occurred to him, whereas in fact it had crossed his mind soon after his arrival, 'have you any intention of gracing the soirée tonight at Globe House, or the Fenchams' ball on Friday?'

The wary look remained. 'No. Why do you ask?'

He shrugged. 'No reason really. It was just that I had considered putting in an appearance at both events myself. What a pity that I shall be denied the pleasure of your company!' and with that he left, almost strutting like a gamecock which had struck first blood, and was savouring the sweet taste of victory.

By the time Julian had arrived back at Berkeley Square the feeling of satisfaction had long since dwindled, and he found himself once again prey to that tumult of conflicting emotions which frequently plagued him these days.

It seemed the more he saw of his Marchioness, the worse his affliction became. Whenever they had attended the same party, he had experienced no difficulty whatsoever in picking her out amongst the throng. It was by no means just those glorious auburn locks which made her stand out like a beacon. The way she moved, the way she talked, the way that rich gurgle of laughter floated in the air set her quite apart from other members of her sex. The simple fact was, of course, he desired her. And what red-blooded man would not? No doubt half the men in London lusted after the supremely lovely Marchioness of Wroxam, if the truth were known. Yet she had betrayed not the smallest interest in any one of those young puppies who gathered about her the instant she set foot inside a ballroom.

The heavy lids lowered as he remained gazing out of the library window across the large patch of green in the Square. Polite Society no doubt continued to speculate, wondering which of them was in fact responsible for the break up of the marriage. He strongly suspected that the finger of suspicion was increasingly being pointed in his direction, for his Marchioness had swiftly gained a deal of respect for her faultless manners, and impeccable behaviour. She never flirted; she never cast out lures; she never betrayed the least partiality for any one of her young admirers. Yet, there had to be someone, somewhere gaining her favours, he reminded himself again. Not here in London, perhaps…but somewhere.

Beneath the half-hooded lids his eyes began to glint ominously, a sure sign to those who knew him well that his lordship was in a dangerously determined mood.

He swung round sharply and went over to the bell-pull beside the marble grate. While waiting for his summons to be answered, he poured himself a glass of wine, and was in the process of sampling its contents when the butler entered in time to see a hint of disapproval flicker over his master's wholly masculine, aristocratic features.

'You rang, my lord?'

'Where did we purchase this burgundy, Slocombe?'

'From the usual vintner, the one we have patronised for a number of years, my lord.'

'In that case I believe it is time we took our custom elsewhere. This wine is decidedly inferior to the glass I was given earlier today.'

'I shall attend to the matter at once, my lord,' Slocombe responded automatically. 'Would there be anything else, my lord?'

'Yes, send Thomas to me.'

The young footman must have been about his duties in the hall, for no sooner had the butler departed than Thomas slipped quietly into the room.

It was not often that his lordship requested to see him personally. Usually he received his orders directly from Mr Slocombe, so he remained hovering tentatively by the door, racking his brain to think of what he might have done to displease his master.

Having seated himself at his desk, Julian was in the process of writing a brief note, and kept his eyes firmly fixed on the task in hand as he said, 'You may recall that two weeks or so ago, I sent you with a letter to a certain house across the river in Greenwich.'

'Yes, my lord.'

'You remember the precise whereabouts of that house?'

'I do, my lord.'

'Excellent! Because I wish you to go there again now. If you should be fortunate enough to find Mr Jonas Finch at home, kindly request him to return with you here at once. If he should be away, then give this letter to his good lady wife, instructing her to hand it to Finch immediately on his return.'

After sealing the brief missive, he placed it into his young servant's hand, instructing him to attain what largesse he might require for the hire of a hackney carriage from Slocombe, and then turned his attention to the neat pile of letters awaiting his attention on one corner of his desk.

It might have been pure imagination, but he suspected that far more mail was being left these days for his personal consideration. No doubt his efficient young secretary had noticed that he had been more willing to take a keener interest in the day-to-day running of his affairs in recent weeks. A wry smile tugged at the corner of his lips, as he reached for the topmost letter. He had needed to keep himself occupied, to try anything to take his mind off that beautifully packaged problem which had been besetting him of late.

He continued to work his way steadily through the pile, responding to some in his own bold, flowing hand, while leaving instructions on others for his secretary to attend to. He had reduced the pile considerably, when the door opened and Slocombe announced the arrival of the person he most wished to see.

'Ah, Finch!' Rising to his feet, his lordship reached out to shake the hand of the small, stockily built individual whose grey eyes were as penetrating as his own, before requesting him to be seated in the chair positioned in readiness by his desk. 'I trust my servant didn't drag you away from urgent business?'

'Nothing that cannot be set aside, m'lord,' he answered, his shrewd eyes following the Marquis's progress across the room in the direction of the decanters.

'Brandy is your particular poison, if my memory serves me correctly.' Julian poured out two glasses of the amber liquid, handing one to his visitor before seating himself behind his desk once more, and taking a moment to study the contents of his own glass.

'You may recall, Finch, many years ago, when you were employed as a Runner, you made an intensive search for my wife.'

'I do, sir.' Nothing in the ex-Runner's weatherbeaten features betrayed what was passing though his mind, as he continued to hold his lordship's steady gaze. Since leaving the Runners some years ago, and setting himself up in business as a private investigator, he had earned himself a reputation for discretion, which was perhaps one of the reasons why he had been so successful in his chosen profession. 'And with no success, as I embarrassingly recall.'

'That was no fault of yours,' Julian responded, thereby assuring his visitor that he held him in no way to blame. 'You were tireless in your efforts, as I remember, for which I was extremely grateful.'

Picking up his glass, Julian went over to stand by the window once again. 'You may or may not be aware,' he went on after a moment's thoughtful silence, 'that my wife has unexpectedly turned up again.'

'Aye, sir. I had heard. Popped up out of the blue, as yer might say,' he quipped, and noticed the faint smile tugging at one corner of his lordship's mouth.'

'It might be more accurate to say, out of the green, Finch. I have discovered that my Marchioness has been living across the sea in the Emerald Isle.'

The ex-Runner's brows rose sharply. 'Little wonder, then, that we never found no trace of her.'

'No, it isn't at all surprising,' his lordship agreed, taking a further moment to study the liquid in his glass, before tossing it down his throat in one appreciative swallow. 'What does amaze me is that she managed to survive. Her past is shrouded in mystery; her present is something of an enigma too. With your help, I intend to solve the conundrum. Both of them, in fact.'

If there was a man under a considerable strain, and doing his level best to conceal the fact from the world at large, then it was the man who was now resuming his seat on the opposite side of the desk, Jonas Finch decided. He had glimpsed the underlying tension in him all those years ago, when the young Marchioness had disappeared without trace. He had detected it again when his lordship had required his services a few weeks before to locate the whereabouts of that unfortunate woman, but it was more noticeable now. His lordship was like an over-wound spring, ready to snap.

'Since my wife's unexpected arrival in London several weeks ago,' his lordship continued, 'she has made at least two trips out of town to my certain knowledge. She intends to make a third.' His grey eyes held the ex-Runner's steadily above the desk. 'I want to know where she goes, whom she sees, where she stays.'

'I understand, my lord.'

'You do, do you?' His lordship's rasping laughter cut through the air like a knife. 'I certainly wish I did, Finch... My God, I wish I did!'

His admirable control did not desert him entirely, and he quickly had himself in hand once more. 'I believe she plans to leave London tomorrow, or the day after.' His eyes narrowed speculatively, as he fixed his gaze on an imaginary spot on the wall behind his visitor's head. 'If she follows the normal pattern, she'll remain away four or five days, and travel by hired carriage. As she has a perfectly good conveyance of her own, I can only assume that she doesn't wish to be recognised leaving the city, and the direction she takes noted.'

'Which would suggest, my lord, that she has something to hide.'

'It does indeed,' Julian agreed. 'Secretive she may

be, Finch, but she's no fool, so do not make the mistake of underestimating her. Find out what you can, but don't take your time about it. If my wife begins to suspect that she's being watched...'

'Don't you worry, my lord. I'm an old 'and at this game. I'll discover what I can and get back to you in a few days.'

Jonas Finch turned out to be as good as his word, and as a result of his findings, the Marquis himself left the city, travelling in a westerly direction, four days later.

Having decided to dispense with the services of his valet, his lordship had ordered a small bag to be packed in the unlikely event that he should remain away overnight. He doubted very much that the need would arise. In fact, he hardly knew why he was embarking on this short journey in the first place.

Staring absently through the window at the last rows of straggling houses on the outskirts of the city, he turned over in his mind the conversation he had had with the estimable Mr Finch just a few hours earlier.

'Are you certain about that?' he had queried, after the ex-Runner had disclosed that her ladyship was staying in a house situated on the outskirts of a small market town some thirty miles from the capital.

'Quite certain, sir. The landlady of the Blue Boar Inn was the friendly sort, a born gossip. The type of person we like to meet in my line of business, as you might say. She told me that the house belonged to Mr Whittam, a lawyer in the town. He and his good lady wife are enjoying a protracted holiday in Scotland, visiting their many relations up there. Seemingly he was only too happy to lease the house during his absence, and a certain Mrs Stapleton, a—er—brave major's young widow, is having the use of it until the owners return in the summer.'

'And there's no one else living in the house?'

'No one, my lord, excepting the servants.' Finch had assured him. 'Apparently, the Whittams' cook-housekeeper remained to take care of the place. And there's also an Irish groom and a boy staying in the house, so the landlady informed me. Seemingly they're your wife's servants, my lord.'

'And no one else visits the house regularly?'

'No, my lord. From my bedchamber window at the inn I had a clear view of the place, and saw no one enter or leave the house whilst I was there. As luck would have it, the landlady is a good friend of the Whittams' housekeeper, so she'd know whether Mrs—er—Stapleton entertains any visitors or not, and, according to what she told me, the young widow sees no one during the short periods she remains at the place.'

Drawing his mind back to the present, his lordship leaned back against the plush velvet squabs, at a loss to understand what could possibly induce his wife to make these frequent visits into the country. There had to be some reason, he told himself. And yet why should he be so determined to discover precisely what that reason was? Why hadn't he simply paid a visit to his lawyers and started proceedings to terminate the marriage? What on earth was he doing here now? Was he hoping to discover his faithless wife lying naked in the arms of another fawning lover…? Or was the opposite, in fact, nearer the truth?

Unanswerable questions continued to plague him

as his powerful team of horses ate up the miles, and it seemed no time at all before his coachman, as previously instructed, drew the carriage to a halt at the outskirts of the small market town of Merton Lacy. His lordship stepped down on to the road, ordered his head groom to await him at the Blue Boar, and then walked towards a red brick house, set a little way back from the road.

The wrought-iron gate creaked on its hinges as he pushed it open, and the gravel crunched beneath the soles of his boots as he walked slowly up the path to the door. He reached out one hand to grasp the highly polished brass door-knocker, cast in the shape of a lion's head, and then let it slip from his grasp, as he detected the squeals of delight from what he assumed must be a garden at the back of the house.

He turned on his heels, and had almost reached the corner of the building, when a small, sturdy object, racing from the opposite direction, cannoned into him.

Julian grasped the young shoulders, steadying the child and preventing him from falling. It was a moment before the boy raised a head covered in dark brown curls to reveal a pair of wickedly twinkling grey eyes, set in an impishly smiling countenance. Every muscle in his lordship's abdomen contracted, just as though he had received a physical blow. There was not the smallest doubt in his mind that he was looking for the very first time upon the face of his own son.

Hurriedly approaching footsteps broke the momentary trance-like state, and his lordship raised his eyes to see his wife's personal maid appear round the corner of the building, and then stop dead in her tracks.

'Holy Mary Mother of God! 'Tis himself, no less!'

'It is indeed,' his lordship responded in a voice that made Mary wish she had donned a thick woollen shawl.

Chapter Five

Seated beneath the branches of a sturdy cherry tree, Jennifer was taking full advantage of the sweetly smelling country air after having suffered the stale atmosphere of the city for more than two weeks. Although engrossed in the sketch she was making of the rolling countryside beyond the garden, she was vaguely aware that someone was approaching across the grass. It was not until the footsteps drew closer, and some detached part of her brain registered that they were too heavy to be those of Mary, that she drew her attention away from the rural landscape, glorious in the late afternoon May sunshine, to cast a glance over her shoulder.

She was on her feet in an instant, the sketch-pad falling from her fingers, forgotten, as she cast an anxious glance towards the house. Then she forced herself to look back at that darkly forbidding countenance looming ever nearer, and knew at once that it was already too late.

'What are you doing here?'

It was a singularly inappropriate question to ask in the circumstances, and seemingly he thought so too, for he made no attempt to answer, to say anything at all. He just continued to stare down at her, eyes hard, merciless, a look she clearly remembered with chilling clarity from years before.

A surge of blind panic left her feeling as if she might swoon at any moment, but she steadfastly refused to grasp the back of the chair for support. The idyllic life she had built for herself might be in imminent danger of being destroyed completely, and she might be denied any opportunity to try to save it, but she would never again belittle herself by attempting to plead with him, or to justify past actions. No, not a second time! she thought determinedly.

Tapping into that deep well of inner strength, she managed at last to break the hold of that implacable gaze, and swung away to stare across at the rural landscape which had suddenly lost much of its charm. 'So, you have been keeping track of my movements,' she announced, stating what ought to have been obvious from the moment she first saw him, like an avenging angel, striding across the grass towards her. Her eyes narrowed. 'Now, why, I wonder?'

His continued silence proved that he hadn't the slightest intention of satisfying her curiosity, so she was forced to draw her own conclusions. 'No doubt you expected to catch me in the arms of some ardent lover.' She might have laughed had the situation not been so dire. 'Wasn't once enough for you, Wroxam?'

She detected what sounded suspiciously like a faint gasp. Had it been anyone else she might have supposed that she had succeeded in inflicting a painful wound, but she didn't attempt to delude herself. Her husband's armour was impenetrable. 'Well, I'm sorry to disappoint you. You'll need to search very much harder if you wish to uncover proof of my continued infidelity. You'll find no languishing beaux here.'

'No, I discovered something far more damning,' he rasped, betraying his mounting rage, and she could not in all honesty say, as she turned to look at him again, that she blamed him either. Had their roles been reversed, had he deprived her of all contact with their child, she would have wanted to murder him.

He looked as if it would have afforded him the utmost pleasure to release his understandable animosity in a display of physical violence, but he made no attempt to strike her.

'Why, Jennifer? Why?' he demanded, his voice still harsh, but noticeably more controlled. 'Was it because you were so determined to extract some perverse revenge that you denied me all knowledge of my son's existence?'

In the face of having such an appalling accusation levelled at her, the fact that he had addressed her by her given name for the first time since her return to England seemed totally unimportant. She was about to assure him that nothing could have been further from the truth when she caught sight of her faithful groom striding purposefully in their direction, concern clearly writ across his handsome face.

'Are you all right, Miss Jenny?'

'I'm fine, Patrick,' she assured him, but he was plainly unconvinced, as his next words proved.

'Are you sure, now?' He darted a distinctly menacing look in his lordship's direction and received a less than friendly one in return. 'It'd be no trouble at all to throw him out.'

She didn't doubt for a moment that her groom,

never having been one to run from a fight, would have enjoyed making the attempt. Whether he would have succeeded or not was a different matter entirely. Both men were of a similar height and build, and although Wroxam was every inch the fashionable gentleman, she didn't suppose for a moment that he wasn't capable of defending himself should the need arise. A contest between the two might prove interesting, but in the present situation it could only make matters worse.

'I'm perfectly all right, Patrick. But I thank you for your concern.' She cast a fleeting glance towards the house. 'Do you happen to know where Charles is at the moment?'

'Mary has him safe. They're in the front parlour.'

'In that case,' his lordship put in, 'you are free to go about your duties. In fact, you can take yourself off to the local inn and inform my servants that they are to return here with my carriage immediately.'

Patrick's expression was openly insolent, as he looked his lordship over from head to toe. 'To be sure now, I could do that if I took me orders from you. Which I don't.'

Jennifer decided it might be wise to intervene. 'Please, Patrick. Do as his lordship requests.'

After taking a moment or two to transfer his gaze to her, he gave a brief nod of assent, and then walked slowly back across the lawn, his lordship following his progress until Patrick had disappeared round the corner of the house.

'I shall take leave to inform you, madam, that your choice of servants leaves much to be desired,' he announced, turning back in time to see her attempting to suppress a smile.

'Both Mary Harper and Patrick Fahy can be out-spoken on occasions, I'll admit, but their unfailing loyalty more than compensates for this defect.' She raised her chin, mimicking his haughty gaze to perfection. 'Furthermore, they are my servants, Wroxam. Kindly remember that in future.'

'Whether they remain so is far from certain,' he countered with a certain grim satisfaction, which instantly sent alarm bells chiming rather loudly in her head.

'What do you mean?'

'Simply this…' He took out his snuffbox and left her anxiously waiting while he made use of its contents. 'You can return with me now to Wroxam Park, or delay no longer in making your farewells to our son.'

The following morning, as Jennifer seated herself in her husband's carriage once again, she remembered vividly the very last occasion she had travelled through this part of the country. She was forced to accept the unpalatable fact that her situation now was no better than it had been then. If anything, it was considerably worse.

She glanced briefly across at her son, all eagerness to continue the journey after their overnight stay at the superior posting-house, before transferring her gaze to the man sitting on the seat beside him. The feeling that surged through her was decidedly hostile.

A choice he had offered her. Bitter resentment, corrosive as acid, coursed through her veins. What choice? There had been no choice! How could she be separated from the person who had become her whole life, even for the short time it might have taken her to come up with some idea to get him back? And it would certainly need to be a foolproof scheme, she reminded herself, for no court in the land would deny Wroxam sole custody of their son, if he chose to seek it. Yes, the law was most definitely on his side. Consequently, when she did attempt to effect her and her son's escape, she must face the fact that she would be doing so illegally. Therefore, it would mean that for the foreseeable future they would need to hide themselves away, perhaps in Europe.

Sadly no scheme had occurred to her as yet; not even after last night, when she had lain awake for hours considering her plight, and thinking about little Charles, under the watchful eye of his father, in the next room. Evidently Wroxam considered that she wasn't to be trusted. Which was most astute of him! She doubted that his vigilance would subside for some considerable time, so she would need to bide hers, and await her opportunity. In the meantime...

'Mama, why aren't Mary and Patrick travelling with us?'

The unexpected question forced Jennifer to abandon her schemes for the future, and she easily managed to smile across at the being who was her sole reason for living. She had wondered how long it would be before he queried both Mary and Patrick's absence; had wondered too just how much Wroxam had disclosed to his son during the evening and night they had spent together.

'I told you yesterday, Charles, before we set out, that Mary and Patrick would be going to London to collect my belongings from the house I have been using in the capital. They will follow in a few days.'

He appeared to accept this readily enough this time,

but she doubted his questions would stop there. Her son had always possessed an enquiring mind, so she was not in the least surprised to be asked, 'Will we be going back to Ireland after we've stayed in his lordship's house for a while, Mama?'

'You shall not be returning to Ireland, Charles. You are to make your home with me,' his lordship answered, before Jennifer could voice a non-committal response.

'Am I, sir?'

Seeking confirmation, Charles turned to her, but Jennifer found herself quite unable to assure him that this was so, when every fibre of her being recoiled at the mere idea of sharing a house with her husband again. Seemingly Wroxam sensed the war raging within, for he stared across at her, looking infuriatingly pleased with himself.

'Indeed, you are, my boy,' he said softly, his eyes never wavering from the lovely, taut features of his wife, 'because I wish it so.'

'Do you, sir? Why?'

A moment's silence, then, 'Because I am your father.'

If there had been a secret compartment beneath her seat, Jennifer would quite happily have made use of it, and hidden herself away. Was Wroxam determined to make her situation as uncomfortable as possible? Why in heaven's name could he not have waited a few days, or at least until they had discussed how best to break the news of his parentage to Charles? But no, he had had to go ahead and blurt it out that way, damn him! Little wonder poor Charles was looking so bewildered!

'But—but my papa is dead,' he announced, his

forehead puckering. 'Mama said so. He was a brave soldier. He died in Spain, didn't he, Mama?'

Jennifer could feel the noose of retribution slowly tightening about her throat. She raised her eyes, well expecting to see the man seated opposite still smugly smiling, thoroughly enjoying her discomfiture, and was surprised to discover what might have been a hint of sympathy lurking in grey depths.

'Your mama, like several others, assumed the worst when I went missing in Spain, but as you can see I managed to return unscathed. I shall tell you all about it one day, but not now.'

Jennifer couldn't have been more surprised. Julian had been in Spain…? Surely not!

Not knowing whether to believe him or not, she watched one shapely hand disappear into the pocket of the elegantly tailored jacket, and reappear a moment later clasping a delicately painted enamel snuffbox. Evidently the taking of snuff was a habit he had acquired during their years apart. The man was certainly full of surprises!

She transferred her attention to her son who, at that moment, appeared lost in admiration for the way his recently acquired sire opened the delicately painted lid with an expert flick of one long finger. Then, quite unexpectedly, she saw lines of disapproval furrow his young brow once again.

'Mama does not approve of gentlemen taking snuff,' Charles remarked, having quickly recognised the contents of the small box. 'She says it makes a mess everywhere, besides turning nostrils a horrid yellow.'

Jennifer didn't know how she managed to stop herself from laughing when long fingers checked in the act of extracting a pinch of the brownish-coloured powder. She doubted that Wroxam was accustomed to having his practices criticised, most especially by candid eight-year-old boys. How very disconcerting for the poor man!

'And shall I like living in your house, sir?' Charles asked, after watching the snuffbox, its contents untouched, being returned to his father's pocket.

'I sincerely hope you do, my son.'

'And is it a big house, with hundreds and hundreds of rooms?'

'Not quite hundreds, no. But it is certainly large enough for you to have a bedchamber of your own. Which, I might add, shall be situated farthest from my own, as you are fast proving to be an unconscionable gabble-monger.'

Charles was not slow to note the faint twitch at one corner of his father's mouth, but his impish chuckle was swiftly checked when his lordship laid his head against the velvet squabs and closed his eyes.

'Why are you going to sleep, sir? You've only just got out of bed.'

'I have not long left a bedchamber, true,' his lordship agreed, keeping his eyes firmly closed. 'But I attained precious little rest there. You even chatter in your sleep, my son.'

Charles turned an indignant little countenance towards his mother. 'I do not talk in my sleep, do I, Mama?'

'I have not frequently heard you, no,' she consoled him, ever the doting mother.

What he might have revealed when asleep was of little concern. What he might disclose during the days and weeks ahead most definitely was, but there was little she could do to prevent it, short of swearing him to secrecy. And that was something she would never do!

She had no wish for him to look upon his father as some kind of ogre in whom he could never confide. Not that she considered there was much chance of this ever occurring, at least not on the evidence of the past few hours. Early days they might be, but amazingly Wroxam was betraying all the signs of becoming a very considerate father. Charles had swiftly lost all vestige of shyness with him. Which, of course, was a good thing as far as her son was concerned, but which might prove disastrous for her, especially if he grew too fond of Wroxam.

'I'm sorry, Charles, what did you say?' she asked, suddenly realising that he had spoken.

'Why did those people back at the inn call you your la-ladyship, Mama?'

'They addressed me in that way because your father is a peer of the realm, Charles. He is a Marquis.'

He appeared to consider this for a moment. 'Am I a mar-marquis too?'

'Not yet, you're not,' a deep voice beside him answered. 'You will be one day. But not, I sincerely trust, for some considerable time to come.'

Charles turned back to his mother, his young forehead puckering again. 'Are you a lady Marquis, Mama?'

'My title is Marchioness.'

'Do Patrick and Mary know that you are a mar... mar—'

'Yes, they do.'

'And did Grandpapa James know too?'

'Yes, Charles. Grandpapa James knew.'

Jennifer looked across at the man opposite. His eyes remained firmly closed, but she knew he was digesting every word. No, she reiterated silently, there was little hope of keeping any part of her past secret from him now.

The coachman turned into Wroxam Park's eastern gateway midway through the afternoon, and as the carriage was brought to a halt outside the main entrance to the impressive Restoration mansion, which had once been her home, Jennifer reflected on just how much one's life can change in a matter of a mere twenty-four hours.

At this time yesterday she had been sitting in the garden of that comfortable little redbrick house she had hired in the country, happily passing an idyllic spring afternoon indulging in one of her favourite pastimes. She had felt perfectly contented, without a care in the world, and yet here she was now, about to take up residence again in the house which held such bittersweet memories, a house which she had never expected to set eyes on again.

Sublimely ignoring her husband's helping hand to alight, she stepped down from the carriage, and walked resolutely into the spacious hall, thankful that Charles was beside her. His excitement and demands to explore each and every room distracted his astute father's attention, preventing those shrewd grey eyes from studying his mother's physiognomy too closely.

After instructing the footman to find a maid to attend her ladyship, Julian turned his attention to Jennifer at last. 'It would appear that I shall be forced to deprive myself of your company, madam, as our son is determined to keep me fully occupied for the remainder of the afternoon, but I'm certain you remember your way about, and can find your way to your own room without the least trouble. We shall meet again at dinner.'

Even though she clearly detected the challenging note in his voice, Jennifer found herself crossing the hall. At the head of the wide sweeping staircase, she automatically turned along the gallery passageway towards the west wing. As she reached her old bedchamber, she paused for a moment before slowly pushing open the door and entering. Then she felt as if she had been transported back in time.

Astonishingly nothing had been touched, nothing had been changed: everything was exactly where she had left it. The silver-backed hairbrush, hand mirror and comb on the dressing table were precisely where she had placed them, beside the delicate crystal bottles which had once held her perfumes. It felt as if she had never been away, and yet she had been absent for more than eight long years, living a completely different lifestyle, where she had been expected to do her share of the work in the running of a house. And she had, enjoying every moment of it!

What, she wondered, throwing wide the delicately patterned drapes which had been left half-drawn across the windows, would she do with herself now that she was back here, against her will, perhaps, and forced to remain for the foreseeable future? What duties would she be expected to perform?

Her eyes suddenly strayed to the comfortable four-poster bed, and her blood ran cold. No, surely not that! Surely even *he* was not so inhuman as to expect her...

A scratch on the door interrupted the fearful conjecture, and she swung round to see a plump, fresh-faced young woman tentatively enter the room, carrying a pitcher of warm water.

'Begging your pardon, my lady, but I was instructed to wait upon you.'

Jennifer, regarding the new arrival keenly, frowned in an effort to remember. 'I do not believe I know you. You were not here before, surely?' she remarked a trifle disjointedly, her mind racing back over the years.

'No, my lady. I took my sister Daisy's place when she left to marry the local blacksmith five years back.'

'And what is your name?'

'Rose, your ladyship.'

Jennifer couldn't prevent a wry smile at the maid's automatic courtesy. Charles had remarked upon it during the journey, and she too had still not grown accustomed to being addressed again in such a fashion, even after all those weeks in London. Mary's presence was partly the reason for this: a constant reminder that she had lived a very different kind of life where courtesy titles had played no part. How she wished Mary were here now!

'Come on, Miss Jenny,' she had said, shortly before they had parted company the previous afternoon. 'Don't you be falling into one of your black moods now. To be sure that won't help at all. You've no choice but to go with the boy. That doesn't mean that you're beaten. Why, you're more than a match for that husband of yours, if you put your mind to it. Stand up to him, Miss Jenny! Don't give him the chance to break your spirit a second time.'

The memory of those parting words acted like a balm on her jangled nerves, forcing her to come to terms with her unfortunate predicament. She might have little choice but to remain here, but that didn't necessarily mean that she would need to kowtow to Wroxam's every whim. She might be every inch the loving mother; she was no longer the meek, obedient wife. Therefore she would never be coerced into performing the duties of one!

The arrival of her boxes certainly didn't deter her from this resolve, but did bring her mind back to the present. When the two footmen had left the room, she instructed Rose to help her unpack.

If the young maid thought it unusual for a lady of such high standing to demean herself by undertaking such a task, she certainly betrayed no sign of it. She wasn't, however, so successful in hiding a faint look of disappointment when she began to examine the contents of the boxes.

'What's the matter, Rose?' Jennifer asked, after noting the slightly disappointed look.

'Nothing, my lady, except…are you in mourning?'

Although she had been living something of a double life in recent weeks—the Marchioness of Wroxam in the capital; the young widow Mrs Stapleton at her rented country retreat—telling untruths didn't come easy to her. Necessity had forced her to keep her identity secret in past years, but now the reason for doing so had literally been taken from her, so there was no further inducement to lie.

'I have not suffered the loss of a close relative, Rose, but I did lose someone last autumn…someone I loved very much.'

The young maid's eyes betrayed a deal of sympathy, as she lifted the carefully folded black gown from the box. 'It would be quite in order for you to go in half-mourning now, my lady,' she suggested, after a moment's consideration. 'There's a pretty mauve gown, and another in pearl grey hanging in the wardrobe.'

'What?' Jennifer didn't attempt to conceal her astonishment before she flew across to the larger of the wardrobes and flung wide the doors to see the evidence with her own eyes. Unbelievably, all her clothes were still hanging there, where she had left them. But why?

She drew out one of the pretty gowns. Old fashioned and a little faded, the dress was one which had made up her trousseau. But why were they still here? The question again filtered through her mind, and she turned to the maid for enlightenment.

'Mrs Liddel insisted that nothing be touched, my lady. She saw to it that the room was swept every week without fail. And in the summer months the drapes were always drawn across the windows in the afternoons to protect the furnishings. It's been that way ever since I came here five years ago.'

Jennifer looked again about the room, this time studying everything in minute detail. The housekeeper might have instructed the maids to leave everything as it was, to treat everything with tender, loving care, but she received her orders from Wroxam. So why had he insisted that the room's contents be preserved? Had he been plagued by a guilty conscience after she had disappeared? Or was it simply that he had felt the need to enter this room from time to time and be reminded of how very foolish he had been in choosing such a faithless creature for a wife?

As though by a natural progression of thought, she

turned to the door which connected their respective bedchambers, and her eyes narrowed as she instantly perceived there was no key in the lock. But then, she reminded herself, that door had never been locked, at least not during the time she had lived in the house. His lordship was undeniably a virile man who had chosen to visit her frequently during those few short months of marriage. Much to her shame, she well remembered how she had welcomed his attentions. Thank the good Lord she had more sense now!

'I rather think, Rose,' she said, dragging her thoughts back to the matter of her dresses, 'that these gowns are no longer suitable for a woman of my advanced years to wear.' A wry smile touched her lips. 'Quite apart from the fact that I am somewhat fuller in the figure now, and would find them uncomfortably tight.' She chose not to add that wearing them would evoke too many painful memories, and that she needed no extra reminders of how very naïve, how very trusting—her eyes automatically strayed to the communicating door—and how very accommodating she had been in her youth.

Her natural thrifty nature coming to the fore, Rose abandoned the unpacking, and joined her mistress by the wardrobe. 'But, my lady, I could easily let out a little material about the bodice. Mrs Liddel has always praised my stitchwork. No one will know the gowns have been altered. I'll take care they will not!'

'I'm sure you would, Rose, but I would never dream of putting you to all that trouble when I have gowns enough.' She waved a hand in the general direction of the boxes on the floor. 'Those make up just a small part of my wardrobe. My maid shall be bringing the rest of my things from London in a few days.'

Jennifer tossed the gown she had been holding down on the bed, but not before she had observed Rose's suddenly crestfallen expression at mention of the personal maid. No doubt she had been hoping that the absent mistress's unexpected return to Wroxam Park would offer the opportunity of improving her lot. And perhaps Rose might be granted her wish if she proved to be both diligent and loyal.

'Mary's apron covers many duties, not just that of abigail, so I do not doubt she would appreciate some help from time to time,' Jennifer disclosed, thereby instantly restoring the young maid's hopeful expression. 'In the meantime, we'll remove these dresses… No, my mind is made up,' she went on, when Rose looked about to protest further. 'They are, however, too good to throw away. Share some amongst those of the household staff who can make use of them, and distribute the rest amongst the estate workers. I'm certain their female relatives will appreciate them.'

'I'm sure they will, my lady,' Rose reluctantly agreed, looking longingly at the array of beautiful gowns, knowing that she would never be able to squeeze her plump curves into any one of the dresses, no matter how many alterations she made.

'Never mind, Rose,' Jennifer consoled, easily reading the young servant's thoughts. 'If my memory serves me correctly, there is a rather voluminous fur-lined cloak in the other wardrobe. You may have that. By the by,' she went on, interrupting the young servant's heartfelt thanks, 'do you happen to know where my son is now?'

'I believe he's in the nursery, my lady, happily playing with the toy soldiers his lordship had when he was a boy.' She gave a sudden start. 'Oh, I almost forgot…his lordship's compliments, and would you join him in the dining-parlour at six for dinner?'

How very cosy! Jennifer thought, but said, betraying her consideration for the servants, 'I sincerely hope our unexpected arrival has not caused you all too many problems, especially not Mrs Quist.'

'Oh, Cook is still in London, my lady, with Mrs Liddel and Mr Slocombe. I think I overheard one of the footmen mention that his lordship has already sent a message to instruct Mr Slocombe to close the town house, and return here at once.'

Jennifer paused in the act of helping Rose remove the clothes from the wardrobes. 'In that case, after we've placed these in another chamber, where you can sort through them at your leisure, remind me to pay a visit to the kitchen, just to assure whoever is preparing dinner not to concern herself unduly over the menu,' she remarked, once again betraying her consideration for others.

By the time Jennifer descended the impressive wooden staircase early that evening, there wasn't a servant in the house who didn't consider her a gracious and considerate mistress. Having had her hair arranged by Rose in a simple yet very becoming style, she looked every inch the mistress of the house, serene and supremely contented. Nothing, however, could have been further from the truth. There was no place in the length and breadth of the land where she would less wish to be. Her thoughts in turmoil, she was dreading the forthcoming meeting with the master of the house, and fearing what might be demanded of her in return for the privilege of remaining under his roof.

Somehow she managed to smile her thanks to the young footman who opened the door for her, but the curl on her lips swiftly faded when she saw the tall, erect figure standing by the dining-parlour window, staring out across the park.

Grudgingly she was forced to own that he was always immaculately attired, and this evening was no exception. His impeccably cut jacket of dark blue superfine fitted like a glove, emphasising the breadth of superb shoulders, and the equally well-made breeches did little to conceal the muscular strength of those long, straight legs.

She was, however, in no mood to appreciate a fine physique and, seemingly, neither was he in a mood to admire the neatness of her appearance, for he turned the instant the footman had closed the door and commented,

'I see you have not chosen to dispense with the mourning attire, Mrs—er—Stapleton.'

She forced herself to return that sardonic gaze. 'I have grown accustomed to widowhood, Wroxam. It offers a woman such freedom.'

His eyes narrowed fractionally, but his voice contained the same amused drawl as he remarked, 'I could have wished that you had bestowed a higher rank on me than mere major when you chose mentally to dispose of me six feet beneath the earth... A colonel at the very least!'

One finely arched brow rose. 'Why aim so low? Why not a general?'

'Oh, no, my dear. All the generals I know are old and infirm, and a mite too fond of their port and brandy if their rosy noses are any indication.'

Her smile could not have been sweeter. 'Give it

time, Wroxam, and I'm certain you'll be taken for one of their number.'

There was a definite twitch at the corner of his mouth, as he moved round the table, but before he could reach her chair, she had seated herself and was shaking out her napkin.

The entrance of the footman, bearing a large tureen, succeeded in bringing the banter to an abrupt end, but the instant their soup had been served his lordship dismissed the servant with a nod and instructions that he would ring when he wished him to return to serve the second course.

'I thought you would feel more comfortable in here,' he ventured when Jennifer, appreciating the tasty broth, never offered to speak. 'The large dining-room is a little impersonal, and I had no intention of making myself hoarse by attempting to hold a conversation down its long length.'

Reluctantly she raised her eyes from the contents of her bowl. Evidently he was in a talkative mood. She could not recall his being quite so garrulous during meal times. One might be forgiven for supposing that age had mellowed him, made him more amenable, but she wasn't prepared to delude herself. Wroxam was like a wild animal, dangerous, unpredictable; always alert, just waiting to strike out at the unwary.

'We always ate our meals together in here,' she reminded him, 'never in the dining-room.'

'Is that so?' For a moment he appeared surprised before his gaze noticeably hardened. 'As your memory is so acute, perhaps you can remember why you quite failed to inform me that you were with child before you chose to disappear off the face of the earth?'

With that one rapier-like barb he had changed from pleasant dinner companion into ruthless inquisitor. How right she had been not to drop her guard! she mused, returning that hard-eyed gaze with slightly raised brows and a faintly contemptuous smile.

'And would you have believed it was yours, if I had happened to conveniently remember?'

Beneath the strong cheekbones his face paled, and the muscles along the powerful jaw grew taut. Her counter-thrust had hit its mark, and yet Jennifer gained little satisfaction from the knowledge that his armour was not impenetrable after all, and that he could be wounded just like anyone else.

Surprisingly enough she found herself experiencing compassion, but quickly suppressed it. Heaven only knew she had no wish to hurt him! None the less, betraying any weakness would not help her cause. If she were to tell him the absolute truth would he understand, might it lead to a cessation of hostilities between them for the short period she might be forced to remain? she wondered, before she recalled that it had availed her nothing almost nine years ago when she had been scrupulously honest in those letters she had written him.

Sighing, she placed the spoon in her bowl, suddenly finding the soup no longer to her taste. 'Would you believe me if I told you that I didn't realise I was with child when I left you?' she asked hurriedly, before she could change her mind.

Patently he did not; the swift rise of decidedly mocking brows was proof enough of this, even before he said, 'Were you so ignorant, then, of the workings of your own body?'

She refused to allow his decidedly sceptical tone to irritate her. 'Might I remind you, Wroxam, that I was only sixteen years old. My mother died when I was ten. These are facts. Even you cannot refute them. I had no one to instruct me on what I might expect to happen, or why, once I became a wife.'

He was looking merely thoughtful now, as though he were silently acknowledging that there was some truth in what she had said, and she didn't hesitate to thrust home her advantage. 'If anyone ought to have known that I was with child, then it was you, Wroxam. You are ten years my senior. And, at the time, you were vastly more experienced than I was.'

In normal circumstances she would never have dreamt of discussing such a topic, especially with a member of the opposite sex. This, however, she silently reminded herself, was no time to be missish or fainthearted. 'Did it never once cross your mind to wonder why I began to miss my monthly?'

'*Touché*, madam!' he exclaimed, gallantly acknowledging this valid point. 'My only excuse, I suppose, is that I did, if my memory serves me correctly, make several trips to London during the months following our marriage.'

The slight curl which instantly appeared on her lips was a masterly display of contempt, but in this instance he considered it completely unjustified. 'Might I remind you, madam, that it was not I who proved to be unfaithful in our short marriage.'

'There is absolutely no need to remind me, Wroxam. It is something I am never likely to forget, even though the reason why I erred will no doubt always remain a mystery to me.'

He frowned in puzzlement, as he watched her rise from the table and go across to the window, wondering precisely what she had meant, but the shout of bitter laughter which suddenly filled the room thrust the desire for an explanation from his mind.

'It is ironic, is it not, that had my son been blessed with blue eyes and golden locks, neither of us would have been allowed to set one foot across this threshold. No amount of assurances on my part would ever have convinced you that I was already carrying your child when I rode out with Geoffrey Wilburn on that fateful afternoon.'

'Perhaps it is fortunate then that no assurances are necessary,' he countered, 'and that I have accepted Charles as my own at face value, as it were.'

'Yes, damn you!' She swung round, eyes blazing, revealing for the first time in his presence that she had not been blessed with that fiery head for no reason. 'How could you not? You would have needed to be blind not to have known at once that he's the fruit of your own loins!'

She turned back to stare sightlessly out of the window, ashamed now that she had allowed his flippancy to goad her into a rare display of temper. 'If you suppose for a moment that it gave me any pleasure to see Charles grow yearly more in your image, you delude yourself. And if you imagine I kept his existence a secret from you out of spite, some petty form of revenge, then you could not be more wrong.'

The fist he brought down hard on the table, sending crockery and glasses clattering, was evidence enough of his own rising ire, as was his voice which cracked through the air like a whip. 'Damn it woman, then why?'

Even in her own highly tense state Jennifer could appreciate that his anger was totally excusable. No matter how she tried to explain it, no matter how justified she believed her own actions had been, the fact remained that she had denied her husband the joys of parenthood for eight long years; and, worse, she had tried to deprive her son of his birthright. Yes, she silently conceded, that had been the hardest decision she had been forced to make; and, yes, perhaps she had been wrong. As for the rest...

She could not prevent a further heartfelt sigh escaping. 'Because I wanted my son to enjoy a happy childhood.'

'And what made you suppose that he would not have attained just that by living here?' he countered with lightning speed, his tone intractable, but she refused to be cowed. She may have been wrong, cruel even, to have denied him all knowledge of his son's existence. Nevertheless, she had believed that she had had no other choice.

'And just what kind of life, Wroxam, could Charles have hoped to have living under this roof? Oh, yes, he would have been cosseted by an army of servants, and given everything money could buy,' she went on without granting him the opportunity to answer, 'but he would have been forced to pass his childhood years in an atmosphere charged with animosity and contempt, where his parents could hardly bring themselves to speak to each other and lived quite separate lives.' Her chin lifted in open defiance. 'Well, he may have been denied many material things, including his title, but at least he was blessed to live in a house where love and mutual respect abounded. And I can never be sorry that I ensured that at least the first eight years of his life were happy.'

'And they shall continue to be so,' Julian assured her after a moment's silence, and sounding so determined, so wholly sincere, that she almost found herself believing him.

'I'm not totally insensitive, Jennifer, no matter what you may think. Nor am I blind,' he went on. 'It took me a short time only to realise that there is a strong loving bond between you and our son. Which is very understandable in the circumstances, and I have no intention of attempting to thrust a wedge between you, now or in the future. Our son's welfare is my prime concern, and that is precisely why I offered you the opportunity of returning here.'

If he expected a declaration of gratitude, then he was doomed to disappointment, and when at last she raised her eyes, all that was discernible in their striking green depths was a strong element of suspicion.

'And what, pray, will you expect of me in return for this rare altruistic gesture of yours? What will be my position in this house?'

'Quite naturally you shall resume your role as its mistress.' He reached for his glass, his gaze becoming noticeably harder as he studied her above its rim. 'It goes without saying that I shall expect you to behave with the utmost propriety at all times.' His voice had hardened too. 'Woe betide you, madam wife, if you should bring disgrace to the name you bear a second time!'

Her reaction again was not quite what he might have expected, and he detected precious little humour in the sudden burst of laughter which echoed round the room.

'So, I may not discredit the proud Stapleford name, but you, no doubt, will continue to do so with all the masculine verve you have displayed for the past nine years.' Raw contempt replaced the suspicion in her eyes. 'Very well, Wroxam, I shall abide by your terms, for they suit me very nicely. I shall manage your house, and run it, I sincerely hope, just as you would wish. But that is all.'

Receiving no response, she turned once again to contemplate the view beyond the window. 'I have already taken steps to ensure my—er—privacy. I paid a visit to the kitchens earlier, and took the opportunity whilst there of discovering the whereabouts of the keys to my room. I was successful in my endeavours, and the door connecting our adjoining bedchambers is now locked…and shall remain so for as long as I reside under this roof.'

She distinctly heard the sound of the glass being placed none too gently back down on the table, but it was already too late. In three giant strides Julian had covered the distance which had separated them and, before she could take steps to avoid it, had imprisoned her in his arms. She had a momentary glimpse of the determined set of his mouth, before it clamped over hers, hard and bruising at first, and then unexpectedly gentle, parting her lips and winning the response she seemed incapable of denying.

There was an unmistakable note of triumph in the deep rumble of laughter, after he had raised his head and released his hold, a taunting reminder, had she needed one, that she was not complete mistress of her emotions where her wholly masculine husband was concerned.

'I do not think, madam wife, that you are as indifferent to me as you would have me believe,' he announced, thereby increasing her mortification at her own weakness. 'But no matter.' He lowered his eyes, gazing with a knowledgeable intimacy at the rise and fall of her breasts. 'A hundred locked doors wouldn't succeed in keeping me from you if I wished to avail myself of your charms. But you need harbour no fears on that score.'

He moved swiftly back to the table, as though her nearness was suddenly abhorrent to him. 'Now that that is clearly understood, let us continue with our meal.'

Resisting the urge to flee from the room, Jennifer gathered together the shreds of her dignity and joined him at the table. It was one thing to be told that one might rest easy in one's bed at night, and quite another to discover that one need not have troubled to take precautions to achieve this objective in the first place.

Chapter Six

Jennifer paused in the letter she was writing to admire the pleasing aspect from the window. Wroxam had willingly acquiesced to her request to be granted this small room at the back of the house for her own private use, a place where she could write her letters, or just sit quietly and contemplate life. And she had been given plenty to think about during the month she had been back at Wroxam Park, not least of which had been the behaviour of its master.

Loath though she might be to credit her husband with any of the finer feelings, she was forced to concede that his behaviour towards her had been exemplary; the perfect gentleman, in fact, solicitous to her every need. Of course they didn't see a great deal of each other. When he wasn't busily engaged with his secretary or steward, discussing estate matters, he spent much of his free time with their son. Except during those few days the week before, when he had paid a short visit to the capital, he had made a point of riding out across the estate with Charles every morning, weather permitting.

She could not prevent a sigh escaping. Daily she

had watched her son growing more attached to his sire, but there had been little she could have done to prevent its happening; and, truth to tell, she wasn't so very certain that, even if it had been within her power, she would have attempted to stop a bond developing between them.

Understandably enough there were certain aspects of her enforced stay which continued to irk her unbearably. Wroxam had decreed that if she chose to stay away for any length of time without first obtaining his consent, she would not be allowed to return. Furthermore, she could not set foot outside the door with Charles to enjoy a pleasant walk in the garden without discovering a servant hovering nearby.

The staff, of course, were faultlessly obeying their master's strict instructions. And it was intolerable! Yet, she could hardly blame Wroxam for keeping a close guard on Charles, for if the truth were known, she would still leave with her son if the chance ever presented itself, and if she had somewhere to go; somewhere to hide where she could be certain Wroxam would not find them.

In the meantime she was forced to be satisfied with her lot which, she couldn't deny, was not too much of a hardship. The servants treated her with the utmost respect, and the kindness of the older members of staff, those who had worked in the house when she had first crossed the threshold as a naïve young bride, was very touching, most especially the deference Slocombe always showed towards her; as recompense, no doubt, for barring her entry to the town house all those years ago. Yes, all in all, she had little cause to complain, and now that her loyal confidante Mary was firmly established under this roof, she was not without feminine companionship and unwavering support.

The subject of her thoughts entered the room a moment later to remind her that she had promised to go through the following week's menus with Cook after luncheon.

Jennifer consulted the ormolu clock on the mantel-shelf. 'Good gracious, is that the time! I do not know where the morning has gone to. I think I shall eat my luncheon with Charles in the nursery today.'

Mary suddenly appeared to find the toe of her right shoe of immense interest. 'I don't think that's such a good idea. Master Charles is feeling a mite sorry for himself at the moment.'

'Oh?' Jennifer paused in the tidying of her writing-desk to cast an enquiring glance over her shoulder. 'Did Wroxam not return in time from his inspection of the cottages to take Charles out for his ride?'

'Oh, his lordship returned right enough. A little later than expected, but he did return. One must give the man his due, he does keep his promises,' Mary acknowledged, betraying a grudging respect for the Marquis. 'Trouble was, Master Charles decided he couldn't wait, and rode off by himself.'

Jennifer experienced a moment's alarm. 'He didn't take a tumble, did he? He isn't hurt?'

'He didn't take a tumble, no,' Mary assured her. 'And the little monkey wouldn't have ventured out by himself at all if Patrick had been about, but Pat had accompanied his lordship.' Her expression betrayed a distinct lack of sympathy. 'Well, you've told Master Charles often enough that he's not to go off by himself, so the truth of the matter is he's only himself to blame.'

'Yes, yes, you're right,' Jennifer was forced to agree, knowing that she would now need to speak sternly to her son, something which she always hated doing. She sighed. 'I suppose I must punish him by forbidding him to go riding for a day or two.'

Mary was not at all successful in suppressing a chuckle. 'Oh, there's no need for you to be worrying yourself over that. I don't think Master Charles will wish to sit on a horse for a while.'

Jennifer was instantly suspicious. 'Whatever do you mean?'

'Well, I don't know all the details, you understand, but from what I can gather from Annie, the nurse-maid—when his lordship arrived back and discovered Master Charles had ridden out, he went in search of him. He found him, no problem, over by the home wood, and by the time his lordship had finished with him, Master Charles couldn't ride, and was forced to walk back to the house, feeling very sorry for himself.'

It took Jennifer a moment only to appreciate fully what she had been told. 'Do you mean that Wroxam had the audacity to beat my son?'

Mary watched the colour fade completely from the delicate features, and then return with a vengeance. She knew perhaps better than anyone else that the lovely Marchioness, although very level-headed and placid as a rule, was quite capable of losing her temper on occasions. Before she could attempt to reason with her, however, to suggest that maybe young Charles had now reached an age when a firmer hand was necessary, Jennifer had stormed from the room and was heading across the hall in the direction of the library.

Without knocking she threw wide the door, and swept into the room in a swirl of pale green petticoats to discover his lordship precisely where she had expected to find him, seated behind his desk, going through his correspondence with his secretary. Not even by the raising of one of those expressive brows did he betray the least surprise, or annoyance, come to that, at the rude interruption; he merely turned to his secretary announcing that they would continue after luncheon.

Julian waited for Mr Aubrey to leave the room, which he did with alacrity and, it had to be said, with a deal more dignity than her ladyship had shown when entering it. Then he fixed his faintly amused gaze on the avenging virago standing on the opposite side of the desk, fists clenched, appearing as though she could quite cheerfully have unleashed her wrath in a physical attack upon him.

After contemplating the neat arrangement of auburn locks, he lowered his gaze to the stormy green eyes. It was abundantly obvious what had brought her here in such a fine fury, and he resisted the temptation to feign ignorance. 'I believe I know why you're here, Jennifer. Perhaps you would care to sit down so that we can discuss the—'

'How dare you!' she interrupted, the faint amusement playing about his mouth fuelling the furnace of her wrath. 'How dare you lay violent hands on my child!'

'Our child,' he corrected gently and, leaning back in his chair, he regarded her in silence for a moment. Like the proverbial she-wolf, Jennifer was a fiercely protective mother. 'I would be the first to admit that you have done a remarkable job in rearing our son on your own, Jennifer. He's a fine boy. If you have been lax in any department, then I suspect it has been a reluctance to discipline him when the need arose.'

'Oh, for heaven's sake!' she exclaimed, not allowing this unexpected praise to sway her. 'He's a boy. He's bound to get into mischief from time to time.'

'True,' he agreed, urbanity itself. 'But had I done what Charles did, I would have felt a birch rod and not the flat of my father's hand across the seat of my breeches.'

She found her gaze instinctively straying to those long fingers gripping the arms of the chair. His hands were elegant and sensitive, like those of an artist, but also strong, and attached to undeniably powerful arms. She found herself wincing at the mere thought of what poor little Charles must have suffered, and raised her eyes to discover him regarding her rather quizzically, as though he knew precisely what had been passing through her mind.

Her chin lifted. 'Then I consider that your father was unnecessarily brutal, and your mother a rare sort of creature to permit her child to be so ill used. I am not of that ilk. And I shall tell you plainly that I've no intention of sitting idly by and allowing you to break my son's spirit.'

'I've no intention of breaking his spirit. Nor, I might add, have I the least intention of allowing him to break his foolish little neck, if I can do anything to prevent it.'

Jennifer regarded him in astonishment, deciding that he must have taken leave of his senses. The aged mare he permitted Charles to ride was incapable of maintaining even a sedate trot. 'Wroxam, really!' she scoffed. 'Old Bessie is the most placid of creatures. I doubt she has ever attempted to unseat her rider.'

'She hasn't,' he readily confirmed, swiftly realising that she was only in possession of half the facts. 'Evidently you're not aware, however, that our foolhardy son attempted to practise his equestrian skills this morning on quite a different animal.'

Although she had thus far declined her husband's invitation to avail herself of one of his hacks, she had frequently paid visits to the stables, and had cast an expert eye over each of the fine specimens he kept there.

A frightening possibility suddenly occurred to her. 'Oh, no! You don't mean he attempted to ride that grey hunter of yours?'

'It is indeed a foolish mother who does not know her own son.' A flicker of admiration added a sparkle to his grey eyes. 'And no one, my dear, could ever accuse you of that failing.'

Fearing her legs would no longer support her, Jennifer made use of the chair recently vacated by Mr Aubrey, silently conceding that there had been some justification for Wroxam's actions.

She sighed and shook her head. 'I suppose I must take my share of the blame for what happened.'

'You are not suggesting, I hope, that you actively encouraged him to disobey my orders by riding the grey.'

'Of course I did not! And I'd like to know what your servants were about to saddle the brute for him.'

'Merely following instructions, my dear.' His smile was faintly sardonic. 'Our enterprising young son informed the head groom that I wished the grey saddled in readiness to accompany him out upon my return.

The moment the groom's back was turned, Charles led the grey to the mounting block, and was riding out of the yard before anyone could stop him.'

There was more than just a hint of regret in his deep sigh. 'I do not enjoy the role of heavy-handed father. I know he's bound to get into mischief from time to time, and it is my place to discipline him. Nevertheless, I believe he'll be less inclined to indulge in foolish starts if his mind is suitably occupied. So, I have decided to engage a tutor for him, someone who will not only prepare him for school, but will endeavour to nurture his love of outdoor pursuits.'

Jennifer found little difficulty in setting aside her own lingering resentment towards the man seated opposite when discussing the matter of their son. Wroxam's proposal sounded ideal. 'And know you of such a person?'

'No, but Aubrey suggested that a friend from his university days might be exactly the young man I'm looking for. Apparently, this friend wishes to study law, but until he attains the age of five-and-twenty, and comes into a legacy left by a maiden aunt, he has not the funds to pursue his chosen career. In the meantime he must earn his living, and according to Aubrey is considering teaching as an option. If you're agreeable I'll write to him.'

She did not need to think twice about it. 'Strangely enough I was seriously considering engaging a governess for him. Perhaps you're aware that I taught Charles myself, but since James's death I'm forced to own that I have been sadly neglectful.' She swiftly found herself the object of an intense gaze. 'Surely you've learned all about James O'Connell by now? I felt sure Charles would have told you all about our life in Ireland.'

The fact that she evidently thought that he would stoop so low as to interrogate their son to discover what she had been up to during their years apart both hurt and annoyed him, but he succeeded in keeping all emotion from his voice as he said, 'Charles has on more than one occasion mentioned a Grandpapa James who, I assume, is this James O'Connell of whom you speak. I also know that O'Connell was a successful horse breeder. But that is all I know.' He found no difficulty in returning her faintly sceptical gaze. 'I have no intention now or at any time in the future of interrogating our son in order to discover how you have spent the past nine years... I would prefer to learn about it from you.'

Whether she believed him or not was difficult to judge, for she merely shrugged slender shoulders before rising to her feet and moving across to the window. She was silent for so long that he thought that he was destined to remain in ignorance, but then she said very softly,

'There is not much to tell.' Statue-like, she continued to stare out of the window, seeing, he suspected, quite a different aspect in her mind's eye. 'When Mary and I arrived in Ireland our money was almost gone. It had been our intention to make our way up country to the home of Mary's parents. Needless to say we never reached the Harpers' humble cottage in County Clare. By the third day we had no money, not even for food. Which did not trouble me overmuch. What little I had eaten during the previous days I had not managed to keep down. Foolishly I imagined that it was merely a combination of lack of food and exhaustion which caused me to collapse by the roadside that evening. Mary, having been far more worldly wise than I, guessed at once.

'Fate chose to look kindly upon me that day,' she continued, her voice soft, her thoughts seemingly locked in the past. 'The occupant of a passing carriage, observing my distress, ordered his coachman to stop. The good Samaritan who offered aid was none other than James O'Connell. He took us both back to his house, and sent for the doctor, who later confirmed Mary's suspicions.'

'And he took care of you all these years?' Julian prompted, when she fell silent once more.

'I think it would be more accurate to say that we took care of each other. At the time James happened to be looking for someone to take the place of his elderly cook-housekeeper, and I was more than willing to take up the position in exchange for a roof over my head. In the end Mary and I shared the duties.'

He noticed the wry smile tugging at the corner of her mouth before she added, 'Those many occasions I ventured into the kitchen during my formative years, and later here with Mrs Quist, were not in vain. I proved to be very skilful in the kitchen. At least my culinary skills satisfied James. Thankfully he was a man of simple tastes.

'As you are aware, James was a very successful horse breeder, but he was not wealthy, at least not by your standards. His home was little more than a large farmhouse, comfortable, but not sumptuously furnished. He was an astute man, and realised almost at once that I wasn't the simple soldier's widow I pretended to be. After a few weeks, during which time I had grown inordinately fond of him, and had learned to trust him implicitly, I did eventually confide in him. James wished to make contact with you, to inform you of my whereabouts, but I would not hear of it. As far as I was concerned our marriage was at an end. I had a new life, and one that I found infinitely more rewarding.'

Julian found himself grasping the arms of the chair so tightly that his knuckles showed white. Harsh words, indeed; none the less, beautifully candid. Although torn between anger and grudging respect, he failed completely to keep sarcasm out his voice as he remarked,

'So you preferred the life of a kitchen-wench to that of a Marchioness… How very singular!'

'Yet very understandable,' she parried. 'James, you see, had been a widower for many years. I believe he swiftly came to look upon me as the daughter he had never been blessed to have, and he treated Charles like a grandson. For eight wonderful years I felt perfectly contented; was protected and loved. James O'Connell was the finest man I have ever known. He taught me so many things. Most of all he taught me to be myself. He died last autumn… And I shall never meet his like again.'

There had been an unmistakable catch in her voice, and when she turned away from the window and walked slowly towards the door, Julian knew she had been on the verge of tears. It occurred to him then that he had never once seen her cry.

He was destined not to do so now, for although she kept her face averted, she sounded perfectly composed as she said, 'If you will excuse me, I shall go to the stables and see Patrick. I know you have been looking for a suitable mount for Charles to ride, but there's no need. I'll ask Patrick to return to Ireland and collect Charles's pony.'

'Does that mean you are now resigned to remaining here?' He saw the slender hand reaching out for the door-handle check for a moment. 'You have only to give me your word, Jennifer, that you'll not attempt to leave with Charles, and the restrictions placed upon you will—'

'No, Wroxam,' she interrupted softly. 'I have never lied to you, and I have no intention of starting now. My arranging for Charles's pony to be brought here is merely an attempt to keep my son out of mischief, and for no other reason.'

Without waiting for a response, Jennifer withdrew. Closing the door quietly behind her, she crossed the hall and left the house by way of the front entrance. As she made her way along the path, she was quite unaware that a pair of troubled grey eyes were following her progress along the path towards the stables, where she discovered Patrick being berated by the woman who had shared so many of her past experiences, both happy and sad.

'Why, you traitor, you!' Mary exclaimed, hands on hips. 'I never thought I'd live to see the day when you'd turn against Miss Jenny.'

Patrick paused in the grooming of one of Jennifer's fine carriage horses to look across at Mary, with that roughish, crooked smile which had melted the heart of more than one pretty colleen over the years, but which had never appeared to have had the least effect on her, and instantly perceived the slender figure in the doorway.

'Did you hear that now, mistress…? 'Tis a traitor

I'm being called. And me the most loyal man who ever drew breath!'

After resorting to her mother tongue in order to utter something most indelicate in response, Mary swept out of the stable, leaving Patrick to follow her stalking progress across the yard with his eyes, and Jennifer to detect a certain look in them which she had never noticed there before. The truth hit her with stunning clarity. He was in love with Mary! Why in heaven's name had she never realised that until now? Was she so obtuse, so blind that she never saw what was going on right under her very nose?

'Well, mistress, I can guess why you're here.' Patrick transferred his gaze from Mary's retreating form to Jennifer's slightly troubled expression, his blue eyes still smiling, but now lacking that special glow. 'Have you come here to tear a strip off me for not protecting that precious son o' yours from his father's wrath?'

He was nothing if not direct, Jennifer mused. That was perhaps why she had always liked and trusted him, even though his reputation where the fair sex was concerned was not precisely stainless. Their association, however, had been somewhat different.

'It was not your place to interfere, Patrick,' she pointed out.

'That's true enough. Though I might have done so had I thought his lordship were enjoying the exercise.' There was a faint rasping sound as he rubbed long fingers back and forth across his chin. ''Tis true I've been thinking that a man who can care so much for the boy, and have such a way with beasts, cannot be all bad.'

Undoubtedly his lordship had risen in this bold

Irishman's estimation during the few short weeks they had been at Wroxam Park. No mean feat as Patrick's respect was not easily won!

'I didn't come here to discuss this morning's unfortunate occurrence,' she told him, swiftly channelling her thoughts to the matter in hand, 'but to ask you whether you would care to return to Ireland to collect Charles's pony?'

It occurred to Jennifer then that she didn't treat Patrick like a servant either. She had no difficulty in issuing orders where Wroxam's staff were concerned, but her relationship with both Patrick and Mary had always been different. In Ireland their close association had seemed perfectly in order. She had done her share of the work, and had found it quite natural to look upon them both as colleagues and friends. Here, of course, everything was different. Whether she liked it or not her position had changed. She was once again a lady of consequence, albeit a reluctant marchioness, and she wouldn't care to be seen showing more consideration to certain members of the household. That, she told herself silently, could quite easily lead to a certain amount of resentment and ill feeling amongst the members of staff.

'To be sure, it'll be a pleasure to be away from this heathen country if only for a short time,' Patrick answered, once again bringing Jennifer back to the present. 'Be it just the pony you'll be wanting me to bring, mistress? Or is it *himself* you be wanting too…? He'll 'ave missed you, I'm thinking.'

A look not unlike that which had fleetingly glinted in Patrick's eyes minutes before flickered now in her own. 'And I have missed him… Yes, Pat, bring my baby too.'

The sound of hooves on cobblestones captured her attention, and Jennifer turned to see a footman leading a chestnut mare, with a lady's saddle upon its back, into the stable-yard. Evidently they had a visitor. A rare event indeed! Only Colonel Halstead and his wife had paid a visit to the house since her return, which was perfectly understandable in the circumstances. The majority of their neighbours were still in town enjoying the delights of the Season. None the less, she couldn't help wondering whether Wroxam himself had not dissuaded any would-be callers.

'Come to the house when you're ready to leave, Pat, and I'll provide you with funds.'

She left him then to make the necessary preparations, and went directly back into the house to be told by Slocombe that Mrs Royston had called, and that his lordship wished her to join them in the parlour.

Jennifer's initial impulse was to ignore the request and seek sanctuary in her bedchamber, but she curbed it. She had no desire to see the woman who had witnessed her shame all those years ago, but knew she couldn't avoid a meeting indefinitely. Melissa Royston and Julian had been friends since childhood, and his nearest neighbour had always been a regular visitor to the house. At the back of her mind memory stirred, and Jennifer vaguely recalled Julian mentioning that Melissa had travelled to Italy several weeks ago to visit her brother Geoffrey. It was safe to assume that, now she was back under her own roof again, she would resume her regular visits to this house.

Tapping into that deep well of fortitude which her dear protector James O'Connell had managed to instil in her during their years together, she walked resolutely into the room to find the half-sister of the man who had had such a devastating effect on her young life sitting serenely on the sofa, sipping a glass of Madeira. At first glance Melissa Royston seemed little changed. She was as slender as she had been nine years before, and her lovely black hair had lost none of its shine. As Jennifer drew a little closer, however, she clearly detected the faint harsh lines about the mouth before the full lips curled into a mechanical smile, quite devoid of warmth.

'Jennifer, my dear! I could hardly believe it when Colonel Halstead informed me this very morning of your return. Where on earth have you been hiding yourself all these years, silly child?'

'Hardly a child any longer, Mrs Royston,' Jennifer responded, swiftly deciding there had been precious little affection in the kiss Melissa had placed upon her cheek; merely a token gesture, nothing more.

'No, perhaps not,' Melissa agreed, re-seating herself, but not before her dark eyes had subjected the younger woman to a swift assessing glance. 'But need we be so formal, my dear? After all, we used to be such good friends.'

Had they? Jennifer wondered. If so, she chose her friends with rather more care these days. Nevertheless, she had no intention of being inhospitable, even though she strongly suspected that Melissa was not so overjoyed by her unexpected return as she was trying to appear.

'Can I tempt you to a glass of Madeira, Jennifer?' Julian asked, and at her nod of assent went over to the decanters. 'I believe I did mention that Melissa has been visiting Geoffrey in Italy.'

As he handed her the wine he searched her face in

vain for any sign of distress at mention of her ex-lover's name. It seemed almost as though she had forgotten his very existence, or had successfully blotted all thoughts of him from her mind.

'Sadly I found him most unwell,' Melissa informed them, after watching her childhood friend seat himself beside his wife on the other sofa. 'He was always a sickly child, never strong, as you may remember, Julian. He went to live abroad shortly after—several years ago,' she corrected, and Jennifer could not help wondering if the sudden check had been quite deliberate.

'I'm sorry to hear that he is unwell,' she responded, aware that her husband's eyes remained firmly fixed on her profile.

'I'm afraid it is consumption. We thought that the warmer climate would benefit his health, and for a short period it seemed to do just that. Time and time again I've written to him, trying to persuade him to return here. But, of course, he won't, not after what happened between you and him, and the disgrace of it all… He still paints, however. You may remember, Jennifer, that art was his ruling passion.'

She did remember very well. It was strange, though, that she retained no memory whatsoever of their one and only illicit coupling. 'I do, indeed,' she responded, refusing to betray the fact that she found the conversation more than just a little disturbing. 'And possessed a certain aptitude, as I recall.'

'Yes, indeed,' Melissa agreed, her gaze alternating between Julian's impassive countenance and his wife's faintly concerned expression. 'He has managed to live quite comfortably on the money he has earned from his paintings. But let us not discuss Geoffrey.'

Once again her lips curled into a smile which no-where near touched the dark eyes. 'I understand you have a son, Jennifer. May I be permitted to make his acquaintance?'

'Of course you may, Melissa,' Julian responded swiftly, as he clearly detected the faint tightening of slender white fingers about the stem of a glass. 'But not today. I'm afraid he's in disgrace.'

'Oh, dear! Suddenly discovering yourself to be a father has not proved all joy then, Julian,' Melissa teased, with a tinkling laugh which sounded distinctly forced, at least to Jennifer's ears.

'On the contrary, fatherhood is very much to my liking.' His lordship then changed the subject, and was successful in keeping the conversation well clear of any topics which might cause the lady beside him further disquiet, until Melissa announced that it was time to take her leave.

He was more than willing to acquiesce to her re-quest to accompany her out to the stables, though he could have wished that she had refrained from pos-sessively wrapping her arm round his before they had left the room.

As they entered the hall they encountered Mary, emerging from the back parlour. With the possible exception of his wife, to whom she was quite touch-ingly devoted, Mary never displayed the least defer-ence to anyone. So it came as no surprise to Julian when she subjected the woman clinging to his right arm like a limpet to one of those bold, assessing dark-eyed stares. What she appeared to see evidently did not please her overmuch, for she frowned dourly and muttered something in Gaelic before quickly mount-ing the stairs.

'Who was that insolent creature, Julian?' Melissa demanded to know the instant they had stepped outside. 'Not a servant of yours, surely?'

'She isn't strictly speaking a servant, Melissa. For want of something better to call her, I suppose you might say she is my wife's companion.'

'You must be mellowing with age, Julian. I wonder you tolerate such a brazen-faced creature in your household,' Melissa commented.

He found himself very much resenting her tone. 'I tolerate her because she took great care of my wife during our long separation. She is utterly devoted to Jennifer, touchingly so. And loyalty, Melissa, is something that one cannot buy. It is earned, and Jennifer appears to have little trouble in winning the respect and devotion of those around her…? I wonder that I never realised that before now.'

She appeared slightly taken aback, but swiftly regained her composure. 'How very like you to say something so noble, my dear friend! When I know what you must be thinking and feeling at this present time.'

'I doubt that you do, Melissa,' he returned bluntly.

'Oh, but I do, my dear,' she countered. 'We have known each other far too long for me not to realise precisely why you allowed Jennifer to return to Wroxam Park. And it is just like you to be so noble and not part mother and son.' Her expression appeared all touching concern. 'But can you be sure, Julian, that the child is yours? After all—'

'There is not the smallest doubt in my mind, Melissa,' he cut in, the harsh tone more marked this time. 'Even if Charles were not my image, I would still believe he was mine, if Jennifer told me it was so.'

Having amazed himself by this completely spontaneous declaration of trust, he guided his equally astonished companion into the stable-yard to discover Patrick on the point of departure.

'Good Lord, man!' Julian didn't attempt to hide his surprise. 'You're not setting off today, surely?'

'No time like the present, sir,' he responded, after having cast his smiling blue eyes over his lordship's very attractive companion. 'The mistress wants the boy's pony brought here, and that's reason enough for me to be on my way.'

Julian couldn't help smiling at this: yet a further example of the unfailing devotion shown by his wife's servants. 'How long do you expect to be away?'

Patrick shrugged, clearly unwilling to commit himself, before he mounted one of the fine carriage horses his mistress had brought from Ireland. 'Difficult to say, sir. If it were just the pony I were collecting, I'd say I'd be back in ten days, two weeks at the most. But the mistress, now, she be pining after that baby of hers, and I dare swear the imp has been doing its share of fretting in return during these past weeks.' There was a flash of white teeth. 'And the baby can be a mite troublesome on occasions, as yer might say, sir. All depends on its mood. So it might take me a while longer to complete the trip.'

Against all the odds Julian found himself smiling as he watched Patrick doff his hat and ride out of the stable-yard. 'Impertinent rogue,' he muttered good-humouredly, much to Melissa's further astonishment.

'Julian, how can you take it so lightly? Jennifer's baby...? Whatever can it mean?'

'Unless I much mistake the matter, the so-called baby will turn out to have four legs, and not two, as you imagine.'

Julian then wasted no further time in helping his visitor to mount her own horse. Melissa Royston was one of the few women in whose company he did not become swiftly bored. She had never to his knowledge ever divulged a word about her brother's sordid association with Jennifer. Whether this had stemmed from a desire not to sully Geoffrey's reputation or out of admiration and respect for himself, Julian wasn't perfectly certain, but would always feel immense gratitude towards her for maintaining a strict silence over the years. None the less, he might have wished that she had displayed more tact during her first meeting with Jennifer. His wife's infidelity might not be easily forgotten, especially not by him, but there was absolutely no need to allude to the distasteful event at the first available opportunity, as it seemed to him Melissa had done. Consequently he was not sorry on this occasion to see his visitor ride out of the stable-yard.

On re-entering the house, he encountered his butler positioning a vase of flowers on the large oak table in the hall. 'Ah, Slocombe! Convey my apologies to her ladyship and inform her that I shall not be taking luncheon with her today.' He then turned, about to enter his library, when he bethought himself of something else. 'Also, be good enough to seek out Penrose. No doubt he will still be busily engaged in my bed-chamber. If so, ask him to give you the small leather case I keep locked away in the cupboard, and bring it to me in the library.'

Evidently Slocombe had little difficulty in running the dapper little valet to earth, for no sooner had his lordship poured himself a glass of wine, and had made himself comfortable at his desk, than the butler entered carrying that all-important leather-bound case.

It was several minutes after Slocombe had placed the requested article on the desk and had left the room that Julian reached out one hand to undo the leather buckle and extract its contents. It had been almost nine long years since he had set eyes on those six letters, one for every week Jennifer had remained by herself here at Wroxam Park, whilst he had tried to find solace in the arms of an energetic and highly resourceful young mistress, whose name escaped him completely now.

The first letter, which he had scanned briefly and then had flung into the fireplace in his library at Berkeley Square, only to rescue it quickly from the flames should it prove useful in attaining a divorce, was crumpled and slightly charred; the rest had their seals intact, never read, almost forgotten until now.

Placing them in strict chronological order, Julian read each one in turn, and then again, digesting every word written in the faintly childish hand which had developed over the years into an elegant, sloping scrawl. In each one Jennifer had professed her undying love for him, had assured him over and over that she had never looked upon Geoffrey Wilburn as anything other than a friend, and again and again had begged his forgiveness. Only in the penultimate missive, when she had evidently begun to accept that their marriage was at an end, had she come anywhere

near offering an explanation for her adulterous behaviour.

*...I realise that you may never find it in your heart
to forgive me, Julian. In truth I cannot forgive myself,
nor understand why I behaved as I did. It continues
to remain so unreal to me, like some horrible, bad
dream. I recall clearly riding out with Geoffrey that
day. I remember too our seeking shelter in the cottage
by the wood when it came on to rain, but that was
the only reason I entered the cottage with him. Please
believe me when I tell you that everything that happened afterwards continues to ·remain just a blur.
Even when I looked up to discover you standing in
the doorway, you seemed so unreal, so very far away,
and yet I know you were there to witness my shame...*

Julian reread the paragraph a third and then a fourth
time. Could it possibly be true? Could Jennifer honestly have retained no memory at all of what happened between her and Geoffrey after they had entered that cottage on that eventful September
afternoon? It seemed highly unlikely, and yet...

'I have never lied to you, Wroxam, and I do not
intend to start doing so now,' she had said, when she
had stood in this very room a matter of an hour earlier. He had had no difficulty in believing her then.
And yet this...

Tossing the letter aside, he went over to stare sightlessly out of the window, striving desperately to recall
every detail of a scene he would far rather forget. Had
she, in truth, appeared a little dazed when he had
caught her in bed with Geoffrey? Had there been a
certain faraway look in her eyes? He was inclined to
think that there had been. She had certainly seemed
lost, almost in a world of her own, when she had

returned to Wroxam Park. His eyes narrowed as a sinister possibility occurred to him for the first time. If she had, indeed, told him nothing but the truth in that letter she had written all those years ago, then what had induced that complete memory loss?

Chapter Seven

'When do you think Patrick will return, Papa?' Having swiftly taken off his own shoes and stockings, Charles helped his father remove the highly polished boots on which Penrose, the valet, always managed to achieve a looking-glass shine.

His young brow puckered as he studied his father's muscular calves, with their covering of dark hairs, before his thoughts returned to the absent groom. 'I want to ride my pony again. Then I can show you how well I can really ride, Papa, and you will let me ride your horses.'

Julian checked for a moment in the act of rolling up his trousers. Not once since he had attempted to try his equestrian skills on possibly the most spirited horse in the stables had Charles alluded to the incident which had earned him his father's severest displeasure, nor had he appeared to bear any ill will for the swift punishment he had received, which Julian considered was very much to the boy's credit.

'I have seen you ride often enough to be certain that you will one day make a fine horseman, my son,

and you may be certain that I shall always keep you
suitably mounted.'

'Patrick said he thought you were a fine rider,
Papa,' Charles disclosed, while reaching for one of
the fishing-rods, and dangling his small feet playfully
in the stream. 'Patrick said that Grandpapa James told
him once that you'd have to go a long way to find
anyone with a finer seat on a horse than Mama.'

Did he now? Julian mused, much struck by this
ingenuous disclosure. Not once since her return to
Wroxam Park had Jennifer availed herself of any of
the horses in the stable. He had assumed, quite
wrongly it seemed, that she no longer cared for riding.
This had not occurred to him as in any way out of
the ordinary. Many females appeared to lose interest
in that particular form of exercise once they had given
birth. Furthermore, he couldn't say that he could ever
recall her betraying any real zeal for being in the saddle. She had been, as far as he could remember,
merely a competent horsewoman, nothing more.

'Evidently your mama acquired a partiality for that
particular form of exercise when you lived in Ireland,
Charles?'

'She was always with Grandpapa James, in the stables or riding about the land with him. He was very
old, and Mama looked after him. She loved him very
much, and cried and cried when he died. And Mama
never cries, but she did then. I sometimes think she
still looks sad now. I don't like it when Mama is sad.'

'No,' Julian responded softly, staring for a moment
at some distant spot on the far bank of the stream.
'Perhaps she'll be happier when Patrick returns with
her horse.'

Excitement glittered in the boy's eyes. 'Is Patrick bringing Mama's horse?'

'I believe so, yes. She is something of a troublesome filly, I understand.'

Charles, casting his father a surprised glance, didn't hesitate to enlighten him. 'But Oriel's a gelding, sir! Mama loves Oriel nearly as much as she loves me. If it hadn't been for Mama taking care of him he would have died when he was a foal. Mama is very clever,' he continued, not for the first time in Julian's presence betraying the deep love he bore his mother. 'She can do anything. She can play cricket, and she can fish too. She caught a trout once, as long...as long as your arm, Papa!'

'Which is more than you will manage to do, my son, if you continue chattering,' a voice from behind remarked, and Julian swivelled round to see Jennifer emerge from the clump of trees by the stream's edge.

Just how long she had been hovering there he had no way of knowing, but he suspected, by the hint of wry amusement pulling at her lips, some little time.

'You should not pay too much heed to everything my son tells you, my lord,' she advised, moving from beneath the shadow of the trees, with a look in Charles's direction which managed to convey a deal of affection as well as mild exasperation. 'Occasionally he is inclined to view his mama through a rosy haze. Furthermore, he appears to have developed an unfortunate tendency to indulge in harmless exaggeration.'

Julian found himself effortlessly smiling too at this further example of his wife's ruthless honesty. To say that their relationship was increasingly improving would, he knew, place him in danger of succumbing to his son's harmless complaint. Thankfully, though, there had been several occasions in recent days when there had been less restraint on Jennifer's part, and her manner towards him had bordered almost on the friendly, most especially when Charles was present.

'I was beginning to suspect it was a whale you must have caught, m'dear,' he teased gently. 'If I'd realised just what an accomplished angler you'd become I would have suggested that you join us.' A gleam of hope softened his eyes. 'It isn't too late. I could easily return to the house for an extra rod if you would care to bear us company for an hour or so.'

'Another time, perhaps,' she responded, after a moment when she appeared as though she might accept the invitation. 'I have one or two letters I must write.'

Jennifer turned to her son, who continued to splash his bare feet playfully in the stream. 'Perhaps if you can manage to sit still for a few minutes, and give your tongue a rest too, you just might succeed in catching some fish which can be eaten at supper.' Her eyes began to twinkle. 'But as I place little reliance on your powers of self-control, I do not believe I shall suggest Mrs Quist change the menu for this evening.'

Jennifer could not forbear a smile at her son's mischievous chuckles as she turned and made her way through the small copse, aware that grey eyes, perhaps still betraying that hint of disappointment, were following her progress.

If the truth were known, she would very much have liked to remain with them, but wiser counsel had prevailed. Although it was impossible to avoid totally the company of the man she had married, she was honest enough to admit that when they were together she felt increasingly vulnerable, increasingly threatened, regarding him as more the man, less the adversary. Increasingly she was finding it difficult to ignore that raw masculinity and abundance of charm he could exert when he chose.

She shook her head almost in disbelief. It was so hard to equate the image she had built up over the years of a cold, aloof monster whose wrath could be quite merciless, with the engaging gentleman who joined her for dinner most evenings and whose charisma was hard to ignore. Little wonder, she mused, why so many women over the years had fallen under his wholly masculine spell and had been very willing to engage in more intimate relations with him. It was just a great pity that she had not been so free with her charms as Wroxam, if common report was to be believed, had been with his during their long separation.

The truth of the matter was, of course, she had been more than content with James O'Connell's company and the platonic friendship and camaraderie she had enjoyed over the years with his people. With hindsight, however, it might have been wiser if she had allowed her chaste mantle to slip from time to time and engaged in the odd affair. Her experience of the opposite sex would then have vastly increased, and she might now find herself more able to resist this ever-growing attraction she was experiencing towards the man she had married.

Oh, yes, her position was precarious indeed, she was forced to concede. She was here on sufferance, nothing more. It may have been an act of generosity on Wroxam's part, a rare altruistic gesture to allow her to remain; but her position was far from secure.

If she disgraced him in any way, if she displayed the remotest interest in any other man, she didn't doubt for a moment that he would turn again into that merciless, intractable man she well remembered.

She would be foolish ever to drop her guard, to allow a closer relationship to develop between them. That could only leave her open to heartache and the searing pain of rejection which she could also well remember.

As she moved towards the steps leading up to the mansion, the door opened suddenly and James the footman stepped out. 'Oh, your ladyship,' he beamed, with every evidence of delight at seeing her. 'I was about to come in search of you. There's a lady in the front parlour wishing to see you.'

'Mrs Royston?' Jennifer queried, with a sudden lowering feeling. She was finding the attractive widow's ever-increasing visits something of a trial.

'No, my lady. Someone you met during your stay in London, I understand. She was reluctant to give a name.'

Intrigued, Jennifer went straight into the sunny parlour, and recognised at once the figure staring out of the window at the wonderful view of the lake. 'Serena, what a delightful surprise!' The wan smile she received in response was not quite what she might have expected, and the disquiet she had experienced during her walk back across the park returned with a vengeance. 'Come, let us sit down, and you can tell me to what I owe the pleasure of this unexpected visit.'

'I doubt you'll consider my unexpected arrival such a pleasure, Jenny, when you know why I'm here,' Serena disclosed, as she allowed herself to be led across to the sofa. 'You might consider that I'm trading on our brief acquaintance. You see, Jenny, I suppose you might say I've run away.'

The admission, far from producing an exclamation of shock or dismay, merely evoked an expression of wry amusement. 'You do not appear in the least surprised, Jennifer. It isn't the normal behaviour of well brought-up young ladies.'

'Oh, I don't know,' she responded, after a moment's reflection, the wickedly wry smile more pronounced than ever. 'I certainly know of one other who resorted to such drastic measures.'

'Who?' Serena demanded to know, momentarily forgetting her own unfortunate predicament.

'Me,' her ladyship answered with simple pride. 'Although, in my case, I suppose it would be more accurate to say that I simply left this house and never bothered to return. One is forced to resort to drastic measures when one's life has become unbearable.' Sympathy and understanding flickered in her eyes. 'I assume that is what has happened in your case, Serena?'

She nodded. 'Life at home has become quite intolerable since I refused to marry Lord Sloane.'

This did manage to elicit an exclamation of mingled shock and dismay. 'Marry Lord Sloane...? Serena, you cannot be serious!'

'Unfortunately, I am,' she confirmed in a heartfelt sigh. 'Shortly after you had left the capital, Lord Sloane's attentions became more marked, and to my surprise Mama seemed actively to encourage him. When I began to find excuses not to attend certain parties where I knew he would be present, she became out of all reason cross, and announced that remaining in town was a waste of time and money, as I seemed determined to end my days a spinster. We hadn't been home a week before Lord Sloane came seeking an interview with Papa.'

Jennifer would have been the first to admit that she didn't hold Lady Carstairs in particularly high esteem, having decided from the first that she was rather a foolish woman, prone to indulging in idle gossip. Nevertheless, she had never considered her unfeeling.

Harder to understand still was Sir Roderick Carstairs's attitude in all this. Serena had mentioned on more than one occasion that she and her father were very close. Surely a loving father would never countenance a union with a man of Lord Sloane's unsavoury reputation?

'But surely your father sent Lord Sloane about his business, Serena?' she asked, at last giving voice to her puzzling reflections.

'I think he most certainly would have done if Mama had not been so set on the marriage.' Again Serena sighed. 'I love my father dearly, Jenny, but I'm not blind to his faults. He's a very weak-willed gentleman in many ways. He always defers to Mama's wishes.' She shrugged. 'Which, I suppose, is quite understandable in the circumstances. You see, years ago he made some unwise investments, and lost a great deal of money. It was only through Mama's family coming to the rescue that Papa was able to keep the estate. Even now he cannot afford to squander money, so having me off his hands is bound to take a weight off his mind.'

'Yes, I can appreciate that. But to a man like Sloane!' Jennifer was appalled, and it clearly showed in both expression and voice. 'Surely your father must know of his reputation?'

'Papa does not go about much in society any more,' Serena responded, once again coming to her father's defence. 'I suppose he's willing to believe that the unsavoury stories concerning Lord Sloane are somewhat exaggerated in view of the fact that Mama is so set on the marriage.'

'So what do you intend to do now?' Jennifer enquired, when her friend relapsed into a melancholy silence.

'I refuse to remain at home, where I'm continually made to feel ungrateful and selfish, and merely a burden on my family. So I have decided, as I have no money of my own, that I must engage in some genteel occupation in order to support myself. And that is why I came to see you, Jenny,' she confessed in a rush. 'I remembered that you had promised someone that you would look about for a governess whilst you were in London.' Her eyes flickered with a glimmer of hope. 'As you left the capital so suddenly, I thought perhaps that you hadn't had the opportunity yet to engage a suitable candidate for the position, and might consider putting my name forward for the post.'

'Oh, I see,' Jennifer murmured, having the grace to look a little shamefaced. 'I'm afraid I misled you somewhat. In fact, it was—'

'I wouldn't expect any preferential treatment,' Serena interrupted, fearing that Jennifer might consider that she was trading on their friendship. 'I received a good education, and have always been an avid reader, therefore I'm certain I could—'

Jennifer herself didn't hesitate to interrupt this

time. 'It isn't that I doubt your capabilities, my dear friend. But I did mislead you. It was I who required the services of a governess…for my own son.'

Serena appeared so sincerely astonished that Jennifer didn't doubt for a moment that she had been completely unaware of Charles's existence up until that moment. 'I would have thought that the whole of the polite world would have known by now that Wroxam and I have a child.'

'It—it may well be so,' Serena conceded, having now recovered from the shock a little. 'But Mama and I left London a matter of two weeks after your sudden departure. I must confess that before we left town rumours had begun to circulate about a possible reconciliation between you and his lordship.'

Jennifer's gurgle of mirth held a distinctly mocking ring. 'So that is what Society surmises?'

'Well, I—er—suppose it is understandable,' Serena suggested, suddenly feeling a little uncomfortable. There was a look in those green eyes which she could not quite interpret and which she did not quite like, a hard, unpleasant gleam that boded ill for someone.

'I can quite see why you might feel a little uncomfortable employing me as your son's governess,' she ventured, hurriedly returning the conversation to the subject that concerned her most at present. 'I shall quite understand if you are unwilling to offer me the opportunity.'

'Whether I might feel uncomfortable or not is irrelevant, my dear,' Jennifer returned gently. 'The case will not arise. His lordship has decided to engage a tutor for Charles. He interviewed a young man several days ago. Mr Granger seems ideal. He's a charming young man, and I certainly put forward no objections to his taking up the post. He will commence his duties in a week's time.'

Serena tried desperately hard not to betray her bitter disappointment, but Jennifer could sense the growing anxiety. She knew well enough what it was like to be abroad in the world with little money and nowhere to go. It was a daunting enough situation for a man, but very much worse for a female, especially if she was without a protector.

'Have you some kind-hearted relative who might take pity on your plight?' Jennifer asked, very concerned.

'There's my godmother, I suppose. You may remember that you met her on the occasion of your uncle's ball. She's frequently asked me to visit her in Bath. But it could only be a temporary arrangement, and I feel I must write first, and not just arrive unexpectedly on her doorstep, especially in the circumstances.'

'Then do so. And in the meantime…' having come to a decision, Jennifer rose to her feet '…you must remain here as my guest until you receive a reply from your godmother.'

'But, Jenny, you cannot possibly have me to stay… I mean—I mean, what will his lordship say?'

'He'll be delighted, of course!' It was perhaps fortunate that Jennifer, making her way across the room to the bell-pull, had her back towards her unexpected visitor, for her expression betrayed something quite different. The truth of the matter was, she had no idea how the master of the house would react to the news that they would be having an uninvited guest to stay for an unspecified time.

Slocombe entered in response to the summons, and

Jennifer, admirably maintaining a self-assured air, ordered him to have a room prepared. Then promptly
dispatched him to find Mary, and to inform her that
her presence was required in the parlour.

'You must be tired after your journey, Serena, and
will no doubt appreciate a lie-down before dinner.
Don't look so worried, my dear. You'll feel much
more the thing after you have had a little nap.'

The door opened, drawing Jennifer's attention
away from her friend's wan expression. 'Ah, Mary!
You remember Miss Carstairs, I'm sure.'

'Of course I do. How are you, Miss Carstairs?'

'In need of your help and tender care, Mary,'
Jennifer responded before Serena could do so. 'She's
tired after her journey, and I require you to see her
comfortably established in her bedchamber, and ensure she has everything she needs.' Her eyes fell on
the rather shabby cloak-bag tucked by the side of the
chair. 'Is that the only luggage you have with you,
Serena?'

'I'm afraid so. I didn't feel that I could bring too
many of my belongings with me.'

'Very sensible,' Jennifer agreed, maintaining beautifully the matter-of-fact tone. 'It is always preferable
to travel light if one can possibly do so.' Reaching
out her hands, she drew Serena to her feet. 'I shall
leave you in Mary's care now, my dear. Try to rest
before dinner. I'm afraid we keep country hours here
at Wroxam Park and dine at six. I look forward to
seeing you again then.'

The instant the door had closed behind them,
Jennifer's bright, reassuring smile vanished, as her
thoughts turned to the master of the house. What
would he say? She experienced more than just faint

disquiet at the thought of approaching him, and then cursed herself for being so spineless. Nervousness when dealing with Wroxam was a sure recipe for disaster. Had she not had experience enough of that in the past? If she had faced up to him before, had not tamely remained here in this house for those weeks at his expressed command, things might have turned out so vastly different between them.

No, the only way to handle Julian was to face up to him. And strangely enough, he seemed to like it, she reflected, remembering clearly that day, not so very long ago, when she had taken him to task over his treatment of Charles. Whether he turned out to be as understanding over Serena's unexpected arrival was a different matter entirely, however. In the meantime, she reminded herself, she had those letters to write to occupy her time until his return from his fishing expedition.

Having Serena's unfortunate predicament constantly intruding into her thoughts, Jennifer took rather longer over the task than expected, and was somewhat surprised when Slocombe unexpectedly appeared in her private little sanctum to enquire whether she wished to delay dinner that evening.

'Good gracious!' Her eyes automatically turned to the mantel-clock. 'I had no notion it was so late. No, Slocombe, we'll dine at the usual hour. I'll go up and change now.' She checked in her progress across to the door. 'I presume his lordship has already returned?'

'Yes, my lady. I believe he is in his bedchamber.'

Realising that there wasn't time to see Serena before dinner, Jennifer went directly to the west wing.

As she approached the door to her room, she saw her husband's pernickety valet, carrying a pile of soiled linen, emerge from the chamber next to her own, and decided that it was more than likely that Wroxam would leave his room before she had had time to change her own attire.

Waiting only for Penrose to go about his duties, she knocked lightly on her husband's door and, receiving no response, entered before her courage failed her to discover Wroxam, dressed only in a full-length robe, emerging from his dressing room, rubbing his wet hair with a towel. Of course she had seen him dressed in very much less on numerous occasions in the distant past; in fact, wearing nothing at all. But catching him now, for the first time since her return, in this casual state rekindled bittersweet memories of more intimate moments they had shared, and reminded her that she was familiar with every inch of the skin hidden beneath that crimson brocade robe.

The instant he noticed her standing there, hand still clutching the doorknob, Julian stopped dead in his tracks, his eyes widening momentarily, before his lips curled into a distinctly provocative half-smile, as he easily detected the hue, not dissimilar to the shade of his garment, suffusing Jennifer's delicate cheeks.

'What an unexpected pleasure, my dear! Do come in and close the door.' His smile grew more pronounced when she made not the least attempt to move, and continued to regard him as though he were some fearsome predator about to attack. 'I am fully aware that only a matter of the utmost importance would have induced you to set foot in this room, and I can assure you that you are perfectly safe. I have never been disposed to ravishing unwilling females, and even if I were, there really wouldn't be time. Penrose will be returning shortly.'

The flippancy restored sufficient courage for her to close the door, but not quite enough to induce her to accept the offer of the comfortable chair too conveniently positioned by the huge four-poster bed.

Julian didn't miss the apprehensive glance she cast the room's most prominent feature, as though it were a hot bed of coals, something perilous and threatening, something to be avoided at all costs. Anyone observing her reaction might be forgiven for supposing that she had never sampled the pleasures of the flesh, let alone given birth to a child. Yet there was something singularly pleasing in the display of pretty modesty; something which had been too spontaneous not to be perfectly genuine.

'You will forgive me if I do sit down, my dear, and finish my toilet. I do not wish to be late in going down to dinner…especially as we have, so I understand, a guest now staying with us.' He met her frankly startled gaze in the dressing-table mirror. 'Yes, Slocombe did inform me upon my return that a Miss Carstairs had arrived.'

'And you do not object to her staying with us for a short period?' Jennifer, quite unable to keep surprise from creeping into her voice, noticed the faintly sardonic lift to one dark brow in the dressing-table mirror.

'I cannot perceive why you should imagine I would raise the smallest objection to having a guest under our roof. The sooner you cease to view me as some kind of unfeeling monster, my dear, the better we shall deal together.'

Receiving no response, he reached for his comb

and proceeded to drag it through his damp locks, while continuing to hold that now decidedly wary gaze through the mirror. 'However,' he continued, once satisfied with the arrangement of his hair, 'I do not for a moment suppose it was to inform me of your friend's arrival that was your sole reason for coming here.'

'Well, no,' she admitted, grudgingly admiring his perspicacity. 'You see, Julian,' she continued, sublimely unaware of the fact that she had addressed him by his given name for the first time since her return to England, 'Serena's arrival was a complete surprise to me, too. Had I written to invite her to stay, I would quite naturally have consulted you first.'

'So?' he prompted, when she began to look distinctly ill at ease.

'Well, not to put too fine a point on it, you might say I offered her a refuge, somewhere where she can safely remain until she is able to find a more permanent place to reside… I suppose you might say she has run away from home, you see.'

'Dear me,' he muttered in a half-mocking tone. 'You and your friend appear to have much more in common than just a similarity in age.'

Jennifer did not misunderstand, and refused to permit this piece of deliberate provocation to go unchallenged. 'I do not consider that in the least amusing, Wroxam!' she snapped, chin lifting. 'And, might I remind you, I did not run away. I merely left you.'

'I stand corrected, my dear.' The hard contours of his face were softened by a surprisingly tender expression. 'May I be permitted to know why Miss Carstairs felt compelled to take such drastic action?'

'Oh, she had a very good reason,' Jennifer assured

him, her annoyance at his earlier flippancy swiftly dwindling. 'Her parents, seemingly, wish her to marry that loathsome Lord Sloane. Quite naturally Serena has refused to do so.'

His expressive dark brows snapped together. 'If that is indeed the case, my dear, then I find it not at all difficult to comprehend Miss Carstairs's behaviour, and am doubly happy to offer the sanctuary of my home…with one stipulation.'

'Which is?'

'That she writes to her parents, informing them that she is staying at Wroxam Park as our guest.' In one smooth movement he rose to his feet, one long-fingered hand reaching for the opening of his dressing-gown as he did so. 'And now, my dear, if there's nothing else you wish to discuss, I'll spare your blushes by asking you to leave, for I am about to disrobe.'

With a rumble of faintly mocking laughter ringing in her ears, Jennifer whisked herself from the room, closing the door firmly behind her before opening the one to the adjoining chamber. Young Rose appeared promptly in response to the summons, and even though Jennifer went down to the parlour with fifteen minutes to spare before dinner, it was to discover Serena already there, appearing quite remarkably composed and cheerful in the Marquis's company.

'Ah, my dear!' he greeted her, with every evidence of delight. 'I had assured our guest that you'd not keep us waiting, and once again you have justified my faith in you.'

Yet another display of that seemingly effortless charm. What in the world had come over the man of late? she wondered, casting a suspicious glance in his direction before turning a smiling countenance to her friend, who was looking very much happier than she had been earlier. Whatever Wroxam had been saying to her, it certainly appeared to have restored the healthy bloom in those thin cheeks.

'Before you joined us, my dear,' his lordship remarked, handing her a glass of Madeira, 'Miss Carstairs was offering her opinion on the latest thespian to have taken the capital by storm and, like myself, is one of the few who doesn't hold Lawrence Merrivale in high esteem. I saw him very early in the Season, and thought his portrayal decidedly unconvincing. In fact, he put me very much in mind of my valet, Miss Carstairs,' he added, turning once again to her, 'with his thin, high-pitched voice and mincing walk. Hardly everyone's idea of the dashing hero.'

Serena laughingly agreed; and it was by no means the only time his lordship was able, with very little effort it seemed, to ignite a spontaneous gurgle.

Throughout dinner, Jennifer noticed, he managed to keep her friend in a high state of amusement with his caustic remarks and less-than-flattering observations on several of Society's most famous figures. Serena appeared to lose every vestige of shyness with him, and seemed quite disappointed when he announced, after the meal was over, that he would not be joining them in the parlour for tea, as pressing estate matters were requiring his attention.

'So I will bid you goodnight now, Miss Carstairs, and hope to see you in the morning at breakfast.'

'I look forward to it, my lord.'

'You sounded as though you truly meant that,' Jennifer remarked, as she led the way back into the comfortable parlour.

'I did,' Serena readily confirmed. 'Your husband is truly a most charming gentleman. I cannot deny that when I discovered only his lordship here earlier, my poor heart sank, but he put me at my ease at once, making me feel so very welcome that you might find it difficult to be rid of me. Why, he's nothing like the cold, autocratic man I've always imagined him to be!'

She gave an uncertain little laugh, as she once again made herself comfortable in one of the chairs. 'I must confess, Jenny, that when I heard all the rumours about a reconciliation between you, I was inclined to dismiss them as ludicrous. How pleased I am to discover that I was totally wrong!'

'You were not in error, Serena,' Jennifer countered. 'There is no reconciliation.'

It was perhaps fortunate that Slocombe entered the room at that moment, carrying the tea-tray which he automatically placed on the low table by his mistress's chair, because Serena was quite unable to stop herself from gaping in disbelief, so stunned was she by the disclosure. Fortunately, by the time the butler had withdrawn, closing the door quietly behind him, she had managed to school her features, even though she was still finding the astonishing admission somewhat hard to believe.

Jennifer, dispensing the tea, was not slow to note the lingering doubt in her friend's eyes. 'You shouldn't be fooled by appearances, Serena,' she advised, handing her one of the filled china cups. 'I would be the first to admit that on the surface Wroxam is charming, seems the perfect host, the most considerate and convivial companion. But I am not fooled. He has a tongue like a viper, can be equally venomous, and can strike with lightning speed when one least expects it.'

Both the look which glinted in her eyes and her smile completely lacked any vestige of warmth. 'I am permitted to reside here simply because I am the mother of his son, and for no other reason.'

'Oh, Jenny, I'm so very sorry,' Serena responded, not quite knowing what to say or what to believe, either. From what she had observed thus far, his lordship's manner towards his Marchioness was one of quite touching tenderness. Anyone might be forgiven for supposing that he was, indeed, a man very much in love with his wife. Yet, if what Jennifer had told her was true...

'I do not deserve your pity,' Jennifer unexpectedly announced, forcing Serena to abandon her perplexing thoughts. 'I brought it all upon myself by making the foolish mistake of underestimating my husband. I really ought to have considered the possibility, before I decided to bring Charles with me to England, that Julian might decide to have me followed. Of course, he expected to find me enjoying the attentions of some ardent lover. Instead, he found me enjoying the company of my son.

'You appear shocked, my dear. But let me assure you that Wroxam had every reason to suspect I had a lover.' Her eyes never wavered from Serena's face as she added, 'It certainly wouldn't have been the first time that he had discovered me naked in the arms of another man.'

'Jennifer, whatever can you mean!' Serena's expression clearly betrayed staunch disbelief. 'I simply cannot believe that you would ever—'

'Behave like a wanton,' Jennifer finished for her.

'That is precisely the reaction I would have expected from such a good friend as you, Serena. Unfortunately in this particular instance I am unworthy of your good opinion, for I did make a cuckold of Julian once... Though why I did so, I have never been able to understand. I was very much in love with Wroxam, whereas I was never in love with Geoffrey Wilburn.'

'Geoffrey Wilburn?' Serena echoed, desperately striving to come to terms with what she was hearing. The name meant absolutely nothing to her.

'He used to live with his half-sister, Melissa Royston, our nearest neighbour,' Jennifer enlightened her, before rising to her feet and going over to the window to stare out at the lake, sparkling now in the late evening sunshine.

It was a view that she had always loved, had always remembered so well; just as she had never forgotten that day when she had happily agreed to accompany Geoffrey out for a ride across the estate. She had not intended to ride so far, but when it had come on to rain, she had not thought twice about seeking shelter in that old cottage by the wood on his sister's land.

'So you went into the cottage with Geoffrey,' Serena prompted when Jennifer fell silent after disclosing this much, 'merely to shelter from the rain and for—for no other reason.'

'And for no other reason,' Jennifer confirmed. 'I remember Geoffrey opening a bottle of wine. I remember sitting with him at the rough wooden table, drinking a glass. But after that I can recall nothing...nothing until I saw Julian, like some shadowy figure, standing in the doorway. For some reason I was unable to bring his face into focus. It was like peering through a haze, like waking from a dream, and not quite knowing what was real and what was not. Which was possibly just as well, because I clearly recall Melissa saying that he looked positively murderous.'

'I do not quite understand, Jenny,' Serena put in quickly. 'Are you trying to tell me that this man's sister was there also? If so, surely everything was perfectly respectable?'

'Melissa didn't accompany Geoffrey and me out riding on that occasion, though she sometimes did. She was busily engaged making last-minute arrangements for a dinner-party she was planning to hold that evening. Geoffrey had promised to be home in good time, and when he failed to return, she rode over to see if he was here. Her arrival coincided with Wroxam's return from London, and they both set out looking for us.

'Melissa remained at the cottage to help me dress after Wroxam had gone. I remember her coaxing me to drink some sort of herbal tea. It tasted very bitter as I recall, but at least it managed to clear my head a little, but not sufficiently for me to remember precisely what had taken place. Melissa put my loss of memory down to shock—distress at being discovered in such a compromising position with her brother.' Jennifer shrugged. 'And who knows, she may possibly have been right.'

'And you still do not remember what took place between you and Geoffrey in that cottage?' Serena asked gently, when Jennifer had returned to the chair opposite.

'No, and I doubt I ever shall. But I shall never forget Julian's look of contempt, or the cold indifference I received when I arrived home. At the time, of course, I didn't realise that that was destined to be the last time I would see him for eight and a half years. He returned to London immediately, and I was ordered to remain at Wroxam Park.'

She then went on to relate her subsequent meeting with Mary, and to divulge a little of the happy life she had enjoyed in Ireland with James O'Connell. 'He was a truly wonderful man. Had he not died last autumn, I certainly wouldn't be sitting here now.'

'And do you intend to remain?' Serena asked, still striving to understand, to come to terms with what she had learned.

'If you had asked me that question several weeks ago, when I first arrived here, I could have given you an answer at once. Now I'm not so certain.' Sighing, Jennifer leaned back against the chair. 'Wroxam gave me no choice—either I return here with him, or give up my son. And during these past weeks I have witnessed a bond developing between them, a rapidly growing affection.'

'I very much look forward to making Charles's acquaintance.'

'Perhaps I'm a doting mother, Serena,' Jennifer responded with a gentle smile, 'but I think he's a fine boy. And in that Wroxam and I are in complete accord. He has become truly attached to his son. So, you see, he is capable of experiencing some of the finer feelings. But where I'm concerned…' She shook her head. 'He never loved me. I realised that a long time ago. The only reason he tolerates my presence here is because I am the mother of his son, and for no other reason.'

Serena was not so certain. If it wasn't love that had brought that tender look into his lordship's eyes for just one unguarded moment when Jennifer had joined them before dinner, then Serena was at a loss to know what it could have been.

Chapter Eight

Jennifer couldn't deny that she enjoyed having another female in the house. Serena proved to be the same charming, witty companion that she had known during her time in London. Charles liked her very much from the first. Having a lively younger brother, Serena was vastly experienced in the ways of very young gentleman, and never fell into the grave error of addressing them as little boys. She frequently accompanied Jennifer to the nursery wing, and was only too willing to join in any games Charles might wish to play, which swiftly earned her the supreme accolade of being thought a 'great gun' by the young heir.

Julian, too, appeared quite content to have another female residing under his roof. That easy charm of manner which he had displayed towards their guest on that very first evening continued, and had Jennifer not considered her friend a very level-headed young woman she might have feared that Serena was in grave danger of falling under the Marquis's destructive masculine spell.

But no, Jennifer mused, studying her friend's animated face across the breakfast-table. Serena, like

herself, was far too sensible to be fooled by any peerless displays of gallantry, though it had to be said her
expression brightened the instant his lordship entered
a room, and she always appeared eager to converse
with him on any topic he happened to raise; just as
she was doing now.

His lordship, of course, was very knowledgeable in
the ways of the fair sex, as the string of mistresses he
had enjoyed over the years proved very nicely.
Although Serena certainly didn't fall into the category
which would normally attract him, her appearance,
under Mary's expert fingers, was most definitely
showing such signs of improvement that one might
almost say that she looked quite pretty this morning,
Jennifer decided.

Mary had encouraged her to wear her hair in a
more becoming style, and now that the use of curl-
papers had been abandoned, her hair lay quite naturally in soft waves. Her dress, on the other hand, had
not improved. In her flight from the family home,
poor Serena had been limited in how much she could
carry, and Jennifer was heartily sick already of seeing
her in the plain grey gown she donned during the day,
and the unflattering pink silk she wore to dinner each
evening.

'Something appears to be troubling you this morning, my dear.' Julian's softly spoken remark succeeded in putting an end to her musings, and Jennifer
turned her attention to him. 'Do you not agree with
what Miss Carstairs and I were saying about the sheer
wanton extravagance displayed by our future king?'

'I'm afraid I wasn't attending. My mind was elsewhere.'

'That you find our conversation not sufficiently

stimulating to hold your attention is flattering to neither Miss Carstairs nor myself,' he remarked, with wry amusement, 'but I suppose we must admire your honesty. May we be permitted to know where your thoughts were precisely?'

She experienced not the least qualms over enlightening him. 'I was thinking that it is high time Serena had some new dresses. I'm heartily sick of seeing her in the same clothes each day, are you not?'

There was just the faintest twitch at the corner of the thin-lipped mouth. 'May I apologise on my wife's behalf, Miss Carstairs. Her innate honesty can be quite ruthless on occasions.'

'Truth to tell, sir, I'm heartily tired of wearing the same dresses myself,' Serena responded, casting a pained glance down at the skirt of her grey gown. 'I could, I suppose, add a postscript to that letter I've written to my parents, asking them to send a trunk of my clothes on to me here.'

'No, don't do that,' Jennifer hurriedly countered, visions of insipid, fussily adorned gowns floating before her mind's eye. 'You are in need of a new wardrobe to complement that very becoming way you now wear your hair. Nothing cheers a lady up more than a new dress or two, and there are several particularly fine shops in the local town, where I'm certain we'll find materials enough to cater for your needs.'

Julian hurriedly rose to his feet, as Serena looked about to protest. 'As I know little of frills and furbelows, I'll leave you ladies in peace. I promised to accompany Charles out riding, before his new tutor arrives.'

He paused for a moment by Serena's chair. 'You could do no better than to listen to my wife's advice,

Miss Carstairs. Perhaps I'm a little prejudiced, but I find her taste in dress impeccable,' and with that he departed, leaving Jennifer staring suspiciously after him as the door closed.

'What, I wonder, have I done to warrant that un-expected praise?'

'He admires you, Jenny, obviously. And with good reason, I might add! You know precisely what suits you. You always look so charming and as neat as wax, whereas I—'

'Have been induced, by your dear mama, I do not doubt, to dress in colours more suited to a schoolroom miss. Well, we can soon remedy that.' Finishing the last dregs in her cup, Jennifer rose to her feet. 'And there's no time like the present.'

After ordering her carriage brought round from the stables, Jennifer wasted no time in ushering her friend upstairs to don outdoor clothes and, deaf to all protes-tations, then led the way outside to discover what promised to be yet another lovely early summer's day.

Mary, who had been invited to join the shopping spree, smiled knowingly as she took her seat in the carriage. 'I'd save your breath to cool your broth, Miss Serena,' she advised, 'because it's certain sure wasted on Miss Jenny. I've known her a good deal longer than you have, and can tell you that once she's taken a notion into her head, there's no moving her. You can support her...you can ignore her...but don't ever try to stand in her way.'

This piece of sound advice earned her a seraphic smile. 'How well you know me, dear Mary! And how sensible you are too! Little wonder I've tolerated that sharp tongue of yours all these years. Now, kindly bend that discerning mind of yours on what colours to choose for the new dresses.'

Thus petitioned, Mary gave the matter due consideration, putting forward such interesting suggestions on precisely what colours and styles would best flatter a Junoesque figure that by the time they had entered a certain shop in the small market town, Serena's resolve was swiftly crumbling.

'Very well, Jenny,' she agreed, the last of her objections crushed by the very obliging Mrs Goodbody who was only too willing to display her finest wares for such a distinguished customer as the Marchioness of Wroxam. 'Perhaps sufficient for two dresses, on condition that the money you are forced to dispense on my behalf is a loan only.'

'Of course,' Jennifer obligingly agreed, before her attention was drawn to a length of lovely amber-coloured silk. 'Which you will pay back as soon as you have managed to acquire a position as a governess.'

Serena was not deaf to the wry amusement in her friend's voice, but before she could extract the solemn vow she required to salve her conscience, Mary drew her attention to some lengths of fine velvet, ideal for making up into spencers.

For several moments Serena began to dwell on the delightful prospect of donning gowns which, although could never miraculously turn her into a ravishing beauty, would undoubtedly flatter a tall, full-figured lady who was not precisely straight out of the school-room, before the tinkling of the shop's bell drew her attention.

Ordinarily she would have bestowed no more than a cursory glance on the slender, handsome woman who stepped inside the shop, had she not turned in time to catch a certain flicker in striking dark eyes as the stranger's gaze fell upon the Marchioness, standing by the counter.

Half hidden by a mannequin, draped in the shopkeeper's finest wares, Serena was able to watch the new customer without being observed in return, and saw her step lightly down the two steps to the shop floor. The hard, venomous gleam in her eyes vanished, and was replaced by a seemingly effortless smile, as she announced with every evidence of delight, 'Why, Lady Wroxam! What an unexpected pleasure!'

It might have been Serena's imagination, but she thought she could detect a slight stiffening in her friend's slender frame before Jennifer turned to face the newcomer. 'Unexpected, indeed, Melissa. Yet your arrival is most opportune. You may help me decide between the turquoise and kingfisher-blue silk for my friend here.'

Once again Serena detected the hard flicker in dark eyes, and thought perhaps her presence was resented, until she realised the unfriendly glance was directed over her shoulder at Mary.

'Serena,' Jennifer beckoned, 'may I make you known to our nearest neighbour, Mrs Royston. Melissa, this is my very good friend, Miss Carstairs, who is staying with us at Wroxam Park at the present time.'

Serena, touching the tips of the fingers extended towards her, realised suddenly that this woman was none other than the sister of the man who had brought such trouble into her friend's life.

'You may not be aware of it, Miss Carstairs, but

you have been singularly honoured,' Melissa informed her, with a return of that seemingly effortless smile. 'It isn't often that his lordship has guests to stay at his country estate. I have been trying to persuade him for years to entertain more when residing at the Park, but his lordship is a gentleman of strict habit, and rarely changes his decisions about anything, unless it is to his own advantage to do so. I suppose also he attains all the companionship he requires from his near-neighbours… Which reminds me,' she added, turning once again to Jennifer who was faintly smiling too, as though at some private thought. 'I have decided to hold a small dinner-party early next month, and should very much like you and his lordship to be amongst the guests…and Miss Carstairs too, if she should still be with you.'

'In view of what you have just told us, Melissa, I'm certain that his lordship will be only too delighted to accept,' she responded, turning to Mrs Goodbody who reappeared from the back room, with a package in her arms. 'I shall also require a length of this kingfisher-blue, Mrs Goodbody, and also some lengths of the velvet.'

'My, my! Are you planning on having a whole new wardrobe, your ladyship?'

'No, Melissa. These purchases are for Miss Carstairs. Unfortunately one of her trunks was mistakenly left behind in Hampshire,' Jennifer responded, lying quite convincingly, Serena thought.

'Woe betide my servants if they forget mine when I set forth on Friday!'

Jennifer raised her brows in exaggerated surprise. 'From where do you get your energy, Melissa? Only just recently returned from Italy and now off again on another trip!'

'Oh, I'm not travelling nearly so far this time. Just into the next county to spend a week or two with my aunt. She has been unwell of late. In fact, that is why I'm here today. I wish Mrs Goodbody to make some slight alterations to my new carriage dress before I leave.'

'In that case I shan't take up any more of the good lady's time.'

Turning to the proprietress, Jennifer informed her that she would return the following day for the remainder of the purchases. 'And do not forward the bill to my husband, Mrs Goodbody. I shall settle the account tomorrow. There are one or two other items I wish to purchase,' and with that Jennifer exchanged swift farewells with her neighbour before leading the way outside.

For a while no one spoke, then Serena, having studied the package which Mrs Goodbody's young assistant had carried out to the carriage, and had placed on the seat, cast a suspicious glance across at her friend, who appeared lost in admiration for the passing countryside.

'This parcel is rather bulky. Did you, perchance, buy some lengths of material for yourself?'

Green eyes glinting with unholy mischief met Serena's suspicious gaze. 'No, I did not. The contents of that parcel are yours and yours alone.'

'Oh, Jenny!' Serena was genuinely appalled, for she was not so foolish as to suppose there was only sufficient for two dresses hidden beneath the wrapping. 'What on earth have you purchased?'

Jennifer frowned for a moment in an effort to re-

member, and then turned to Mary. 'What did we select in the end, can you recall?'

'The gold silk and the russet. Also the lavender and
the kingfisher-blue... No, the kingfisher-blue is being
collected tomorrow, together with the lengths of velvet. I believe there are also several lengths of muslin,
and a selection of laces for trimming in the parcel.'

'What a memory you have, Mary!' Jennifer was
genuinely impressed. 'You must remind me tomorrow
to collect the remainder of our purchases. Such a pity
our spending spree was interrupted! I was just beginning to enjoy myself.'

These latter remarks turned Serena's thoughts from
the appalling problem besetting her of how precisely,
and when, she was going to manage to repay the
money for the materials, and she gazed intently at her
friend. 'Am I correct in supposing that you do not
care very much for Mrs Royston, Jenny?'

'I much preferred her brother,' she admitted, and
then smiled as Serena darted a faintly wary glance at
the carriage's third occupant. 'I have no secrets from
Mary,' she assured her. 'Like yourself, she is completely trustworthy, and would never disclose to a living soul that it was I who was responsible for the
break-up of my marriage.'

Serena experienced a surge of sympathy, just as she
had done when Jennifer had taken her into her confidence a few days before. Although her friend had
spoken about that time in her life with little emotion,
anyone with the least sensibility would have known
that she still retained bitter regrets and deep shame
for the way she had behaved.

'Do you suppose Mrs Royston holds you entirely
responsible for what happened, Jenny?' she asked

gently, and watched slender shoulders rise in what might have been a shrug of complete indifference.

'At the time I wouldn't have said so, no. I believe I mentioned that, although Melissa appeared deeply shocked at finding me and her brother in such a compromising situation, she was immensely kind, and accompanied me part-way back to the Park. But,' she frowned suddenly, 'since my return I have sensed a certain resentment in her attitude towards me. She never fails to allude to my adulterous behaviour, as she did today by making the point that his lordship rarely changes his mind about anything, once it is made up. Which, of course, was simply her way of letting me know that Wroxam is never likely to forgive or forget the humiliation I inflicted upon him. I believe she was fond of her half-brother. So perhaps she does blame me for his moving away. I do not know, of course, but I would imagine that Geoffrey found it extremely difficult, after what had occurred between us, to face Wroxam again. No doubt that is why he decided to live abroad permanently.'

'Yes, you may be right,' Serena agreed. 'But his lordship has at least one thing to be thankful for—neither Mrs Royston nor her brother ever breathed a word about the affair. I never heard the least rumour, except about your disappearance, of course.'

'Wroxam's continued silence is quite understandable,' Jennifer responded, after giving the matter a moment's thought. 'He's a very proud man. I know of only one person in whom he ever confided—his good friend Mr Dent.' Once again she shrugged. 'And I can only assume that Melissa's lips have remained sealed out of regard for Julian. After all, they have been friends since childhood. No one seeing them together could fail to see her fondness for him.'

Mary cast a disapproving look across the carriage. 'To be sure, Miss Jenny, there are times when I think you see what you want to see, and no more. The way that woman behaves when she visits the house, anyone would think she was the Marchioness of Wroxam.'

'And you, Mary,' Jennifer countered, 'can be quite bigoted when you take someone in dislike. You made up your mind not to like Mrs Royston the first time you set eyes on her.'

Mary didn't attempt to deny it. 'She's evil, that one. Her eyes are cold and soulless. And I'll tell you something else, Miss Jenny, she don't like you. Her friendliness is as false as her smiles!'

'I'm inclined to agree with you,' Serena put in. 'There is something about her I don't quite like. And I certainly wouldn't trust her, Jenny. Perhaps Mary is right, and she is in love with his lordship. Not that I believe for a moment that her feelings are reciprocated,' she added hurriedly. 'As they have known each other throughout their lives, his lordship has been granted ample opportunity to cement a closer bond between them than mere friendship, had he ever chosen to do so.'

'Perhaps,' Jennifer conceded, sounding a little doubtful, and received a questioning glance from her friend. 'Melissa married Josiah Royston, a man more than twice her own age, shortly after her father died. I seem to recall Geoffrey telling me that the only reason his sister married Royston was for his money. Seemingly, their father died leaving heavy debts, and it was only by marrying Royston that Melissa was able to retain the family home. Wroxam, of course, was rich enough to have settled the family's debts, but as he had only just attained the age of two-and-twenty at the time, perhaps marriage never entered his head.'

'Has she been a widow for very long?' Serena asked, after digesting what she had learned.

'Oh, yes. She had been a widow for well over a year when I first met her. Her sigh contained a deal of sympathy. 'Whether one likes her or not, one cannot help but feel sorry for her. She lost her mother when she was very young, and didn't deal very well with her stepmother, I understand. She spent much of her formative years with the aunt she intends to visit at the end of the week. It was only when her stepmother died that she returned to the family home, but even then she continued to spend many weeks each year with her favourite aunt. Since Geoffrey's departure she has spent most of her time in that big house living quite alone. I suppose that is why I don't resent her close friendship with Wroxam. She must be very lonely.'

'If that is so, why then hasn't she married again?' Mary suggested, voicing the very question which was passing through Serena's mind. 'I might not like her, Miss Jenny, but I'd be the first to admit that she's a handsome woman. I'm certain most gentlemen must find her most attractive. Which makes me wonder whether she's been waiting for just one certain gentleman to make her an offer... If so, then your return, Miss Jenny, must have come as a bitter blow.'

'If your suspicions are correct, Mary, then Melissa has good reason to dislike me. Nevertheless, if his lordship does think of her as rather more than just a friend, then it is up to him to do something about it, and start proceedings for our divorce.'

'Oh, no, he won't do that, Miss Jenny... at least, not now,' Mary responded, with a secretive little smile, which did not go unnoticed by at least one other occupant of the carriage.

Serena turned her head to stare out of the window as the carriage passed through the estate's western gateway. Like herself, Mary obviously suspected that his lordship's feelings for his wife were very strong. She also suspected that Jennifer was not so indifferent to him as she would have people suppose. There was no denying, however, that her manner towards him was certainly guarded, courteous rather than friendly.

Perhaps, Serena mused, as the carriage came to a halt outside the impressive front entrance, and she led the way into the house, Jennifer was wary over dropping her guard, thereby making herself vulnerable once more. Undoubtedly she had been bitterly hurt years ago, and although she had fully understood his lordship's subsequent actions after discovering her in such a compromising situation, she had never forgotten his ice-cold and total rejection. Yes, it was quite understandable why her friend experienced the need to retain a firm grasp on her emotions. But that, Serena reminded herself, did not prevent one from experiencing them, and she could not help wondering for how much longer Jennifer could withstand the Marquis's undoubted charm and ever-increasing regard.

'I shall not be accompanying you upstairs,' Jennifer announced unexpectedly, arresting Serena's progress across the hall. 'I would be the first to admit that I am no seamstress, so I shall leave you in Mary's very capable hands, and see you again at luncheon.'

After divesting herself of bonnet and pelisse, Jennifer paused before the mirror in the hall to tidy one or two errant curls, and then left the house again by way of a side entrance in order to pay her daily visit to the stables. Not once since her return to England almost four months ago had she sat on a horse. She smiled wryly. It felt more like four years. How she had missed her daily ride! Her own fault, of course, she reminded herself. Undoubtedly she had grown foolishly stubborn in recent years. One might even go so far as to say cussed. Cutting off her nose to spite her face, Mary would have said, simply because she was too proud, too obstinate, to accept favours from Wroxam!

And he owned some fine animals, she was forced to admit, moving down the row of stalls, and stopping at each one in turn to stroke the animal it contained. He had always been a fine judge of horseflesh, of course. It wasn't until her return to Wroxam Park that she had appreciated just how fine a judge he was, however. Every one of his animals was in prime physical condition, and she was forced to own that any man who ensured his livestock received the utmost care could not be totally heartless.

The clatter of hooves on cobblestones interrupted her thoughts, and she went out into the yard once again to see the subject of her thoughts returning from his ride. The smile when he saw her seemed to come effortlessly to his lips, but her own was directed solely at his young companion.

'You look very pleased with yourself, Charles,' she

remarked, stroking the neck of the steady mare he was still forced to ride.

'Papa and I went over to visit Colonel Halstead. He asked Papa if he would care to buy the grey mare his daughter used to ride. She's very pretty, Mama, but I told Papa that she wouldn't suit you.'

'Yes, you did, but you didn't explain why,' his lordship reminded him, dismounting. 'I thought that if your Mama was given her own mount she would be more inclined to join us when we go out. Although,' he added, squinting against the sun's bright rays, as he noticed a distant figure making his way down the long sweep of the drive, 'I may have been a little previous.'

Charles, following the direction of his father's gaze, uttered a squeal of delight. 'It's Patrick, Mama! He's back!'

Whilst Charles continued to jump up and down in excitement, Jennifer moved into the centre of the yard, and waved a hand in welcome, as the distant figure came to a halt.

'Let him go, Patrick!' Charles called. 'Wave again, Mama. Wave again so that he can see you!'

'I believe my baby already has,' Julian heard her respond, before returning his gaze to the driveway in time to see a power-ful black hunter break free from the little cavalcade and come galloping towards the stable.

'No, Papa. No!' Charles clung to the sleeve of the beautifully tailored coat, as his father made to dash forward. 'It's Oriel…Oriel would never hurt Mama! You see…you watch, Papa!'

Easily shaking off the restraining little fingers, Julian remained ready to hurl himself into the big hunter's path, until he saw Jennifer suddenly raise her hands and hold her arms outstretched in welcome. The big black checked his speed, slowing to a mere trot. Then Julian was privileged to witness a spectacle he had never seen before. The powerful hunter entered the yard and walked straight into the outstretched arms, whinnying softly as Jennifer placed her face against his gleaming black neck. He remained thus, as still as a statue, until finally she raised her head. Then he frisked about her like a playful colt, stopping from time to time to nuzzle her neck and cheeks with his velvety lips.

'Well, I'll be damned!' The head groom, having emerged from one of the stalls to investigate the commotion, took off his hat to scratch his grizzled hair. 'If I'd paid a visit to Molly Pike's tavern,' he announced to no one in particular, 'I'd swear the ale had gone to me 'ead!'

Chuckling impishly at this sally, Charles darted forward to greet Patrick, as he came trotting into the yard, leading a fine chestnut pony. Julian joined them, nodding his head in approval, after a brief examination of his son's mount.

'Aye, he's a dandy little fellow,' Patrick agreed, before turning his attention to the by-play still taking place in the centre of the yard. 'And what be your opinion of the baby, sir?'

'Some baby!' Julian scoffed, experiencing a pang of envy at the affectionate way Jennifer was treating the horse. How he wished those slender arms would reach out to him and hold him so lovingly! His expression, however, swiftly changed to one of unmistakable concern. 'You don't mean to tell me that that powerful animal is my wife's usual mount?'

Patrick appeared mildly surprised. 'To be sure he is, sir! And no one can handle him better. Always been that way since he were a foal. Belongs to the mistress body and soul, the boy does. Why not go and make friends with the lad, sir? It's always best to give 'em a minute or two alone together, but he'll be all right now.'

Julian required no further prompting and, with Charles skipping happily alongside, he moved forward to make the powerful black's acquaintance. Oriel, with a soft whinny of welcome, lowered his neck so that Charles could stroke his handsome head, then he raised it again, hesitating for a moment before accepting the treat in Julian's outstretched hand.

'He's a fine animal, madam wife,' he announced after running his hands along the gleaming flanks. 'But not what I'd call a lady's mount,' he added, voicing his concern.

'Oh, we understand each other well enough,' she responded, and Julian shook his head as the horse once again whinnied softly as he nuzzled her cheek.

'I've witnessed it many a time in dogs, but never in horses, at least not to this extent.' He shook his head, still amazed at the display of affection. 'You reared him from a foal, I understand. Which, of course, might account for it.'

'Are you going to ride him today, Mama?'

'No, Charles. He's had a long journey. Maybe I'll consider it in a day or two.'

'And then will you come out riding with Papa and me?' he asked, before a gleam of excitement suddenly brightened his eyes. 'I know! You and Papa could have a race.'

'We'll allow him to settle in first,' Julian said, his

lack of enthusiasm quite evident, and he received a slightly mocking glance.

'Faint-hearted, Wroxam?' Jennifer spared a moment to watch his favourite mount being led into the stables. 'I'm certain that grey of yours would give a good account of himself.'

'I'm certain he would too, madam wife,' he agreed, desperately striving not to be provoked into foolish actions by the challenging gleam in a pair of lovely green eyes. 'I shall consider the matter whilst I'm away in London during the next few days. In the meantime,' he added, turning to his son, 'we must change our attire. We cannot sit down to luncheon smelling of the stables.'

Jennifer watched them disappear into the mansion by way of the side door, wondering why the bubble of happiness at being reunited with Oriel had suddenly burst. It oughtn't to matter a whit to her whether Wroxam wished to journey to the capital, more than likely to visit his mistress. No, it oughtn't to matter at all...but it did.

Chapter Nine

It was a pleasant late June evening, not too hot now that the oppressive heat of the day had been tempered by a refreshing south-westerly breeze. London at this time of year had been suffocating, and Julian had been heartily glad to leave the capital, with all its noise and stale atmosphere, behind him. Had it not been for the fact that he had deemed it necessary to make urgent and drastic changes to his will, and to visit his lawyers in person in order to assure them that Charles Julian Stapleford was undoubtedly his son and legal heir, and to ensure that his wife was financially secure for the rest of her life, nothing would have induced him to leave Wroxam Park at such a time.

Although his trip to the capital had been made for purely business reasons, it hadn't lacked its lighter moments. Naturally rumours of a child now living at Wroxam Park had begun to spread, and surprisingly enough he had been more amused than annoyed by the number of times the subject of raising children had been introduced into conversations. One person, however, hadn't attempted to touch upon the current domestic situation presiding at Wroxam Park.

He smiled faintly, as he drew his attention away from his idle contemplation of the familiar landscape, and fixed his gaze on his sole travelling companion who, he had noticed, had become increasingly quiet during the journey.

'You appear to be in a world of your own, my dear Theo. I might even go so far as to suggest faintly bored.' He paused to remove a speck off the sleeve of his jacket. 'If you were experiencing reservations about accompanying me back to the ancestral pile, you shouldn't have accepted my invitation. I wouldn't have been the least offended. You above anyone should know I'm remarkably hard to wound.'

Mr Dent held that faintly sardonic gaze without so much as a blink. 'At one time I might have wholeheartedly agreed. You were always a cold fish, Julian, but now...' He noted the quizzical arch of one dark brow, and smiled. 'Well, perhaps you haven't changed completely. And I certainly haven't been bored,' he assured him. 'I was merely thinking what a lovely part of the country this is, and how much of a relief it is to be away from stuffy old London.'

His lordship contemplated his friend in silence for a moment. 'I fail to understand, Theo, why you continue to live in the capital all year round. By your own admission you much prefer peace and quiet. And it isn't as if you cannot afford a country residence.'

'True enough,' he readily agreed. 'And I've certainly considered doing just that on more than one occasion. The trouble is though, Julian, I'd find little pleasure in living in the country entirely on my own. It's different in town, of course. There's always so much going on, even when the Season is over. People are always paying visits. If I were married, I wouldn't need to think twice about the matter.'

'Yes. Yes, I can understand that,' Julian responded, after giving the matter a moment's consideration. 'One can be surrounded by servants, can receive numerous visits from neighbours, and yet it isn't quite the same as sharing your home with another human being. Your life, even your outlook, begins to alter.'

Yours most certainly has, Theodore mused, smiling to himself.

Yes, there had been some notable changes in the Marquis, he reflected, staring through the window at countryside which never failed to gladden his heart. His good friend had appeared remarkably more tolerant during his recent stay in town; more inclined to be amused by the absurdities of his fellow man than irritated by their folly. He seemed—yes—almost more human. Was this the result of discovering himself a father? Or was it, perhaps, due entirely to the fact that Wroxam Park had at last seen the return of its mistress?

'I'm very much looking forward to making your son's acquaintance, Julian,' he remarked, when his lordship remained silently staring out of the opposite window, that same soft smile returning to soften the hard contours of his face.

'He's an impertinent imp, Theo, who has rather winning ways, so do not allow him to tease you.'

This less-than-flattering assessment of the young heir's character was uttered with such indulgence that Mr Dent frankly laughed. Yes, he mused, the Marquis of Wroxam, against all the odds, had adapted to fatherhood like the proverbial duck to water, and the deep affection in which he held his only child was patently obvious. But did this depth of feeling encompass the boy's mother?

'And Jenny…? Is she happy to be back at Wroxam Park?'

The instant he had voiced the question passing through his mind, he regretted his inquisitiveness, for his lordship's smile faded and an expression which seemed to betray both annoyance and concern flickered over the aristocratic features.

'It would be more accurate to say that she is daily becoming more resigned to living at the Park,' he admitted, his voice revealing clearly a faint hint of regret which Theodore did not quite understand.

Was it simply that Jenny was having a little difficulty in adjusting to married life once again? Or was the truth of the matter merely that she had been allowed to return to Wroxam Park because she was the mother of Julian's son, and for no other reason? For her sake, he sincerely hoped that the latter possibility was totally inaccurate. If not, then her future was uncertain to say the least.

'Here at last!' Julian announced, clearly betraying his delight at arriving back at the ancestral pile, as the carriage turned into the impressive eastern gateway. 'I sincerely trust you didn't find the journey too tedious, my dear Theo, and are not wishful to retire early tonight.'

Assuring his lordship that he had no such intentions, Theodore followed into the house which, apart from the butler who had admitted them, seemed unusually quiet and deserted.

'Welcome home, my lord,' was the butler's polite greeting, though whether the sentiment was entirely genuine was debatable, for there was certainly a slight restraint in his manner and a faint look of unease.

As Julian divested himself of hat and cane, he enquired about his son's whereabouts, and was not unduly surprised to discover that, at this hour, he had already retired for the night. 'And her ladyship...? I trust she has not already sought her bed?'

'Er—no, my lord. Will you be requiring refreshments, sir?'

'Only the liquid variety, Slocombe. We dined on the road.'

The butler appeared faintly relieved to learn this, a fact that didn't escape his lordship's notice, though he chose not to remark upon it, and merely enquired his wife's whereabouts.

'I believe that her ladyship is still to be found in the—er—barn.'

Julian was halfway across the hall, heading in the direction of his library, before his butler's disclosure struck him as rather odd. 'Now what the deuce can have taken her out there at this hour, I wonder?' he muttered to himself, checking as he reached for the door-handle. 'Theo, I'm certain Jenny will be delighted to see you. You've always been a firm favourite of hers. Let us go and seek her out before we become too comfortable.'

The instant he entered the stable-yard, his lordship detected the strains of music, a spry tune which he immediately associated with lively country dancing. Voices raised in cheerful discourse and sounds of general merriment were plainly to be heard too, so he was not unduly surprised, as he rounded the corner of the yard, to discover several of his household servants, together with a number of estate workers, sitting on bales of straw, happily supping ale which had undoubtedly come from his own cellars.

One eagle-eyed merrymaker, at least, noticed their approach. 'Holy Mary, Mother of God! 'Tis himself returned!' Mary's voice carried, and Julian couldn't forbear a smile at the reaction his unexpected appearance always seemed to have on the outspoken but touchingly loyal servant.

The exclamation of dismay was heard by most of the other revellers too, and by the time his lordship had reached the large barn's open doorway, the volume of noise had lessened noticeably, and several sheepish glances were being cast in his direction. Only those dancing continued to remain oblivious to his presence, and he was able to observe his wife, looking happier than he had ever seen her appear before, tripping lightly over the dirt floor, partnered by that impudent, handsome groom of whom she was so obviously fond.

Only when the music began to fade did Jennifer become aware of the change in atmosphere, and turned immediately in the direction of her guests' faintly wary glances.

'Good heavens! I didn't expect to see you back so soon.'

Certainly not appearing noticeably disturbed, she came smilingly forward. Julian, however, was not so foolish as to try to suppose that his return was what had prompted the expression of delighted surprise.

'And Theo!' Jennifer held out her hands which were swiftly captured in those two massive ones. 'Julian never mentioned that you would be returning with him. But then, as you are probably aware yourself, he has never been one to disclose his intentions.'

The slight narrowing of grey eyes, which had appeared somewhat softer of late, confirmed Theodore's worse fears: all was not as it should be between husband and wife.

'Truth to tell, it was a spur-of-the-moment decision on my part,' he admitted. 'Wroxam invited me to return with him, and I simply couldn't deny myself the pleasure of seeing you again. You look positively radiant, m'dear.'

The smile of welcome, still hovering about her mouth, turned fractionally crooked. 'I've long considered you the supreme master of gallantry, my dear Theo, but on this occasion I cannot accept such a pretty compliment. For the past hour I have been instructing my very good friend on how to perform Irish country dances, and know I must look a positive fright. Which reminds me...'

Turning briefly she beckoned Serena forward. 'You remember Miss Carstairs, of course?'

Having lived permanently in the capital for most of his adult life, Theodore prided himself on the fact that he knew most everyone in polite society, but he was forced to think long and hard before he realised that the statuesque female moving gracefully towards him in a charming gown of dull yellow, which emphasised the golden-brown tints in her prettily waving hair, was none other than Sir Roderick Carstairs's eldest offspring with whom Jennifer had struck up a surprising friendship when she had been in London.

Being something of a connoisseur of beauty, Theodore had never considered Miss Carstairs even remotely pretty, and he was in no danger of revising his opinion now, but he was struck by the warmth of the full-lipped smile, as she held out her hand in greeting, and the rather becoming twinkle of mischief in the fine eyes.

'Of course he does not remember me, Jenny,' Serena answered, rather liking the way the hand which clasped hers with surprising gentleness made hers feel so small and delicate. 'I am one of those people who can attend a party and very few people remember that I was ever there. Not that I have ever objected to being overlooked,' Serena continued, not granting any of her listeners the opportunity to negate this. 'It has afforded me the utmost pleasure over the years to study, quite unobserved, the frequently ludicrous behaviour of my fellow man.'

'Which is often more amusing than being the centre of attention,' Jennifer remarked, before turning to Julian, who was regarding Serena in the usual mixture of amusement and respect. 'I organised this little party by way of a thank-you to the men who kindly brought some of my belongings over from Ireland. They are wishful to make an early start in the morning, so I do not envisage the party continuing for very much longer, but you are quite welcome to remain if you wish.'

For a moment it seemed as if his lordship might accept the gracious invitation, but then he shook his head, much to Theodore's intense disappointment, for he would very much have liked to remain if only to sample the barrel of home-brewed ale which all the men appeared to be enjoying.

'Good gracious, Wroxam!' he muttered, as they made their way back across the stable-yard towards the house. 'Surely you ain't that fatigued after the journey? It wouldn't have done any harm to remain for a while.'

'On the contrary, my dear Theo,' he countered, 'it might have done just that. My wife appears to have acquired the ability to put people from any walk of life instantly at their ease. Unfortunately I do not possess that gift. My presence would undoubtedly have placed a restraint on proceedings, and I didn't wish that. Besides, I was very much hoping that you would join me in the library to sample a rather fine burgundy which Jennifer managed to acquire during her stay in London earlier this year. You see, not only did she master the art of handling people during our time apart, she also acquired an excellent palate. She never ceases to astonish me with her accomplishments!'

Aye, and you can still manage to astound me on occasions too, Theodore mused, accompanying his host into the library, and accepting the promised glass of burgundy.

Although he had never made any secret of the fact that he held the Marquis in the highest esteem, he had never been blind to his friend's faults. Undue consideration for the feelings of others had never numbered amongst his lordship's virtues, and yet he had shown rare understanding by refusing the invitation to join the merry gathering in the barn. Was it Jennifer's return which had wrought this change in a man who had been considered by many of his peers to be just a mite too high in the instep on occasions? Theodore could not help wondering, as he settled himself in one of the comfortable chairs.

'Will Jenny and her charming friend be joining us later, do you suppose?

The instant he had voiced the innocent enquiry, Theodore realised that something was wrong, for there was just the faintest tightening of the muscles about his lordship's thin-lipped mouth, clear evidence that he was not totally happy about something.

'Highly unlikely, I should imagine. Jennifer does not actively seek my company if she can possibly avoid it.' Julian had tried to sound sublimely unconcerned, but one glance at Theodore's thoughtful expression was enough to convince him that his surprisingly acute friend was suspicious.

Leaning back in his chair, he surveyed the homely face in silence for a moment. 'I never imagined that you number amongst those who foolishly suppose that I and my Marchioness are now reconciled.' His shout of laughter held a distinctly bitter note. 'Come, come, my dear Theo! Surely you know me better than that?'

Theodore's protracted sigh revealed his disappointment even before he said, 'Truth of the matter is, I've not known what to think. I had hoped, of course, that—'

'That I had learned to forgive and forget,' Julian finished for him, the cynical glint in his eyes fading as he stared fixedly down at the contents of his glass. 'Whether or not I am capable of such altruism is irrelevant in the circumstances. Jennifer is not here because she wishes to be, but because I gave her no choice in the matter. Had she not returned with me, she would have forfeited all contact with our son.

'Good god, man, don't look at me like that!' he ground out, easily recognising the recrimination in Theo's kindly blue eyes. Tossing the fine burgundy down his throat with scant regard for its excellence, Julian stalked over to the decanters to replenish his glass. 'She had kept my son's existence secret from me for eight long years. How I managed to stop myself from throttling the life out of her I'll never know! I was angry, bitterly angry at having been denied all knowledge of Charles's existence.' A moment's silence, then, 'But not so angry as to demand anything more from her other than that she return here to Wroxam Park.'

'And now?' Theodore dared to ask, as he watched him resume the seat opposite.

'Now I'm merely confused, at a loss to understand why the event which resulted in our long separation ever occurred in the first place,' Julian answered, while staring intently into concerned blue eyes, 'just as you yourself have always found my wife's adultery difficult to believe. Have you not, my dear Theo?'

He nodded, his expression grave. 'Not that I ever doubted the truth of what you told me. It was just…'

'Just what?' Julian prompted, his gaze more intense than before.

'It was just that I would never have believed Jenny capable of such behaviour. She was never a wanton, not even remotely flirtatious as a girl. What she did seemed totally out of character to me. Added to which, I could have sworn that she was in love with you.'

His lordship's clasp on the stem of the glass tightened noticeably. 'She was…once,' he murmured. 'I foolishly took that love for granted, and it has cost me dearly.' The protracted sigh was clearly audible. 'The problem is, though, if Jennifer herself is at a loss to understand why she committed adultery, it isn't likely that I'll ever be able to uncover the mystery.'

'Evidently you've discussed the matter, then,' Theodore remarked, feeling suddenly quite optimistic.

After all, only by being open and frank about the past could they ever hope to be reconciled in every sense.

His hopes, however, were swiftly dashed when his lordship disclosed, 'Jennifer has never once attempted to broach the subject, except when I met her for the first time in London. It is to her credit that she didn't attempt to make any excuses for the past, and was generous enough to accept total blame. No, I learned of her thoughts, of her complete bewilderment over the incident, from some letters she wrote to me just before she decided to leave the protection of my home all those years ago.'

Leaning back against the chair, Julian took a moment to study the contents of his glass before sampling a little of the fine wine, and taking his time to appreciate its excellence this time. 'Why I kept those letters I'll never know,' he admitted. 'I did, in fact, take the trouble to cast my eyes over the first one, but naturally I was in no mood then to appreciate its contents. Unlike the other week, when I was disposed to study every written word with extreme care, and found the missives most illuminating, if also faintly puzzling.'

'Jenny didn't attempt to—er—deny what had taken place between her and young Wilburn, I trust?' Theodore prompted when Julian fell silent, and stared fixedly at the empty grate.

'Naturally not. What she did make abundantly clear, however, was the fact that she was never in love with Geoffrey Wilburn. And, more interestingly still, that she could remember little of what took place on that fateful afternoon.'

Sandy brows drew together. 'Dueced odd, wouldn't you say? Do you believe her?'

'Surprisingly enough, Theo, yes, I do. During these past weeks I've become acquainted with my wife, which, to my everlasting shame, is something I didn't take the trouble to do nine years ago, and have come to the conclusion that she is one of the most innately honest people one could ever be blessed to know.'

Getting to his feet once more, Julian went to stand before the marble grate, resting his right arm along the length of the mantelshelf as he gazed once again down into the empty hearth. 'She is also a most loving and caring mother, who has earned the unfailing devotion of those who shared her life in Ireland. Since her return here she has swiftly won the respect of my own servants. She is quite simply a rare creature, hard working and touchingly loyal to her friends. Not the type of person one could ever imagine indulging in a meaningless affair with a man she didn't love. And I'm absolutely certain in my own mind, after spending many hours thinking back to that time, that she wasn't in love with young Geoffrey Wilburn. She was friendly towards him, but nothing more. In fact, unless I much mistake the matter, apart from a gentleman called O'Connell, a man she loved and looked upon as a father, men have played no part in her life at all during these past years.'

Theodore was not unduly surprised to learn this. 'She certainly betrayed little interest in any member of our sex during her time in the capital.'

'Ah! So you noticed that too, did you.' Julian betrayed the faintest hint of approval as he cast a glance over his shoulder. 'Very observant of you, Theo!' His expression grew more pensive. 'None the less, even though her affections are not engaged, she has no desire whatsoever to embark on a reconciliation with me.'

Theodore could easily detect the suddenly tense set of those powerful shoulders, and had not missed, either, the note of bitter regret in the refined voice which betrayed clearly enough the state of his lordship's mind.

More than just a modicum of hope returned. 'Look on the bright side, old fellow. At least there's no rival for her affections.'

The shapely hand raising the glass to his lips checked for a moment. 'Oh, I wouldn't go so far as to say that,' Julian enlightened him, faintly smiling now. 'In fact, I do have a rival, a magnificent specimen that is both powerful and handsome. That the object of his evident devotion just happens to be a Marchioness does not, believe me, matter a jot to him.' The smile grew more pronounced. 'Come, I'll take you to meet him. There's still light enough to see, and there's no time like the present.'

Displaying scant appreciation for the excellent wine, either, as he finished the contents of his glass in a hurry, Theodore followed the Marquis outside once more, experiencing the most uncomfortable feeling of unease as a vision of the handsome, golden-haired man with whom he had seen Jennifer dancing a little earlier appeared before his mind's eye. He could not in all honesty say that his lordship had betrayed even a hint of jealousy when admitting to having a rival, but Julian was remarkably adept at disguising his feelings.

He gained a little comfort when his lordship did not head in the direction of the barn, from where the sounds of music and happy chatter still emanated, but he felt a little puzzled when his friend led the way into the large stable, where most of the prized animals were housed.

'Why the deuce have you brought me in here, Wroxam?' he demanded to know, after looking about him in vain for any two-legged creature lurking in the shadows.

'You know full well why,' his lordship answered, leading the way down to the far end of the long stone building. 'I wish you to make the acquaintance of my rival. And here he is!'

'Good gad!' Theodore exclaimed, after peering into the very last stall. 'So that's your rival!'

'He is, indeed. And a worthy one, do you not agree?'

'Magnificent!' A concerned frown swiftly erased the amusement in Theodore's eyes. 'But surely he ain't Jenny's horse? She could never control such a powerful animal!'

'I have yet to see her ride him...I have only been privileged to observe the bond which exists between them. Only before have I seen such affection in a dog for its master. Believe me, Theo, it is something to witness.'

Julian turned his attention to the hunter, and after a moment managed to persuade the beautiful black to move away from the back of the stall. 'Come, Oriel, my handsome fellow. You remember me, surely? Here see what I have for you,' he coaxed and, after a moment or two, velvety lips removed the treat from his outstretched hand.

A rare, wistful and lopsided grin tugged at his own lips. 'Unless I much mistake the matter, apart from our son, only this fellow holds a place in my wife's heart... Now, how the deuce can I ever compete with him?'

Chapter Ten

Three facts became abundantly clear to his lordship during the following days: the first, and very gratifying one, was that his good friend Mr Dent was betraying a marked partiality for Miss Carstairs's company; the second, and equally gratifying, was that Charles had taken an instant liking to his tutor Mr Granger, and the third, and far less satisfactory one, was that his occasionally irksome young son betrayed no immediate signs of forgetting the notion of promoting a race between his mother and father.

Charles, being something of a cunning little rogue, never failed to broach the subject with his father when others were present, and although Jennifer herself never betrayed the least interest, both Miss Carstairs and Theodore were very enthusiastic. Which, of course, was sufficient encouragement for Charles to continue plaguing his father until, albeit most reluctantly, his lordship acquiesced.

'Why the long face, Julian?' Accompanying his lordship out to the stables on the morning the race had been arranged, Theodore could not fail to notice his friend's rather grim expression. 'Surely you don't suppose that you might lose the friendly contest? Why, you're one of the finest horsemen I know!'

'I thank you for that vote of confidence, and the compliment, Theo. But to be perfectly honest with you, I don't give a damn if I win or not. I can only wonder at myself for weakening and allowing myself to be cajoled into doing something I have not the least desire to do by that impish son of mine!'

'But why?' Theodore was genuinely at a loss to understand the reason behind this display of reluctance. 'There's no denying that Oriel is a powerful animal, and not what I'd call a lady's mount, but we've been assured by both Miss Carstairs and Patrick that Jenny is equal to the task of handling him.'

'Perhaps, but I have yet to witness her skill. Not once since we've been here has she attempted to take him out. In fact, I've never seen her on horseback since her return to Wroxam Park.'

His deep frown was clear evidence of a troubled mind, though it cleared somewhat when he noticed Patrick leading an unsaddled Oriel from the stable. 'Not one-hundred-percent fit this morning?' he enquired, but his hopes were swiftly dashed by the groom's assurance.

'To be sure the boy's fine, sir, and raring to be off, as you might say. It's just that I ain't certain sure whether the mistress is taking your challenge seriously or no. When I am sure, I'll know which saddle to put on his back. Joseph and his lads brought all three of the mistress's saddles from Ireland.'

'Three?' Theodore's sandy brows rose sharply. 'A trifle extravagant, wouldn't you say, Patrick?'

'No, sir, not when you consider the mistress has

three ways o' riding—like a lady, training and serious.' His lopsided grin appeared as he glanced towards the house. 'And it looks as if she intends riding serious today.'

Julian, following the direction of the groom's amused gaze, saw Jennifer emerging from the mansion's side door, with both Miss Carstairs and Mary at her heels. Her long auburn hair was for once simply styled, merely confined at the nape of her neck with a bright green ribbon, and she was dressed in a flowing dark green skirt, which he had never seen her wearing before, and a loose-fitting blouse of a lighter hue.

Patrick, having released the reins in order to collect the saddle from the tack-room, left Oriel free to greet Jennifer in his usual affectionate way, earning himself a scold from Mary as he did so for nearly trampling on her foot.

'Good gad, Wrox! Does the beast always behave in that fashion with Jenny?' Theodore asked, amazed at the spectacle.

'I'm afraid so. One might have expected him to have outgrown such coltish adoration by now.' He shuddered. 'Nauseating, is it not? The animal's besotted. Quite besotted!'

Theodore frankly laughed. 'Why, Wrox, old fellow, if I didn't know better I'd swear you were jealous!'

'Stop showing off and behaving like a commoner, Oriel,' Jennifer scolded lovingly. She made no attempt to grasp his reins as she made her way across the yard to join the gentlemen, but then there was absolutely no need for her to do so, for Oriel automatically followed like some adoring puppy.

'It isn't too late to change your mind, Jenny,' Julian surprised her by announcing.

'Oh, but it is,' she countered, secretly moved by the obvious concern she could easily detect in his voice.

When she had first been forced to return to Wroxam Park, nothing would have induced her to accept her husband's offer to ride one of his horses. Then, later, when she had discovered that if she wished to go out riding with Charles, she could do so only in the company of one of his lordship's grooms, stubborn pride had kept her out of the saddle. Since Oriel's arrival, however, the temptation to ride again had been too strong to resist, and she had enjoyed the hours she had spent with him, during his lordship's absence from home, galloping across the Somerset countryside. Since her husband's return she had refrained from riding, simply because she had suspected that Charles would continue to badger his father until he had agreed to the contest, and some perverse inner demon had prompted her to keep her equestrian skills a secret from him, for this was a contest she was determined to win.

'I decided, after our—er—slight disagreement the other week, that I would never again interfere in your handling of our son.'

It was not the admission itself which brought a tender smile to his lips, but the fact that for the first time ever she had acknowledged that Charles belonged to them both.

'Though I must say that I think you were extremely foolish to give way to him over this. Charles has very winning ways, I'm afraid, and can persuade people to do precisely what they have no real desire to do.' She

darted a slightly disapproving glance at the portly figure standing beside her husband. 'Besides which,
there are those who chose to lay bets with certain
persons on the outcome of this race, giving me little
choice but to take the challenge seriously. Which I
sincerely trust that you will also do, Julian.'

This time her glance was directed at her mount who
was now being saddled. 'I just hope Oriel behaves
himself. I'm afraid he can be the most appalling
show-off on occasions. Quite headstrong! But I'll do
my poor best to prevent him from getting too far
ahead of you, Julian. I wouldn't wish for it to be a
totally one-sided contest.'

Theodore could not prevent a chuckle as his
friend's look of concern was replaced by one of astonished outrage. 'You appear to think that the race is a
foregone conclusion, Jenny. Let me remind you that
Wrox, here, is no mean rider.'

'I sincerely trust you're right, Theo, otherwise
Charles will be most disappointed. He's hoping to see
a fine race.' She had some difficulty in suppressing a
smile at the indignant glance his lordship bent in her
direction, and could not resist the temptation to goad
him a little more. 'You must remember, Julian, that I
have yet to see you ride at a neck-to-nothing pace. If,
however, you have any desire to win, you are going
to need to do just that.

'By the by,' she went on without giving him the
opportunity to respond to her taunting, 'I observed on
the diagram of the route you decided upon that you
intend to skirt the home wood. I see no reason to do
so. When I rode out in that direction last week, I
noticed the main track through the wood is perfectly
suitable. Cross-country races are no fun at all if riders

do not need to negotiate obstacles, and I do not consider the banks of the stream cutting across that particular path would pose any real degree of difficulty.'

'Perhaps not, but had you forgotten the five-bar gates at either end of that particular track? Or do you intend to waste time by stopping to open and close them?'

The sarcasm was too blatant to be ignored, and Jennifer raised her finely arched brows in exaggerated surprise. 'Well, you can do so if you consider them a problem, but I fully intend to jump them both, otherwise Charles will be most dreadfully disappointed. He's dragged poor Mr Granger up to the home wood already to watch that part of the race.'

Deciding not to delay the start further, Jennifer took a hold of Oriel's reins, and got into the saddle, revealing as she did so that her skirt had been cunningly fashioned and divided in the middle so that it resembled nothing so much as a pair of rather baggy trousers as she sat astride her mount.

Knowing that his friend was a stickler for the proprieties, Theodore cast his lordship a fleeting glance, but discovered much to his surprise that, apart from slightly raised dark brows, there was no visible evidence that the Marquis disapproved of his wife's apparel or, indeed, her mode of riding.

'Shall we—er—get this contest underway?' Theodore suggested. 'You haven't forgotten, Julian, that you promised to accompany me out later to view Colonel Halstead's place?'

Although Julian would have dearly liked to have his friend residing close by, looking for a suitable country residence for Theodore to purchase was the last thing on his mind at the moment.

Mounting his grey, he accompanied Jennifer out of the yard, avidly watching Oriel's playful antics as they made their way to the starting point, which had been decided would be on the driveway at the front of the house. The powerful black was undeniably restless this morning, eager for a good gallop, and although Jennifer appeared to handle him easily enough, whether she would be able to do so at full gallop was a different matter entirely. Oriel, Julian very much feared, could be temperamental. He was also spirited and, as any seasoned rider knew, spirited horses were difficult to control on occasions.

'It would appear, Julian, that a great many of the servants have found themselves tasks at the front of the house,' Jennifer remarked wryly, and his lordship, momentarily abandoning his concerned thoughts, glanced up at the house to see peering faces at several of the windows. 'I wonder which of us they expect to see take a tumble?'

She could not fail to notice that high, intelligent brow darken, and began to experience pangs of conscience. She ought, she knew, to have proved to him that she was now a highly competent horsewoman, instead of weakening to that inner feminine demon which had prompted her to amaze him with her skills.

'I've always considered it faintly vulgar, Julian, to blow one's own trumpet, and am reliably informed that self-praise is little recommendation. None the less, I have been lucky enough to receive instruction during these past years from a true master. Believe me, James O'Connell would never have given Oriel to me if he had considered that I wasn't capable of handling him. I do not believe that I am being overconfident when I tell you that no one can handle this boy of mine nearly so well as I can. So, if you're ready…?'

She didn't wait for any response, but turned to Theodore, who stood, handkerchief raised, and gave the faintest of nods. The square of fine lawn floated to the ground, and the race was underway.

As soon as they had ridden up the sweep of the driveway, and were heading over the wide stretch of rising pasture land which led to the home wood, Julian was convinced of two things: Jennifer was possibly the finest horsewoman he'd ever seen in his life, better than most men, and certainly his equal in the saddle; and that his chances of winning the contest were zero, a fact which surprisingly enough didn't trouble him in the least, even though he was a man who didn't like to lose.

Lost in admiration, he was happy to watch Oriel gradually increasing the slight lead he had held from the start, and was convinced that Jennifer was not allowing the powerful black to have his head quite yet. They were as one, both horse and rider in perfect accord. The hunter had indeed been well named, for he seemed to fly across the ground like some unearthly creature. Or perhaps, Julian mused, admiring the superb way Jennifer checked her mount's stride before effortlessly clearing with inches to spare the five-bar gate leading to the wood, Oriel felt as if he were carrying a mere fairy on his back, so light was the weight, so slight the control of those slender, expert hands.

He began to fall further and further behind as they rode along the woodland path. He vaguely heard the cheers from his son, urging him on, but he knew the race was lost. As his excellent mount easily cleared the second gate, he was content to watch the peerless display of equestrian skill as Jennifer, at last giving her superb mount his head, galloped across the beautiful park back towards the house.

By the time Julian arrived back at the stable-yard, Jennifer had already dismounted and was receiving heartfelt congratulations from both Theodore and Miss Carstairs, together with those of several of the stable-lads who had witnessed the fine ride.

Julian found it impossible not to smile at the cheeky wink he received from Patrick as the groom led the superb black hunter back into the stable. Patrick had mentioned on more than one occasion just what a fine horsewoman Jennifer was. Charles too had not infrequently praised his mother's equestrian skills, and Jennifer herself had admitted to being no mean rider. And Jennifer did not lie; a fact that he had accepted for some little time.

'Ah, Wroxam!' Theodore, noticing him at last, voiced his commiseration. 'But you were up against superb competition, what?'

'Indeed I was.' Dismounting, he handed his grey over to one of the stable-lads before turning to the victor, his eyes betraying the unalloyed admiration he was experiencing. 'I was comprehensively beaten, madam. I congratulate you.'

Once again Jennifer felt moved by the sincerity she clearly detected in his voice. 'The outcome might have been different had you taken the challenge seriously, Julian, and had not allowed me to take the lead at the start.' She turned in time to see his favourite mount being led into the stable. 'That grey of yours is no slug. I do not believe there is much to

choose between him and Oriel, and he was handi-
capped by extra weight.'

'Perhaps next time we might exchange mounts?'
he suggested, swiftly warming to the notion of a re-
match, but Jennifer, surprisingly, wasn't so enthusiastic.

'Much will depend on Oriel, I'm afraid. He can
be a contrary demon on occasions, and is quite particular whom he allows on his back. You'll need to
win his approval first, then we'll see.' She turned towards the house. 'In the meantime, I must change my
attire.'

'Yes, and so must I. I'll meet you back here in
fifteen minutes, Theo,' his lordship assured him, leaving Serena with just Mr Dent to bear her company.

Not that she objected to this in the least. He might
not be every female's idea of the perfect male companion, but he was swiftly becoming hers. Although
he was large, slightly on the portly side and not remotely handsome, he was every inch the gentleman,
both affable and charming. He was also a most entertaining conversationalist, whose occasionally
vague, rather childlike gaze concealed a keen mind
and razor-sharp intelligence.

Since his arrival at Wroxam Park she had grown
very partial to this large man's company, and experienced no reticence now in remarking, as she
watched her host and hostess disappear into the
house, 'What an ideal couple those two make. At
least, they would be remarkably compatible if ever
they manage to put past events behind them.'

She glanced up at him and knew by his faintly wary
expression precisely what was passing through his
mind. 'It is all right, Mr Dent,' she assured him. 'I

know all. Jennifer confided in me shortly after I arrived here. I know, also, that you are one of the few in his lordship's confidence. What do you make of it all?'

They had begun to walk towards the gateway leading to the shrubbery. It was unlikely that any one of the stable-lads could manage to overhear. None the less, Theodore waited until they'd passed through the gateway before he said, 'Yes, it was all very sad.'

'And very perplexing too, do you not think?' Again she shook her head. 'I cannot imagine dear Jenny ever doing such a thing.'

Massive shoulders rose and fell. 'She was very young. And it must be said that Julian has been known to be selfish, inconsiderate on occasions. At least he used to be. He wasn't perhaps as sympathetic towards his young bride as he might have been. So I suppose it is quite understandable, when you come to think about it, why Jenny sought companionship elsewhere.'

'Companionship, yes,' Serena readily agreed. 'But that, I suspect, was all she sought. She's admitted that she was very much in love with his lordship when they married.' Serena raised both hands in a helpless gesture, at a loss to understand. 'And why is it that she can remember so little about what took place between her and Mr Wilburn that afternoon?'

Theodore drew his sandy brows together as memory stirred. 'Yes, Julian, I recall, mentioned something about that… Yes, it is most odd.' He shrugged again. 'I suppose it is quite possible, though, Miss Carstairs, that the incident is something Jennifer might have preferred to forget.'

'Might have lied in an attempt to save her marriage,

you mean,' she responded, putting his thoughts a little more bluntly than he might have wished. She nodded. 'Yes. Yes, I can understand why you might think that. It is the most obvious explanation—lie in order to save face. But that doesn't answer the question of why now she still claims not to remember. When she returned to England earlier in the year, it was for the sole purpose of requesting his lordship to take steps to terminate their union. There was no reason for her to continue to try to excuse past behaviour... And I, for one, do not believe that she ever did lie.'

Theodore digested this for a moment. 'You may be right, but I think it would be futile trying to speculate on what happened. Besides which, I do not believe that the events of that day are important to that extent any longer.'

'Not to his lordship, no,' Serena agreed, smiling faintly. 'Jennifer, on the other hand, is a different matter entirely.' Her smile widened as she glanced up at the kindly, rounded face. 'But you're quite right—it is futile to speculate. And I must not keep you. No doubt his lordship has returned to the stable-yard by now.'

Reluctantly, it seemed to her, he bade a hurried farewell, and for a moment she followed his progress along the path leading back to the stables, then she turned and walked in the opposite direction. Soon she found herself in the formal gardens at the back of the house and, enjoying the pleasant morning sunshine, continued along the path, arriving at the front of the magnificent Restoration mansion in time to see an all-too-familiar carriage pull up outside the front entrance. Her heart sank.

Chapter Eleven

Jennifer was made aware of the unexpected arrival by Slocombe, who came up to her apartments to inform her that Miss Carstairs was entertaining her mother in the front parlour, and that he had taken it upon himself to furnish the visitor with refreshments. For a moment Jennifer toyed with the idea of hurrying downstairs in order to offer her friend moral support, but then decided against it, and instead seated herself at the dressing table, informing Rose that she might take all the time she required to dress her mistress's hair.

The purpose behind the visit was obvious: Lady Carstairs had undoubtedly made the journey to Somerset in order to persuade her daughter to return home. But would Serena wish to go? That was the all important question. If she did not, then there was absolutely no reason why she should do so. She could be in no doubt that she was welcome to remain at Wroxam Park for as long as she wished. Julian had raised not the least objection to her remaining under his roof. In fact, he had made her most welcome from the start, betraying a surprising bent for her company, so she could be under no illusion whatsoever that her presence in the house was anything but welcome. Furthermore, since Mr Dent's arrival, Serena had not once broached the subject of moving on to Bath to take up residence with her godmother. Which, of course, had been her original intention.

Jennifer smiled to herself as the last curl was neatly pinned into position, and she nodded dismissal to the young maid. Julian was by no means the only one to betray a fondness for the sensible Miss Carstairs's company. It had been a delight to witness the friendship developing between Theodore and Serena during these past days. They had gone along famously from the start. Which was most surprising, really, now that she came to consider the matter, because they were both essentially very reserved people who were not given to indulging in idle chatter. Yet, she had come upon them on several occasions, sitting together, discussing some topic or other, both seemingly remarkably content in each other's company.

It was too early to tell at this stage whether a deeper relationship might develop between them, and she certainly had no intention of interfering in such a personal matter. None the less, Jennifer couldn't help feeling quite optimistic. After all, Theodore had suddenly developed a keen interest in finding himself a suitable country residence, and had dragged Julian off to visit the Grange, the fine country house which Colonel Halstead had decided to sell.

The clock in the bedchamber chiming the hour interrupted her pleasant musings. She judged that Serena had been alone with her mother in the parlour for half an hour, and felt that she couldn't possibly ignore the unexpected visitor's presence in the house

any longer. Hopefully, Lady Carstairs had finally
come to her senses, and had decided to abandon her
foolish attempt to coerce poor Serena into marriage
with a man that she found abhorrent. If this was indeed the case, then Serena had nothing to fear, and
perhaps might now wish to return to the family home.

A sigh escaped her as Jennifer moved across to the
wardrobe to collect one of her lightweight silk shawls.
She would miss her friend's company very much.
Serena's presence in the house during these past two
weeks or so had made her own position far more tol-
erable, almost pleasurable. She could, of course, invite Serena to return a little later in the year.

The idea had been such a natural one that it was a
moment or two before she realised in which direction
her thoughts were leading. What made her suppose
that she would still be residing at Wroxam Park later
in the year? Her present position was tenuous to say
the least. Even supposing Julian was content with his
present domestic situation, there was no guarantee
that he would continue to be so. More importantly,
was she, without being aware of it, becoming more
reconciled to the idea of remaining under this roof,
foolishly looking upon Wroxam Park as her home?

Before she could decide upon an answer, her reflections were interrupted by a gentle tapping on the
bedchamber door. A moment later Serena herself entered, appearing remarkably cheerful on the surface.
Beneath the bright smile, however, Jennifer thought
she could detect just the faintest hint of tension, and
began to suspect that the reunion between mother and
daughter had not been wholly joyous.

'Jenny, can you possibly spare me a few minutes
of your time?'

'As much as you like, my dear,' she responded, striving to sound cheerful herself when, in fact, her misgivings were swiftly increasing. What on earth had Lady Carstairs been saying? Surely she hadn't travelled all the way to Somerset merely to take Serena roundly to task for having left the family home? Sadly that wasn't beyond the realms of possibility. Lady Carstairs could on occasions, Jennifer reflected, experiencing a stab of irritation, be a remarkably tiresome and foolish female! She decided not to waste time in trying to avoid the issue.

'Naturally I have been apprised of your mother's arrival, but thought you would appreciate some time alone together. I trust that Slocombe has seen to everything in his usual, efficient way, and has had a room prepared for her?'

Serena shook her head. 'Mama is putting up at the local inn. She has, in fact, already returned there. She intends to leave for Hampshire directly after luncheon, and is hoping that I shall accompany her.'

'And will you?' Jennifer enquired, uneasiness mounting.

'But of course! Mama swiftly made me realise how very foolish I had been to run away in that dramatic way. More the actions of a silly schoolgirl than a sensible woman, wouldn't you say?'

Jennifer found herself quite unable to say anything, and merely stared rather thoughtfully across the room, until Serena, lowering her own gaze, went across to stand by the window.

'Mama has made me realise too that I've been foolish to turn down Lord Sloane's offer of marriage, without giving the matter some serious thought. And upon reflection I have decided to reconsider. After all,

Jenny, I shall be a titled lady if I marry him, able to command respect. I'll be mistress of my own home too. There's a great deal to be said for that… So, you see, I have experienced a change of heart, and have decided to marry the Baron.'

Serena's unexpected gurgle of laughter before she turned to look across the room sounded more than just a little forced. 'Well…? Are you not going to congratulate me?'

'I might if I thought for a moment that your heart was truly involved.' Jennifer thought she could detect a suspicion of tears before her friend, once more seeming unable to meet her gaze, turned to stare out of the window again.

'I would be the first to admit that it is less than sensible to make snap judgements on our fellows,' she went on, when Serena didn't attempt to speak. 'None the less, I took an instant dislike to Lord Sloane when I met him in London. You were given the opportunity to become better acquainted with him than I was, and you came to the conclusion that he was the very last man you would ever wish to marry. It is my considered opinion that you haven't changed your mind. It is also my considered opinion that up until the interview with your mother a short while ago nothing in the world would ever have induced you to marry Lord Sloane. Furthermore,' she added, with a flash of inspiration, determined to get to the truth, 'I have witnessed a sincere regard developing between you and a certain other gentleman—'

'Don't! Please don't!' Serena cut in, her voice an agonised cry. 'I have no choice, don't you see!'

'No, my dear, I do not see,' Jennifer returned, unfailingly truthful, before she bridged the distance between them and coaxed a now silently weeping Serena to sit on the chaise-longue.

This rare display of emotion was confirmation enough for Jennifer to be sure that her suspicions hadn't been mere fancy. Serena was no fickle young woman, given to changing her mind at the drop of a hat. Unless Jennifer misunderstood the situation entirely, Serena still had no desire to become Lady Sloane. So what on earth could Lady Carstairs have disclosed to force poor Serena to reconsider?

'May I ask you something?' She paused a moment, waiting for the tears to subside. 'Does your mother truly wish you to form an alliance with this man?'

Appearing utterly wretched, Serena shook her head. 'She loathes him… Poor Mama! She looked so ill…is at her wits' end.'

Jennifer could gain little comfort from this. 'I see,' she murmured. 'In that case, I can only assume that Lord Sloane has some hold over your family…at least, over your mother.'

Serena, wisely, didn't attempt to deny it. 'Apparently, he has in his possession certain letters written by my mother to a gentleman she knew years ago. If their contents were ever made known it would bring shame to my family, and total ruin to my poor dear sister.'

Serena didn't attempt to explain further, but there was absolutely no need for her to do so, for Jennifer was fairly certain she had grasped the all-too-obvious implication. She sighed. 'Your sister Louisa is not, I assume, your father's child?'

Appearing as if she carried the cares of the world on her shoulders, Serena gave a distinctly weary shake of her head this time. 'Because of the family's opposition, Mama was unable to marry her childhood sweetheart, Francis Deacon. Years later, after she had married Papa, and had given birth to me, she went to London and stayed in my uncle's house in Berkeley Square. I believe I once mentioned to you that Papa was not one for socialising on any grand scale. He soon tired of the social whirl and left Mama alone in the capital to enjoy the remainder of the Season.'

Serena took a moment to take out her handkerchief and wipe away the evidence of tears. 'Mama assured me that she didn't go out of her way to be in the company of Francis Deacon, Jenny, and I believe her. Inevitably, though, their paths did cross, and...'

'And they had an affair,' Jennifer finished for her, thinking how achingly familiar it was all beginning to sound.

'Don't think badly of her, Jenny. I honestly do not believe she intended to have an affair with this man.'

Smiling wryly, Jennifer rose to her feet, and went across the room to take up her friend's former position before the bedchamber window. 'I'm the last person to pass judgement.'

Utterly desolate though she was, Serena found sufficient spirit not to allow this to go unchallenged. 'There is absolutely no comparison between what my mother did and what happened to you, Jenny. None whatsoever! My mother was our age when her affair took place. She admitted quite openly that she knew precisely what she was doing, and that she and Deacon met secretly on more than one occasion. It is to her credit, I suppose, that she didn't attempt to condone her behaviour, although I believe she truly thought that she was in love with Francis Deacon at the time.

'Of course, she swiftly came to realise her mistake,' Serena divulged after a moment's silence, 'and was forced to acknowledge that he was nothing more than the feckless fribble her family had always considered him. After she had returned to Hampshire, she did inform him that she was carrying his child, but he didn't attempt to respond to any of the letters she wrote him.'

Once again Jennifer was reminded of the heartrending comparison in her own life, but swiftly thrust the painful memory aside. 'And somehow your mother's letters came into Lord Sloane's callous hands?'

'That isn't so difficult to understand when one considers that Sloane and Deacon were close friends. Deacon passed away last year, and Mama seems to think that he must have appointed Sloane his executor. We can only speculate on why Deacon chose to keep the letters. It is highly likely, however, that Sloane came upon them when he was going through his friend's papers, and decided that they might come in useful.'

'For a spot of blackmailing. Yes, I can see that,' Jennifer readily agreed, before drawing her brows together in a puzzled frown. 'Except that the blackmailer's usual motive is financial gain. And as you've mentioned yourself, on more than one occasion, your parents are not so very plump in the pocket, and your dowry is small.'

Much struck by this, Serena frowned. 'And what is more, I'm hardly the type of female to appeal to a man of Lord Sloane's stamp.'

'You underrate yourself, my dear,' Jennifer countered, conveniently forgetting that that was precisely what she herself had once thought. 'I know of at least

one man who finds your company most pleasurable.'
The remark brought a highly satisfying return of colour to Serena's thin cheeks. 'But you're right in thinking Sloane's behaviour most odd. And why, I ask myself, this urgency on his part to secure a bride?'

Again she consulted the mantel clock, and saw that time was pressing. 'I mustn't delay your departure further. Your mother will be understandably anxious. My carriage, of course, is at your disposal.'

Reluctantly, Serena went slowly across to the door. 'You will, I trust, make my farewells to his lordship and—and Mr Dent? I have no wish for you to lie on my account, Jenny. But if you could possibly conceal the truth for as long as possible. Perhaps you might say that I've received word that my father is unwell, and so feel I must return to Hampshire.'

'You may rely upon me, Serena,' Jennifer assured her, before adding, 'and I would advise you not to be in too much of a hurry in contacting Lord Sloane and accepting his offer of marriage. Delay for as long as you can.'

If it was possible for someone to appear both hopeful and puzzled at one and the same time, Serena certainly looked it now. 'Well, I shall of course, if you think—'

'My dear, I do not know what to think,' Jennifer interrupted. 'But I mean to discover, if I can, why Lord Sloane is intent on having you for a wife. You have my word, Serena, that I shall do everything within my power to keep you from marrying that man!'

Later, when Jennifer went downstairs to the dining-room to join the gentlemen for luncheon, and explained the reason for her friend's absence from the table, reactions to the news were both varied and interesting.

Julian said nothing at all, merely raising his brows whilst subjecting her to a prolonged and searching stare, which left her in no doubt whatsoever that he was not entirely convinced that the explanation offered was the true one. Although Theodore did not comment very much either, merely voicing the hope that Serena would find her father much improved by the time she arrived home, Jennifer gained the distinct impression that he was far more upset by Miss Carstairs leaving than he was revealing. Consequently she was not in the least surprised when, a short time later, he announced his intention of returning to London the following day.

Jennifer was naturally saddened to see him go, but as she stood outside, waving a last farewell before the post-chaise hired for the journey began to move away, she felt sure it would not be too long before she saw the large gentleman again.

During the past twenty-four hours she had been granted ample time to consider how best she could help poor Serena out of her unfortunate predicament, and had come to the conclusion that only by travelling to London herself could she possibly discover what might have prompted Lord Sloane's surprising proposal of marriage. The more she had considered the matter the more certain she had become that prim, sensible Serena was hardly the kind of female to appeal to the bawdy, lascivious Lord whose tastes, if common reports were to be believed, ran to the more exotic. So what possibly could be the motive in his relentless pursuit of Miss Serena Carstairs?

'Something appears to be troubling you, my dear,' Julian remarked, not slow to notice the furrows creasing her white brow, as he accompanied her back into the house.

Jennifer didn't attempt to deny it. With Theodore's departure the need for secrecy had gone. 'I know you are extremely busy this morning, Julian, and wish to catch up with your work now that both our friends have left us, but could you possibly spare me a few minutes of your time before you start wading through that mountain of papers awaiting your attention in the library?'

He didn't take even a moment to consider the matter, which gave her every reason to suppose that he might be sympathetic. Her hopes were swiftly dashed, however, when he looked coolly across the desk at her, after she had made known her intention of travelling to London that very afternoon, and responded softly,

'Have you, perhaps, forgotten the bargain we made the day you moved back to Wroxam Park?'

She was nonplussed for a moment, then memory returned. 'But surely, Julian, you will not hold me to that agreement in these circumstances? I do not wish to travel to the metropolis for pleasure, but to help Serena out of her present predicament.'

'I'm afraid you will need to explain a little more fully.' The distinctly sardonic curl to his lips did not precisely boost her confidence. 'I understood Miss Carstairs returned to Hampshire because of her father's ill health.'

He was being deliberately provoking; there was not a doubt in her mind about it. 'Oh, come now, Julian! You knew that wasn't the truth. Serena asked me to say that because…well, because she didn't wish her real motive for returning to become common knowledge. But it would seem I have no alternative but to inform you of it now.'

She felt strongly inclined to keep him guessing, but knew that contrariness wouldn't serve her cause, and promptly relayed all that Serena had revealed.

His lordship betrayed not the smallest hint of sympathy; if anything his look was faintly derisive. 'Letters, I assume, of a highly delicate and personal nature?'

Jennifer did not attempt to deny it. 'Yes. Letters written by Lady Carstairs years ago to a certain gentleman of her acquaintance whom she had once hoped to marry, and for whom she had once retained a strong regard.'

'Very delicately put, my dear,' he announced, the derision more marked than before. 'And did their affair bear fruit, by any chance?'

Jennifer was forced silently to concede, as she rose from the chair and went over to the library window, that her husband was nothing if not extremely astute.

'Yes, Serena's sister, Louisa,' she confirmed softly. 'So you see, Julian, why I must get my hands on those letters.'

'Without wishing to appear vulgarly curious, how do you propose to do that?'

'I have money…I shall offer to—'

'Don't be ridiculous, girl!' he cut in sharply, making her start. 'You may think yourself up to snuff, but you're no match for a man of Sloane's stamp! He would demand a small fortune in return for those letters.' His expression darkened, before his lip curled in a clear display of contempt. 'And perhaps a great deal more from you besides.'

The implication was perfectly plain, and Jennifer experienced both humiliation and anger in equal measures, before anger became the clear victor. Not once had she ever attempted to deny that she and she alone had been responsible for the failure of their marriage. She had paid dearly for her fall from grace, and the shame she had experienced remained with her even after all this time. She needed no cruelly taunting reminders of that one immoral lapse, especially not from this man whose own behaviour in recent years was certainly not beyond reproach.

'Might he, indeed?' she responded, with deceptive mildness, as a desire to hurt him in return swelled like an unstoppable torrent of water.

She moved back across to the desk and, placing her hands on the highly polished wood, leaned forward so that he could not fail to notice the dangerous glint in her eyes.

'In that case he is doomed to disappointment. Since my return to this country not one gentleman has crossed my path on whom I would gladly bestow my favours…as well you know.'

She had the satisfaction of seeing the contemptuous smirk disappear. The gratification she gained from the knowledge that she had succeeded in piercing that masculine armour was, none the less, short-lived, and she swiftly realised that, like a predatory beast, he was far more dangerous when wounded.

'Your fastidiousness undoubtedly does you great credit, my dear. Let us hope that you are as exemplary when it comes to pledging your word.' He learned forward so that his face was only inches away from hers, his eyes glinting every bit as brightly as her own. 'Leave this house without my consent, and you will never be allowed to return.'

Only by dint of tapping into those strong reserves of self-restraint did Jennifer stop herself from lashing out at him with her fists. That and the knowledge that no physical attack could ever possibly succeed in hurting him enough to quench her sudden thirst for revenge.

Raising herself up to her full height, she stared down at him, the contempt she was feeling clearly mirrored in her eyes. 'You are utterly despicable,' she told him, her voice amazingly steady considering she was inwardly trembling with rage. 'How right I was to question, to doubt your displays of thoughtful concern and gestures of friendship during these past weeks. You haven't changed, Wroxam—no, not a whit! You are still the same cold, heartless automaton I married nine years ago.'

With one angry sweep of her hand she sent the pile of papers neatly stacked on the corner of his desk cascading to the floor. 'But this I swear, as God's my judge, that one day, no matter how long it takes me, I shall make you suffer the same agonising torment as you are putting me through now by callously denying me the opportunity of at least attempting to help my friend!'

Chapter Twelve

Without granting him the opportunity to utter anything further, Jennifer stormed from the room, too angry to notice that behind the glinting annoyance in his eyes at her childish display of temper, lurked an emotion closer to desolation than satisfaction at having foiled her plans to visit the capital.

Mary, coming upon her young mistress at the head of the stairs, realised at a glance that all was far from well, but knew better than to try to dissuade her mistress from leaving the house. When Miss Jenny was in one of her black moods she was best left alone until her temper had cooled and she had been given time to think things through.

Patrick was of a similar mind when, attired in her elegant bottle-green habit, she appeared in the stable-yard a short while later, demanding that Oriel be saddled at once. He would have much preferred, as he stood at the imposing arched entrance to the stables, following her progress up the long sweep of the drive, to have been granted permission to accompany her. None the less, he consoled himself with the knowledge that, no matter how black Miss Jenny's mood, her love of horses, and of Oriel in particular, would always ensure that she would never dream of riding in a manner that would put her mount at risk.

His faith in her was fully justified, for although she gave her precious black hunter his head over the rising pasture land, the area she and his lordship had crossed during that memorable race, she checked to a canter well before entering the wooded area which formed part of the border with Melissa Royston's land.

Jennifer had never ridden this way, nor this far, since her return to Wroxam Park. The excellent neighbourly relations which existed between Mrs Royston and his lordship ensured that Melissa would never object to any one of his lordship's relations or friends trespassing on her land; this knowledge, coupled with a need to be alone with her thoughts for a while longer, persuaded Jennifer to venture further into the wood.

Whether or not it was a subconscious desire, or the fact that she had merely kept to the wide track cutting through the wood from east to west, Jennifer wasn't perfectly certain, but eventually she arrived at the old cottage which Melissa's half-brother years before had frequently used as a shelter whenever he had taken it into his head to enjoy a day's shooting.

Slipping lightly to the ground, Jennifer released her hold on the reins, confident that Oriel would not wander very far away, and then turned her attention to the small thatched building which she had visited only once before in her life, a visit she wished with all her heart she had never made.

How neglected, how very shabby it looked now! she thought, momentarily focusing her attention on the poor condition of the thatch, before studying the patches of grime on the lime-washed walls and the rotting window frames and door. She doubted very much that the place had been used since Geoffrey's departure. Which was such a shame, such a waste! After a few necessary repairs, it would make a working man and his family a comfortable home, she decided, reaching for the latch.

The door creaked open on rusty hinges, and Jennifer entered to discover a film of dust everywhere, and cobwebs hanging from the ceiling and clinging to every object in the large single room. The air was stale, heavy with the unpleasant odour of damp and decay. Yet, she had ventured into places during recent years which had been more dilapidated than this one, she reminded herself, staring about with interest.

After a few moments her eyes came to rest upon the small table, tucked away in the corner by the large inglenook, where she and Geoffrey had sat on that grey September afternoon, waiting for the rain to stop. She could not prevent a faint, bitter smile tugging at her lips. A soaking wouldn't have done her a mite of harm, so why on earth had she allowed Geoffrey to persuade her to seek shelter here until the shower had passed? How well she remembered that it was indeed his suggestion that they sought refuge from the rain here. How well she remembered, too, sitting at that small table, enjoying a glass or two of wine. Her eyes automatically turned towards the object in the opposite corner of the room. Try as she might, though, she could not recall climbing into that box bed. Yet, she had undeniably woken to find herself there, with Geoffrey lying beside her—irrefutable evidence of adultery.

Woken...? Narrow-eyed, Jennifer stared at the bed more intently. Yes, she had been asleep. How strange that she should have suddenly remembered that very interesting fact after all these years. She had woken to find Julian, looking as grim as a thundercloud, framed in the doorway, and to discover Geoffrey beside her in the bed. Had their lovemaking so exhausted her that she had sought refuge in sleep? It seemed the most obvious explanation, and yet, if that were indeed the case, why did she retain no memory whatsoever of the energetic coupling?

She shook her head, at a loss to understand what might have prompted her to behave in such a debased fashion. Well, no matter the reason, that moment of weakness, that one occasion when she had succumbed to baser desires, had cost her dear. Sins, as she had once remarked to Slocombe, cast long shadows, and she doubted very much that she would ever step out from beneath hers; at least, if her husband had his way she most definitely would never be allowed to do so.

Her mind automatically returned to their confrontation earlier. He had quite evidently been suspicious of her motives in wanting to go to London. The truth of the matter was, of course, that he simply didn't trust her. What other reason could there have been for denying her the chance to help poor Serena?

Suddenly feeling stifled by the stale atmosphere, she went back outside to discover a rapidly darkening sky. Again she could not prevent a wry smile. History, it seemed, had a habit of repeating itself; only this time she had no intention of sheltering here until the approaching storm had passed, and went directly across the small clearing to where Oriel waited happily beneath the shading trees, munching clumps of sweet grass.

By continuing along the wood's main track, she quickly reached the lane that a little further along divided: the left-hand fork leading to Melissa Royston's home; the other leading to Wroxam Park. By taking this route she would lessen her journey by some twenty minutes or so which, she hoped, would be sufficient to spare her a soaking.

She was on the point of turning Oriel onto the lane when she heard a vehicle approaching, and a few moments later a familiar carriage came bowling round the corner. She decided to wait for it to pass, but wasn't in the least surprised when it drew to a halt just after passing by, and the owner of the elegant equipage poked her head out of the window.

'Why, Jennifer! What a pleasant surprise! I was only speaking to Colonel Halstead and his charming wife this morning, and was hearing all about a certain race between you and Wroxam.'

'How are you, Melissa?' Jennifer asked, more out of politeness than any undue interest in her neighbour's welfare, as she drew Oriel to a halt alongside. 'I did not realise you had returned from your visit to your aunt. I trust you left her much improved in health?'

A faint look of surprise flickered for a moment in dark eyes. 'Oh, yes… Well, she was as robust as one could expect a woman of her advanced years to be.' The dark eyes then focused on Oriel's proud head. 'So, this is the beast I've been hearing so much about. A fine animal indeed!'

As Melissa's knowledge of horseflesh was minimal, this could hardly be considered a glowing compliment. Oriel, at any event, seemed not to think so, or he had taken an instant dislike to the stranger, for he shied away, seemingly eager to bring the encounter to an end.

Jennifer certainly felt inclined to do just that also, and so decided to oblige her beloved mount. 'The boy here is not fond of storms, and as there appears to be one brewing, I must get him back to the safety of his stable as quickly as possible.'

'Oh, surely not!' Melissa countered, looking surprisingly disappointed. 'I'm certain we'll only catch the edge of it, if that. Come to the house and partake of a glass of wine. We've never been granted the opportunity to enjoy a comfortable coze alone since your return, and I'm simply longing to catch up on all your news. My groom will take care of your horse.'

To have refused would have seemed churlish, Jennifer reluctantly decided. Added to which, relations between her and Julian had reached an all-time low. It would be foolish to make the decidedly fraught situation even worse by snubbing his favourite neighbour.

So, accepting the invitation with as much grace as she could muster, she rode beside the carriage to Melissa's home, and after leaving Oriel in the care of an eager young stable-lad, who betrayed every evidence of delight at being left to take charge of such a fine specimen of horseflesh, Jennifer crossed the threshold of a house she had not entered for nine years.

Whether or not she was more observant now that she used to be she was not perfectly certain. However, the first thing that struck her most forcibly was the tasteful elegance of her surroundings. She might not hold Melissa in particularly high regard, but she wasn't so prejudiced that she could not acknowledge that Julian's closest neighbour had impeccable taste. Although the house could not compare with the grandeur of Wroxam Park, it was none the less a well-maintained residence that had been charmingly decorated and handsomely furnished, with no expense spared. Which was not so surprising when one came to consider that Melissa's late husband, Josiah Royston, had been a wealthy nabob, making a fortune out in India before returning, well into middle age, to the land of his birth to enjoy his wealth.

After being shown into the comfortable parlour, Jennifer seated herself on one of the elegant Sheraton chairs, and frowned slightly as she recalled a remark Mary had passed not so very long ago.

Yes, it was most odd, now that she came to consider the matter, that Melissa, an undeniably attractive and well-heeled woman, had chosen not to marry again. Wealthy young widows were, of course, prime targets for heartless fortune-hunters which, understandably, might make Melissa wary of any gentleman singling her out for particular attention. Nevertheless, it was strange that, having ample funds to do so, she had never attempted to acquire a town house, or one even in Bath, which lay within easy reach, less than a day's journey away. A change of scenery, even if one chose not to socialise to any great extent, was always very heartening, and yet Melissa seemed content to remain at Wilburn Hall throughout the year, paying and receiving visits from neighbours, and holding the occasional dinner-party.

Having removed her bonnet and pelisse, the object

of Jennifer's thoughts came into the room, her full lips curled into that smile which never seemed to soften the penetrating directness of those dark eyes.

'Oh, did not my servant furnish you with refreshments? How exceedingly remiss of him. I shall speak to him later.'

'No, please do not take him to task over such a trivial matter,' Jennifer countered. The butler was old, and would be unlikely to attain a new position if he was dismissed. 'I am requiring nothing, thank you.'

'Oh, but surely you'll join me in partaking of a glass of wine?' Seemingly refusing to take no for an answer, Melissa went over to the table on which several decanters stood. 'Are you still entertaining guests at the Park? I understood from what Colonel Halstead was saying that Mr Dent has been with you, and has shown an interest in purchasing the Colonel's house.'

As Jennifer had no intention of addressing Melissa's back, perfectly straight though it undeniably was, she waited until she had been furnished with a glass, and her neighbour had seated herself in the chair opposite.

'From odd things he said during his stay, I gained the distinct impression that he's no longer content to remain in the capital all year round, as he once was.' Jennifer paused to sample the contents of the glass, and found it not at all to her taste, but managed to suppress a grimace. 'Theo left us this morning, without confirming for certain that he intends to buy the Grange.'

'And your friend—I'm afraid I cannot recall her name—is she still with you?'

'No, Miss Carstairs unfortunately was forced to cut

her visit short. She received news that her father is unwell.'

Jennifer suffered a further sip of wine before placing her glass on a conveniently positioned table nearby, conscious as she did so that Melissa was avidly watching her like a cat vigilantly guarding a mouse hole, just waiting for the hapless inhabitant to appear.

'In that case I insist that you accept the invitation I issued before I went to visit my aunt to dine here with me one evening very soon. You have never done so since your return. It was extremely remiss of me not to have insisted long before now. My only excuse is that I gained the distinct impression that Julian seemed disinclined to socialise to any great extent when he first brought you back to Wroxam Park. No doubt he was giving you the opportunity to settle yourself. Such a considerate man!'

Considerate? Jennifer reached for her wine once more. Dear Lord! She braved a further sip, unable to decide which was worse—Melissa's inability to pick a wine, or her misguided assessment of a certain someone's character. 'Perhaps now that our guests have left us, he will begin to socialise a little more. Most of our neighbours, I believe, have returned to their country homes now that the Season is over.'

Over the rim of her glass, she had little difficulty in returning that dark-eyed scrutiny. 'I'm rather surprised, Melissa, that you spend so much time here,' she remarked, giving voice to her earlier thoughts. 'Do you never wish to visit the capital, or spend the summer in Brighton?'

Shapely shoulders rose in a shrug. 'I'm content enough here, Jennifer, although there are times, even after all these years, when I do miss dear Geoffrey's company.'

Jennifer couldn't help smiling to herself. She had wondered how long it would be before Geoffrey's name was mentioned. It was possible, of course, that Melissa genuinely missed her young brother and, granted the opportunity, was always eager to talk about him with someone who once looked upon him with affection. Somehow, though, Jennifer didn't think that this was the reason. It was much more likely that she held Lady Wroxam wholly responsible for what had occurred, and had no intention of allowing her to forget it.

Nerves still raw after the pounding they had received earlier that morning, Jennifer was in no mood to be reminded further of past sins. She had never tried to make excuses for what she had done, nor had she ever been afraid to shoulder her share of the blame. None the less, she hadn't been wholly responsible for what had happened that day, and she had no intention of being branded the sole villain of the piece.

'Yes, I'm sure you must miss him, Melissa.' She took a further sip of wine, quickly deciding that it didn't improve with sampling. 'How long has he been living abroad?' In truth, her interest in Geoffrey now was tepid at best, but she flatly refused to allow Melissa to suppose that she was in the least reluctant to talk about him. 'I believe you mentioned that his health is not good. Is that why he chose to live in Italy?'

'In part, yes. Art, as you may remember, was his ruling passion, and he always wanted to paint in that country.' Again she shrugged her shapely shoulders before adding, 'And after what happened, it seemed an appropriate time to leave and fulfil his dream.'

Jennifer hadn't missed the glint of malice which just for one unguarded moment flickered in those dark eyes before they lowered. Oh, no, Mrs Royston was certainly no friend of hers, and it was doubtful that she would ever wish to be. Was it merely that she considered the Marchioness a heartless seductress who had brought shame on her brother, and had forced him to move away? Or did something else lie at the root of her malice?

Swiftly abandoning her puzzling conjecture, Jennifer placed her glass on the table, and rose to her feet. 'Well, Melissa, it is time I was on my way.'

'Not so soon, surely!' The look of disappointment might have convinced most people, but Jennifer was not fooled. 'You haven't even finished your wine.'

As luck would have it, the aged butler chose that moment to enter the room, bearing a letter for his mistress on a silver tray, and while Melissa's attention was momentarily diverted, Jennifer grasped the opportunity to tip the remaining contents of her glass into a conveniently positioned vase of flowers nearby.

'I really must be on my way now,' she announced, determined to be gone, 'otherwise I shall be late for luncheon.'

Melissa focused her attention on the empty glass for a moment, and then glanced towards the clock on the mantel-shelf. 'Dear me, yes. You're right. I didn't realise the hour was quite so advanced.'

To Jennifer's surprise Melissa chose to accompany her out to the stable-yard, and shooed away the stable-lad, who had taken good care of Oriel, with an impatient wave of her hand. 'I think perhaps you were wise not to prolong your visit,' she remarked, glancing skywards. 'I was wrong in my prediction, I fear. The storm does now appear to be heading in this direction. You will save time by cutting across the long meadow. With any luck you'll make it back before the rain starts.'

Jennifer decided to take this advice and, not lingering over farewells, was soon heading across the meadow which formed part of the boundary with Julian's land.

No landowner in the area had ever objected to the local villagers crossing their property in order to reach the market town some four miles away. Melissa's father had been no exception and had even gone so far as to permit a footbridge to be erected over the wide stream which meandered its way across his land, and which in winter months, or after any periods of prolonged rain, could quickly swell to double its size.

It was just as Jennifer was nearing this wooden structure that she experienced the first searing pain. It was as if all the muscles in her abdomen had suddenly decided to twist themselves into knots. She had never experienced anything like it before. The pain was excruciating and grew steadily worse. If that was not bad enough, she suddenly felt very hot, and her head began to swim.

It had not been her intention to try to coax Oriel to use the narrow bridge. During the summer it was no hardship to cross the stream. By the time she had reached the bridge, however, she was in so much pain that it was as much as she could do to remain in the saddle, let alone find a suitable spot to cross the stream, and Oriel, wary of the unfamiliar structure, reacted instinctively by shying the instant his front hooves met the first wooden slat.

The sudden sideways movement was all it took to unseat Jennifer. Hitting her forehead on the bridge's wooden handrail as she fell, she went tumbling down the slight bank, quite oblivious to the fact that she had come to rest half lying in the stream, or that her unconscious body was partially hidden by the bridge.

Julian glanced out of his library window, pleased to see that the heavy rain had finally passed, and that a late afternoon sun was breaking through the last lingering clouds. He then turned his attention to the mantel-clock which clearly showed that it wanted only an hour to dinner. He wasn't feeling particularly hungry. Nor was he looking forward to sitting down to the meal alone, come to that. Which, if Jennifer's mood had not improved since morning, would undoubtedly be his fate.

He could not prevent a wry half-smile as he glanced at the pile of papers which had been restored to order, and returned to the corner of his desk. His darling wife, it seemed, had acquired something of a temper during their years apart. Not that he could blame her for behaving with less restraint than normal that morning, he reflected, striving to be fair. After all, she had only wished to be granted the opportunity to help her friend. And yet he had resorted to the most underhanded means to prevent her from doing so.

Thrusting impatient fingers through his hair, he rose from the chair and moved across to the window, feeling acutely ashamed of himself now. It wasn't that he objected to Jenny becoming involved in her friend's concerns. Nothing could be further from the truth! Serena Carstairs was a most likeable young woman, intelligent and charming. She most certainly didn't deserve the cruel fate life was about to inflict on her.

Lord Simeon Sloane was an utter blackguard, totally unscrupulous and a menace to any decent woman. Which, in part, was precisely why he didn't want Jennifer having any dealings with the disreputable Baron. But that, Julian was forced silently to concede, was by no means the sole reason for his reactions that morning. What had really disturbed him, had made him behave in a totally unreasonable fashion, was the very great fear that if once she had left Wroxam Park, she might choose not to return.

And yet had he not by his insensitive reactions given her more reason to leave? he couldn't help asking himself, before he was disturbed by a faint scratch on the door, and turned to see Mary enter.

'May I speak with you, my lord?' She did not wait for a response, but closed the door and took a further step into the room. 'I thought you should know that Miss Jenny has not returned from her ride.'

Dark brows snapped together. 'Do you mean she's been out in that storm? Why wasn't I informed of this before!'

'She's been out since the morning, sir,' Mary was not slow to enlighten him, despite his evident annoyance. 'I've known Miss Jenny a deal longer than you have, sir. She's best left alone on occasions.' The defiant look faded from her eyes and was replaced by one of concern. 'But I've never known her take this long to shrug off one of her black moods.'

Julian hardly waited for her to finish speaking before he stalked past into the hall, issuing orders which sent his servants into a flurry of activity. Guilt and worry weighed heavily on his mind, and his anxiety certainly didn't lessen when his worst fears were confirmed by Patrick who verified that Jennifer had, indeed, taken Oriel, and that he himself had already ridden out during the storm, unsuccessfully searching for her across the west section of the estate.

'But if you've no objection, sir, I'd like to keep you company. Two pairs of eyes are better than one. And I've changed my clothes and have a fresh mount ready saddled, so I'll not keep you waiting.'

Julian didn't object in the least and, after issuing instructions to the head groom to have the men search the southern pastures, headed out with the Irishman towards the eastern section of the estate.

'Of course, she may have sought shelter from the rain with one of the neighbours,' his lordship suggested, but Patrick swiftly dashed his hopes.

'She would have sent word, sir. Besides, the rain stopped an hour since. Miss Jenny wouldn't stay away, leaving folk back home worrying about her. And she'd never miss the time she spends in the afternoon with young Charles, if she could help it.'

This was disturbingly all too true. Julian knew that she never missed paying an afternoon visit to the schoolroom to speak with Mr Granger and discover what Charles had been learning that day. He refused to delude himself any longer.

'You think she's met with some accident...taken a tumble from her horse?'

'I'm thinking she's met with some accident, yes,' Patrick concurred grimly. 'It's where that's bothering me. I've already been over all her usual rides.'

'In that case we'll begin our search to the east in Ravens Wood.'

The instant Julian had made the suggestion that heartfelt memory, chillingly vivid, returned with a vengeance. He had never once ventured into that particular wooded area since the afternoon he and Melissa had set out to discover the whereabouts of the young truants. Apprehension gripped like a vice. What might he discover this time? he couldn't help asking himself, as he turned his grey hunter on to the track which led to that infamous trysting place.

But, no, that was unfair, the voice of conscience was swift to remind him, crushing the sudden threat of anger. It had happened only once; he no longer doubted the truth of that. His Marchioness, as she had proved on numerous occasions in recent weeks, was one of the most innately honest people he had ever known.

With these charitable and reassuring thoughts in the forefront of his mind, Julian entered the cottage, and was surprised to discover that he experienced none of the virulent anger he had felt when he had stood on the threshold of the one-room dwelling all those years ago. After a cursory glance across at the box-bed, which no longer held pride of place directly opposite the door, but had been tucked away, rather insignificantly, in one corner, he concentrated on the footprints clearly visible on the dusty floor.

'So, someone's been here,' he remarked. 'And by the size of the prints I'd guess it was a woman.'

'Perhaps Miss Jenny came here to shelter from the rain,' Patrick suggested, but Julian, unable to suppress a crooked half-smile, shook his head.

'Oh, no. She wouldn't do that again,' he responded

with certainty. 'She would be too concerned that lightning just might strike twice in the same place. No, it is much more likely that she came here in an attempt to lay a ghost to rest. But mine is already at peace, so I've no need to remain.'

Conscious that Irish blue eyes were regarding him with keen interest, Julian led the way back outside to the horses. 'Wilburn Hall is only a short ride from here. We'll call there next to see if anyone has seen her ladyship.'

As luck would have it they were spared the trouble. As they emerged from the wood, and turned onto the lane leading to Melissa's home, they came upon an elderly man, walking in the direction of the village. Ordinarily his lordship would have passed without speaking, but something in the stranger's demeanour caught his attention. The man seemed to be in something of a hurry, and appeared, also, faintly disturbed.

'A word with you, my good man.' He drew his mount alongside the stranger, who cast the grey a faintly wary look. 'Have you by any chance seen a lady on a horse during your travels this day?'

'Not seen no lady, sur. But seen a beast. Great black brute of a thing back yonder, rearing and stomping, and stopping honest folk using the footbridge. The gentry folk ought not to leave dangerous beasts to roam about to frighten honest folk. Why, I very nearly ended up in the stream!'

Julian didn't wait to hear more grumbles, justified though they might have been. After one glance in Patrick's direction, he urged his mount forward, leading the way to the bridge which he knew well.

As he turned into the gateway leading to the long meadow, he experienced a mixture of elation and despair. Oriel was there, just where the old man had said he'd seen him, hovering near the far side of the bridge and seeming in a high state of agitation. But where in the world was Jennifer?

'Easy young fellow, easy,' Patrick soothed, managing eventually to catch hold of Oriel's reins. 'You're in a right taking, lad, ain't you?' He turned to Julian who, still mounted, was scanning the landscape with anxious eyes. 'What beats me, sir, is why the lad stayed here. He's none too fond of storms, and yet he remained out in the open.'

'Possibly didn't know where to run. Remember, he isn't familiar with the—' Julian broke off abruptly, as he caught sight of what appeared to be the hem of a woman's skirt poking out from beneath the bridge. 'Good Lord! She's here!'

Patrick, still trying to soothe the disconcerted Oriel, watched his lordship dart nimbly down the slight bank, and return a few moments later carrying his wife, limp and dishevelled, in his arms. As his lordship laid her gently on the damp grass, Patrick could clearly see the livid bruise on her forehead, the only trace of colour in the lovely, ashen face, and could hardly bring himself to ask, but forced the words past suddenly parched lips as he watched his lordship raise his head, after placing his ear against his wife's chest.

'Yes, Patrick, she's alive.' There was not a trace of emotion in the deep, refined voice, but the look in his eyes, as he turned them towards the groom, betrayed clearly enough his emotional state. 'Go back and collect the carriage, and inform Slocombe what has happened. He'll know what to do.'

Although Jennifer didn't regain consciousness during the time his lordship remained with her waiting for the carriage, nor when he carried her, swathed in fur rugs, up to her room to leave her in the capable hands of Mary and his housekeeper, his anxiety of mind was marginally relieved by the prompt arrival of the doctor.

Julian considered Dr Arnold a credit to his profession. He was an immensely experienced man who had spent several years out in the Peninsula caring for Wellington's troops, before retiring from the army and setting up a practice in the West Country. He had earned himself the reputation of being extremely thorough, a practitioner who always took considerable time over his examination. Consequently, after changing out of his soiled clothes, Julian went down to his library to await the results.

There were letters still requiring his attention on the desk, but he didn't attempt to resume any work. Instead, he tried to relieve his anxiety of mind by sampling the contents of the brandy decanter. Needless to say the remedy did not work, but he was prepared to persevere, and was on the point of pouring himself a second glass, when the door opened and the doctor came striding purposefully into the room.

His grave expression did nothing to improve Julian's state, but with praiseworthy self-control he resisted plying the doctor with questions until he had furnished him with a glass of the amber liquid, and they were both seated comfortably on opposite sides of the hearth.

'By your expression, Doctor, I can only assume that my wife's condition is indeed serious.'

'As you are fully aware, my lord, she's had a nasty fall. But apart from the blow to her head, which she tells me she received when she fell against the bridge, she has sustained no other serious injury, a few bruises, nothing more.'

'She has regained consciousness?' The relief was almost more than Julian could bear. 'And she seemed lucid?'

'Extremely so, my lord…unfortunately,' the doctor assured him with a flash of wry humour. 'At one point during my examination she comprehensively consigned me, together with all other members of my profession, to the devil. I don't suppose for a moment that she will sustain any lasting damage from the accident. She has a severe headache, but that is only to be expected.'

He paused to fortify himself from the contents of his glass. 'I've requested that young Irish woman to remain with her overnight. Seems an eminently capable female. I've given her instructions, and she knows to send for me at once if further complications should arise.'

Julian frowned, genuinely perplexed. 'I'm sorry, Doctor, I do not perfectly understand your concern. Didn't you just say that you considered my wife had sustained no serious injuries from the accident?'

'I did,' he concurred, his gaze suddenly intense. 'But what does concern me, my lord, is why your wife should be displaying all the symptoms of having been poisoned.'

For perhaps the first time in his life his lordship was almost bereft of all power of speech 'What! But—but…when? How?'

'That has yet to be discovered, my lord. Although Lady Wroxam was definite about the details surrounding the accident, recalling quite clearly experiencing violent abdominal pains and a feeling of dizziness just prior to her fall, she was decidedly vague about what occurred shortly before. Only mentioned a ride in Ravens Wood, nothing more.' Slightly stooping shoulders rose in a shrug. 'It wasn't the time to plague her with questions. She may recall precisely what befell her in a day or two. Or it is quite possible she may never remember. The mind, you see, can be most accommodating on occasions.'

His lordship was suddenly very alert. 'What do you mean, precisely?'

'There were many atrocities committed on both sides during the war with France, my lord. A great many men saw and took part in certain actions they would rather forget. I've come across cases where experiences were so traumatic that the people involved cannot recall even the remotest detail.'

Once again he fortified himself from the contents of his glass. 'I remember a case years ago, when I first went into practice, of a young woman who was violated, severely beaten, and left for dead. When she regained consciousness she remembered nothing about the incident at all. Perhaps it was just as well. The mind, you see, sometimes protects.'

'So what you're saying, in effect, is that it's possible for a person genuinely not to remember something that happened on a certain occasion?' his lordship enquired, his mind momentarily locked in the distant past.

'Certainly, my lord. Most especially if the person suffered some sort of trauma. But I don't envisage this will be the outcome in your wife's case. She has certainly suffered an ordeal, and received a nasty blow to the head. But she's young and strong, and will recover fully, I'm sure.'

The doctor's optimism was undeniably heartening, but it didn't prevent Julian from paying several visits to his wife's bedchamber during the evening; and that night, after collecting a book from his library, he went to the bedchamber once again.

Mary, seated in the chair by the bed, quietly plying her needle, glanced over her shoulder as the door opened, a look akin to approval flickering for a moment in her eyes when she saw who had entered.

'She has not been sick again,' she assured him, 'and has been soundly asleep for the past two hours. Sleep is the best thing for her.'

'And you could do with getting some yourself. I'll take over.'

'Oh, but—'

'Do as I say, Mary,' his lordship ordered, quiet but determined. 'I need you to remain vigilant tomorrow. I want you and that young maid her ladyship seems particularly fond of to take it in turns to sit with her until she has fully recovered. With the exception of Charles and myself, you are to ensure that no one enters this room. And I want you, personally, to collect all her meals from the kitchen.'

'I'll do as you say, of course.' Mary raised troubled eyes to his. 'All the servants here seem devoted to her. It's hard to imagine that any one of them might...'

'I don't think it, Mary,' he assured her. 'My wife consumed nothing at breakfast that I did not sample myself. But I'm not prepared to take any chances until

I have discovered how the poison was administered, and whether it was done with malice aforethought.'

He moved silently over to the bed, and stared for a moment at the silky swathe of dark red hair stretching across the pillow, before focusing his attention on the delicate cheekbones, which earlier had glowed a bright crimson when she had been feverish. She appeared better now, and her breathing was certainly more regular.

He managed a semblance of a smile. 'I cannot blame Oriel for this. We can be fairly certain that he wasn't responsible for her fall. I've at least been spared the torment of deciding whether to put a bullet through his brain.'

Mary gaped up at him in astonishment, as though she feared that the strain of the past hours had been too much for him, and that he had taken leave of his senses. 'Oh, dear Lord! Don't even think of doing such a thing, sir...ever! Even if the big lad had been responsible, Miss Jenny would never have blamed him.'

Gathering together her sewing, Mary went across to the door. 'It isn't my place to say this, sir, but I'll give you some advice, all the same.' She held his full attention. 'I've known Miss Jenny a good many years. And it's my belief that she'll forgive you most anything in time. But she'd never forgive you, no, not even at her last breath, if you ever harmed that big lad of hers... Either of her boys, come to that.'

Julian watched the door close quietly behind her before turning once again to the figure in the bed, reflecting as he did so that less than six months ago he would never have permitted a person of Mary's station to offer advice, let alone pay her the common courtesy of listening to what she had to say. His wife's unexpected reappearance in the polite world had certainly given rise to many changes, not least of which had been changes in his own attitude to many things.

What a rarity the woman he had married had turned out to be! The surface trappings of lovely femininity concealing an iron will and determined spirit. That much he had discovered during their weeks together. He knew also that she didn't bestow her affections unwarily, but her love once given was intense, and her loyalty unbending. If Mary was right, and he did one day manage to rekindle his wife's tender regard, he would take great care never to risk losing it again.

The slender fingers resting on the pillow moved slightly, drawing his attention, and a moment later eyes flickered open. 'I'm thirsty, Mary.'

He only just managed to catch the words, so softly did she speak, and the look in her eyes as she gazed up at him seemed puzzled, as though she were having difficulty in bringing his features into focus.

Seating himself on the edge of the bed, he slid an arm beneath her shoulders, and gently raised her before placing the glass vessel to her lips.

'Mary has returned to her own room to rest for a while,' he informed her, once she had drunk her fill.

'Julian?' she queried, her voice uncertain.

'Yes, it is I.'

'You—you came back?'

He was momentarily startled, and more so when she seemed happy to rest her head against his chest. Evidently in her dreamlike state she was locked in the past, and he was happy to allow her to remain there.

'Yes, my darling,' he responded softly, cradling her

against him. 'I came back. And here I mean to stay. And so shall you... You see, I do not think I could ever bear to be parted from you again.'

He laid his cheek gently against the soft curls, treasuring this first moment of tender contact, and did not notice the figure standing silently in the doorway, or hear the door close softly again a moment later.

Chapter Thirteen

Mary waited until the nursery-maid had taken Charles from the room before addressing the figure standing before the window. 'You're going to have to decide what you're going to do. You cannot possibly carry on like this, you know.'

Jennifer continued to stare out across that section of park land with which she had grown very familiar during the past week or so. It had long since lost its power to hold her interest, but even so she made no attempt to turn her back on the view. 'I cannot imagine what you mean.'

'You know full well what I mean,' Mary countered, as plainspoken as ever. 'You've been up and about for almost three weeks, and yet here you are, still keeping to your room much of the time, like some feeble invalid. His lordship has the patience of a saint to put up with your megrims, so he has! To be sure he's the most kindly, considerate soul!'

This pronouncement certainly succeeded in capturing her attention, and Jennifer swung round. 'Kindly, considerate soul?' she echoed, regarding her normally very sensible companion with narrowed, assessing eyes. 'Have you been at the gin bottle again, Mary?'

'Well, upon my...' For perhaps the first time ever, Mary seemed momentarily lost for words. 'What a thing to suggest! Not a drop of that demon spirit has ever touched my lips, let alone passed them, as well you know, Miss Jenny!'

'Well, don't rip up at me, you ill-natured shrew,' Jennifer responded, half laughing. 'Something must be amiss with you to say such a ridiculous thing. Wroxam a saintly man indeed!' she scoffed. 'You've certainly changed your tune.'

Mary didn't attempt to deny it. 'To be sure, since coming here I've begun to see his lordship in a different light. Any man that can love a child the way he loves that boy of his cannot be all bad. Furthermore,' she went on, without offering her faintly bemused mistress the opportunity to argue, 'any man that goes out searching the moment he learns that his wife is missing, continues searching until he finds her, and then remains by her bedside throughout the night, is hardly a man lacking in feelings.'

Jennifer was clearly taken aback, and it showed. With the possible exception of recalling feeling extremely nauseous when she had finally regained consciousness, she retained little memory of anything else until she had woken the following day.

'Yes, I thought that might surprise you,' Mary announced, with smug satisfaction, a clear image of that touching little scene she had very nearly intruded upon appearing before her mind's eye.

Jennifer swiftly overcame her astonishment. 'Guilty conscience, Mary, nothing more,' she ventured, raising a shoulder in a gesture of indifference. 'After his behaviour that morning, I suppose he felt he must go in search of me. Besides which, his concern didn't last very long. He took himself off to London the very next day, might I remind you.'

Mary, easily detecting the peevish tone, suppressed a smile. 'So he did. But that wasn't until after he'd been assured by the good doctor that you were over the worst, and no longer giving cause for concern. His lordship informed me that he needed to pay an urgent visit to the capital in order to see someone without delay.'

'Yes, I bet he did need to see someone urgently—his mistress!' Jennifer scoffed. 'He must have been sorely missing her attentions after several week's abstinence!'

'Oh, you're hopeless when you're in one of your stubborn moods!' Mary retorted, raising both hands in a despairing gesture. 'And if it concerns you that much, perhaps you should start thinking about becoming a wife, because carrying on this way won't solve anything.'

She swung round, about to leave, when she bethought herself of something, and delved into the pocket of her apron to draw out a letter. 'I almost forgot… This came for you this morning, and it quite slipped my mind.'

In his favourite chair, Julian sat, empty glass in hand, staring forlornly at the gradually dying embers in the hearth. The early August day had been both bright and sunny, and yet he had felt decidedly chilled after eating dinner on his own yet again, and had requested Slocombe to light the fire in his library.

It had been his intention to occupy the evening hours by working on some estate matters but, as had happened all too frequently of late, he had found it impossible to keep his mind on his work. How could he possibly concentrate when his thoughts continually dwelt on his less-than-idyllic domestic situation, and he was tormented by feelings of guilt? Perhaps if he hadn't tried for so many weeks to convince himself that a combination of wounded pride and a thirst for revenge for keeping his son's existence secret from him was what had prompted him to force Jennifer's return to Wroxam Park, he might have faced reality far sooner. The truth of the matter was, of course, that he had at some point since their first encounter in London fallen deeply in love with his own wife.

Placing his empty glass on the table by his elbow, he ran his hands down his face, contorting his features. He was arrogant enough still to believe that he would one day succeed in winning her regard. None the less, what he could no longer continue to do was force her to remain under this roof against her will. He had to release her from that cruel bargain he had obliged her to make, to leave her free to come and go as she pleased and to allow her unlimited access to their son. But, dear God, by doing so he ran the risk of never rekindling her love or, worse, perhaps one day losing her to someone else!

He detected the faint click as the door opened. Supposing it to be Slocombe entering to light the candles, he didn't immediately attempt to turn his head. When, however, no one passed his field of vision, he did take the trouble to look round.

'Jenny?' he murmured, uncertain, not quite able to

believe the evidence of his own eyes, and fearing that he had consumed one brandy too many.

The fear was well founded, for he felt himself swaying slightly as he rose to his feet, a circumstance that his unexpected visitor was not slow to note. She had never seen him the worse for drink, but she guessed by the slight glint in his eyes, and the empty glass on the table, that he was not perfectly sober.

'I wished to speak with you, Julian, but if it is inconvenient, I—'

'No, no, not at all. As a matter of fact your arrival is most opportune, for there is something of importance I wish to discuss with you,' he interrupted, his voice reassuringly steady, and so she decided to remain.

Seating herself in the chair opposite the one he had just vacated, Jennifer watched him position himself by the hearth, resting one arm on the mantelshelf, and placing one foot, encased in a highly polished top-boot, on the solid brass fender. He might not, she supposed, have been considered handsome by the vast majority of her sex, his features being a little too sharply defined and faintly harsh for masculine beauty, but no one could deny that he was a fine figure of a man, his physique wonderfully proportioned and muscular.

'What is it that you wished to see me about, Jenny?' he asked, forcing her to raise her eyes from their contemplation of his strong, shapely legs, and reminding her of the reason she had sought this interview.

From the moment she had apprised herself of the contents of the letter which Mary had given to her a short while ago, she had guessed the truth, and had felt so very ashamed. Seeing him had only strengthened her belief that it was indeed he who had been responsible, but she needed to be sure. Furthermore, she wished him to confess and explain his reasons for acting as he had.

'I received a letter from Serena today,' she confided, deciding to come straight to the point. 'It would appear that Lord Sloane has withdrawn his offer for her hand.'

His lordship received this information in silence, not even by the raising of one of those expressive brows betraying the least surprise. 'She must be feeling excessively relieved.'

His tone was dry, almost bordering on indifference. Surprisingly enough this display of sublime unconcern, far from making her doubtful, only succeeded in strengthening her belief that he had wrought the miracle.

'Indeed she is. What she cannot understand is why he should have experienced this change of—er— heart. Moreover, she finds it impossible to comprehend what must have prompted him to return all her mother's letters.'

There was no response at all this time, but Jennifer was not deterred. 'One might almost suppose that Lord Sloane had suffered an attack of conscience... But I doubt very much whether he is the type of person to be troubled by that condition. Or from remorse, come to that. Therefore I'm forced to the conclusion that someone persuaded him to change his mind, or induced him to do the honourable thing.'

Jennifer rose from the chair and went across to stand before the window. Although the evening was now well advanced, there was still sufficient light for her to see across the park. This view certainly made a welcome change from the one she had been surveying from her bedchamber window during the past days, but even so it failed completely to capture her interest.

'Serena seems to suppose that it is I who am responsible for saving her from a disastrous union. But I know differently.' She turned again to look at him, and this time glimpsed a hint of irritation flickering over those harsh, aristocratic features. 'I believe it was you, and that is why you paid that recent visit to the capital.

'You're not the only person to admire honesty, Julian,' she continued, when once again she failed to elicit a response. 'You might not wish to disclose what took place between you and Lord Sloane, but I do insist upon knowing precisely what sum you were forced to disburse on my behalf.'

'You owe me nothing, Jennifer,' he responded, after a further lengthy silence, during which he moved over to the decanters and poured out two glasses of wine. 'I didn't part with a penny piece, and I had no intention of you doing so either.'

Automatically accepting the glass he held out, Jennifer re-seated herself. 'Is that the reason why you objected so strongly to my paying Lord Sloane a visit?'

'In part, yes.' Taking up his former stance by the grate, he looked down at her, the saturnine smile which she always found faintly unnerving curling his lips. 'As I mentioned once before, I believe Lord Sloane would have demanded more than just money from you in return for those letters.'

'Yes, and you thought I would have willingly paid

his price!' Jennifer returned, hackles rising at the all too vivid recollection.

'No, I did not,' he didn't hesitate to assure her. 'However, I had no intention of allowing my wife to place herself in a situation whereby she would of necessity be forced to be alone with a man of Sloane's unsavoury reputation.'

Not quite knowing whether to feel touched by his evident concern, or annoyed by the fact that he obviously considered her unequal to the task of dealing with a man like Sloane, she said, 'I would be the first to admit that my experience of such men has been virtually non-existent, but I believe I know the type. I'm therefore quite certain that you didn't appeal to his better nature in order to induce him to hand over those letters, because Sloane simply doesn't possess one.'

'Very true, my dear,' he concurred, smiling down at her in a way that sent her pulse racing. 'And when dealing with such persons one must learn to ignore one's own conscience.'

He paused to sample his wine. 'I know something to Sloane's discredit which, if it should become common knowledge, would ruin his reputation completely. Out of respect for his late uncle, who used to be a close friend of my father's, I have remained silent. However, I made it perfectly plain to him, when I called to see him in London, that if he didn't return all those letters to Lady Carstairs forthwith, and retract his offer for her daughter's hand, I would have no hesitation in revealing the particularly unsavoury event in his past to the world at large.'

Jennifer, following his example, sampled the contents of her own glass. It was quite evident that he didn't wish to divulge any details, and she decided not to press him for more information. Instead, she said, 'What I quite fail to understand, Julian, is why he should have selected Serena as a prospective bride in the first place. I would have thought pretty simpletons were more in his style.'

Not for the first time he found himself admiring the brutal honesty. 'That is easily explained, my dear. The previous holder of the title, the present Lord Sloane's late, lamented uncle, was both honourable and shrewd. Having produced no legitimate heir, there was nothing he could do prevent his disreputable nephew from stepping into his shoes. He could, however, ensure that he didn't inherit his private fortune. It was common knowledge that he held his nephew in low esteem, but he was not a vindictive man by any means, and decreed that should his heir contract a marriage, within six months of coming into the title, to a lady of good birth and unquestionable virtue, he would receive the lion's share of the private fortune. If not, the money was to be divided between various other family members.

'And given his unsavoury reputation,' his lordship continued, 'I suppose he felt not too many avenues would be open to him. So he looked about for a female who was unlikely to capture the interest of many gentlemen, or receive a more advantageous offer for her hand than his, and his eye fell upon Miss Carstairs. Also time was not on his side, and he had in his possession the means by which he could force the union.'

Jennifer's lips curled into a faintly satisfied smile as she refreshed herself once more from the contents of her glass. 'Well, he was certainly wrong about one thing, because unless I much mistake the matter, Serena has captured the interest of an extremely discerning and very likeable gentleman. By all accounts Theo is staying with a friend in Hampshire, and has paid several visits to Carstairs Hall.'

She glanced suspiciously up at him. 'That, I suppose, was not at your contrivance?'

'My dear, you must think me omnipotent!' He watched one finely arched brow rise even further, and relented. 'I may possibly have mentioned during that evening when Theo and I dined together at our club that he was looking faintly bored with life, and that a short visit to our mutual friend Sir Percy Phelps might succeed in restoring his spirits.'

'And I do not doubt that Sir Percy, a gentleman quite unknown to me, just happens to be a close neighbour of Lord and Lady Carstairs.'

'Now that you mention it, yes, I do believe he is.'

Hurriedly finishing off the contents of her glass, Jennifer rose to her feet, feeling more ashamed than ever now for the way she had behaved recently, incarcerating herself away in her room for much of the time, sulking like some spoilt child who had been thwarted, and treating his lordship like some kind of pariah on the odd occasion their paths had happened to cross. She could never possibly repay him for what he had done, but at least she could relieve him of one anxiety which must be continually lurking at the back of his mind.

She looked gravely up at him. 'You asked me once to give you my word that I would never remove Charles from Wroxam Park...I give it to you now, Julian. I shall never take Charles away from here without your knowledge or consent.'

She received no response, not even the faintest visual sign that her pledge had gratified him, and moved over to the door, but turned back as something suddenly occurred to her. 'Did you not say that there was a matter you wished to discuss with me?'

He looked across at her, his expression as before totally inscrutable. 'Thankfully, my dear, I no longer think that will be at all necessary now.'

The promise had not been an easy one to make and Jennifer was well aware that she had burnt all her bridges by giving her word. The decision she came to make three days later caused very many hours of soul-searching, and was a far harder one to reach, because it meant losing the daily support and companionship of two people she had come to look upon as far more than mere friends. However, she was determined not to change her mind and, in consequence, summoned both her loyal companions to her private parlour to inform them of their fate.

Patrick, not totally unhappy to learn he was to return to the land of his birth, cast a hopeful glance in Mary's direction before asking, 'You wish us to take care of the property in your absence, Miss Jenny, is that it?'

'No, Patrick. I have no intention of becoming an absentee landlord. I promised James O'Connell I never would. I am giving both the house and the stud to you, providing you promise to run it together.'

'But you can't, Miss Jenny!' Mary exclaimed, having been the first to overcome stunned surprise. 'Master James left the place to you.'

'Exactly! That is why I'm at liberty to do just as I wish with it. And I have decided to give it to you.'

Although she raised her hand against further argument, she could not forbear a smile. 'It would make matters a great deal easier, however, if you two were to wed.'

If possible Mary appeared more stunned than before, while Patrick's expression changed to one of comical dismay.

'Miss Jenny, what a thing to suggest!' Mary reproved, eventually finding her voice. 'Patrick Fahy is the most rascally womaniser who ever drew breath. No female in her right mind would ever wed him.'

'His faithfulness has yet to be proved; his love has not. He has been in love with you for years. And you are not indifferent to him, Mary—a fact I should have realised some time ago, and perhaps would have done had I not been so selfishly wrapped up in my own concerns. However,' she went on, moving over to the desk to collect a letter, and a purse of money for their journey, which she handed to Patrick, 'the decision, naturally, is yours, and yours alone.'

'When do you want us to leave, Miss Jenny? We could be on our way this very day if you wish.'

'Yes, I think that would be for the best, Patrick.' She placed a sisterly salute on his cheek. 'Go now and pack, and arrange for one of the stable lads to take you to Bristol in my coach. I would appreciate a few moments alone with Mary.'

Julian walked round from the stables to discover Jennifer sitting on one of the benches in the rose garden. She had chosen not to see her friends on their way, and he understood perfectly the reason why. Although he had raised no objections whatsoever when she had discussed her intention of parting with the property in Ireland, he had known full well that parting from her friends would cost her far more.

'They're now on their way to Bristol,' he informed her softly, sitting down beside her.

He longed to take her into his arms and offer some comfort, but refrained. During the past days their relationship had improved immeasurably. They now talked together quite without reserve, frequently laughing and joking. Physical contact, however, remained frustratingly lacking thus far. It would happen, though, given time; he felt certain of it. He would just need to be patient a while longer. Once she felt safe, once she began to trust him completely, realise that he didn't wish her to remain merely to be a mother to their son, she would then dispense with those final barriers of reserve.

'Both Mary and Patrick quite understood why you didn't wish to see them off, and have promised to write as soon as they arrive back at the house. I don't think either of them can believe their great good fortune. They will, of course, once I've arranged all the details with the lawyers.'

'Yes, thank you, Julian, for taking care of the legal aspect. You have been wonderfully supportive over this.' She paused to cast him a grateful smile. 'You could have prevented my parting with the stud, I know.'

Without thinking he reached for her hand, and was relieved when she made no attempt to remove it from his clasp. 'I have my faults, I know, but I'm not an avaricious man, Jenny. I had no desire for a property in Ireland, and in truth I have never once considered it as mine. As far as I was concerned it was yours to do with as you wished.'

Once again she betrayed her appreciation by a slight smile. 'I believe I did the right thing. Neither of them belonged here. I never once looked upon either of them as a servant, and I had no intention of ever treating them as such. Being propertied people, they can now visit here as our guests, avoiding any awkwardness. Although Patrick's leaving has brought about a further problem—namely, who is to look after Oriel.'

The perfection of her brow was suddenly marred by a troubled frown. 'Your grooms are all excellent fellows, Julian. Sadly, though, Oriel hasn't betrayed a particular liking for any one of them, and I'm afraid he can be something of a handful if the mood takes him. Since he came here, I've only ever witnessed him betray a marked partiality for one stable-lad's attentions, and unfortunately he works over at Wilburn Hall.'

His lordship's eyes narrowed fractionally. 'I didn't realise you had paid a visit to our neighbour, Jenny? I had gained the distinct impression that you were not particularly fond of her. When did you go to Wilburn Hall?'

He could not fail to notice the faintly wary look, and guessed the truth at once. 'Was it by any chance on the day of your accident?' If possible her expression became more guarded. 'Why didn't you tell anyone?' he demanded, feeling slightly annoyed. 'When I taxed Mary on the subject shortly after my return from London, she assured me that you'd merely gone for a ride in the wood. Why did you lie, Jenny?'

'It wasn't a lie,' she returned, faintly defensive. 'I did go into the wood.'

'I know that. You went to the cottage,' he responded, drawing a look of surprise from her. 'So, you went to Melissa's house afterwards, I take it?'

She nodded, looking a little shamefaced now. 'I partook of a glass of wine, if you must know. But as Melissa had a glass too, it could hardly have been that.' She shrugged. 'I know Melissa doesn't like me. I can only imagine that she blames me for her brother's leaving. But is that reason enough to try to poison me? It's ridiculous, Julian!'

Although he was forced to agree, uncertainty remained. Nevertheless, he decided not to discuss the matter further, and changed the subject by announcing that it was high time they held a dinner-party.

'You've been back at the Park for three months,' he continued in response to her faintly surprised look, 'and not once during that time have we entertained, at least not on any large scale.'

Rising, he drew her to her feet, and was further gratified when she didn't attempt to disengage her arm when he slipped it through his own, before heading back towards the house. 'I wasn't contemplating a grand affair, just an informal dinner with our neighbours. A table set for thirty or forty guests should suffice, I think.'

'Thirty or forty...?' Jennifer found herself gaping up at him. 'Julian, you cannot be serious! I've never organised anything of that kind before. We never did any entertaining when we were first married,' she didn't hesitate to remind him. 'Although I did arrange several dinner-parties for James O'Connell when I lived in Ireland, they were just for half a dozen or so of his friends.'

'Then it is high time you learned, my girl!' he announced, betraying, she considered, a sad lack of understanding and sympathy. 'When we open the town house next spring, you'll be entertaining as many as five hundred at the ball I intend to hold.'

After escorting her as far as the door, Julian returned to the stables, and ordered his horse saddled. Although he might have succeeded in giving Jennifer something to think about which, with any luck, would stop her brooding over the loss of her friends quite so much, the prospect of playing host to their neighbours would not clear his mind of the niggling suspicions which had begun to plague him. He decided to pay a visit, therefore, to Wilburn Hall.

Although Melissa had been a fairly regular visitor to the Park, Julian had never made a habit of paying frequent visits to the attractive widow, even though they had known each other since childhood. Consequently Melissa betrayed no little surprise when his name was announced and he walked into the parlour.

'Why, this is an unexpected pleasure, Julian!' Setting her sewing aside, she rose to her feet, holding out both hands in welcome, which he captured and then held momentarily in his own. 'Is this just a social call, or had you a specific reason for coming here?'

Had there been just a touch of wariness in her voice, or was he allowing doubts and faint suspicions to make him fanciful? 'I'm here on both counts,' he disclosed, making himself comfortable in one of the chairs, while at the same time watching her closely as she went over to the decanters to pour wine. There seemed nothing in the least sinister in her actions, he was forced to concede.

After a moment's hesitation he sampled the contents of the glass she had handed to him. Apart from its inferior quality, it tasted quite innocuous. Perhaps Jennifer was right, he mused, and it was foolish to suppose that Melissa had tried to poison her. Jennifer, however, was in no way fanciful, he reminded himself, and if she suspected that Melissa genuinely didn't like her, then in all probability it was true.

'We are holding a dinner-party at the end of the week, and hope that you'll number amongst the guests,' he remarked, once she had resumed her seat.

'I'd be delighted, Julian,' she responded, before making a great play of rearranging her skirts. 'Jennifer, I assume, has fully recovered from her accident? I did call as soon as I heard the terrible news, but was informed that she was too ill to receive visitors, and yet when I bumped into Dr Arnold the following day, he assured me that she had fully recovered.'

'The servants were acting on my strict instructions, Melissa. I was forced to go to London on urgent business, and didn't wish Jennifer to over-tire herself whilst I was away. She had had a nasty fall and needed to rest.'

'Well, I cannot say I'm surprised, Julian!' she returned, betraying, he felt, a sad want of sympathy. 'That black hunter of hers looks an unruly brute.'

'Ah, yes, a timely reminder!' He regarded her over the rim of his glass. 'She paid you a visit that day, did she not?'

A moment's silence, then, 'Why, yes! Yes, she did.'

'Did she, perhaps, complain of feeling unwell?'

She appeared to take a moment to consider the matter. 'She seemed fine, as far as I can recall, although

I vaguely remember that she was in something of a hurry to get home before the storm. Why do you ask?'

'It was just that Dr Arnold seemed rather puzzled over certain aspects of her condition.'

Her laughter sounded faintly strained. 'Great heavens! I think it's high time he retired, poor man. She merely took a tumble from her horse, surely?'

'Perhaps,' he conceded, wondering why he had never noticed before that her smile was singularly lacking in warmth. 'And it was concern over her horse which has also brought me here today. I understand you have a young lad working in your stables.'

She looked nonplussed for a moment. 'Oh, you must be referring to my head groom's young relation. Yes, I do believe he comes here from time to time to help out.'

'So he is not, in fact, in your employ?'

'Oh, no, I do not pay him a penny piece. I keep very few animals, Julian, as you know. I have no need for a large staff.'

'In that case, Melissa, I have learned all that I came here to discover.' He had the satisfaction of glimpsing a look of unease in her eyes before he finished off the contents of his glass and rose to his feet. 'Therefore I shall take up no more of your time, and will wander round to the stables to have a word with your groom.'

He discovered his quarry busily engaged in cleaning out one of the stalls. The groom was happy to pause in his task, though he appeared faintly surprised by his lordship's enquiry.

'That'd be my nephew, my sister Meg's boy, Jemmy, m'lord. He's about somewhere.'

'Do you suppose your sister would be willing for him to come to work for me?'

'I'm certain sure she would, m'lord.'

'I understand he took care of Lady Wroxam's mount when she paid a visit here not so long ago. Her ladyship seems to suppose that her horse took a liking to your nephew.'

'Wouldn't surprise me none, my lord. He's only twelve, or thereabouts, but he's good with beasts, so 'ee is... Ah! Here he is now.'

Julian turned as the boy came into the stable, and couldn't prevent a slight smile as he studied the young snub-nosed face, with its liberal covering of freckles, and the mop of bright red hair.

'Ah, yes,' he murmured, 'one begins to appreciate the attraction.'

Chapter Fourteen

Jennifer couldn't help experiencing a deal of satisfaction, and—yes—pride too in herself for the splendid way her first dinner-party was progressing. At least, she amended silently, it was her first dinnerparty where her skills as a hostess were undoubtedly being assessed by ladies far more experienced than she was herself at organising such events. Strangely enough, though, she didn't care a whit. She was determined, after all the planning and hard work, to enjoy herself, secure in the knowledge that all her care over choice of menu had been worthwhile, for she had been complimented on the excellence of her table by most everyone present.

'You cannot afford to sit back on your laurels quite yet, madam wife,' the teasing voice of her husband whispered in her ear. 'A good hostess does not skulk away in corners, guzzling champagne. She circulates, spending a little time with each of her guests, ensuring that the shyest amongst them is not left to her own devices.'

Much to his lordship's amusement he discovered that a pair of lovely green eyes, more often than not glinting with teasing laughter these days, were still quite capable of darting a dagger-look.

'It's a little late to be offering crumbs of advice now, my lord!' she hissed. 'You gave me four days, just four days to organise this affair,' she reminded him, aggrieved. 'And not once, not once when I approached you for a little guidance, did you put yourself to the trouble of instructing me on the finer points, not even over what we should serve our guests at dinner. I was obliged to spend the whole of one afternoon poring over menus with Cook.'

'And time well spent it was, too,' he announced, not above adding insult to injury. 'The dinner was excellent. Everyone thought so.'

The praise, though gratifying, in no way lessened her feelings of ill-usage. 'And then on the evening of the event you compound your shortcomings by lingering over the port and brandy, leaving me to entertain the ladies!'

White teeth flashed in a smile of pure provocation. 'And you'll be glad I did, my beautiful scold, when you hear what I have to tell you.'

Although quite unable to prevent the sudden rush of colour to her cheeks at the unexpected endearment, she managed to retain at least sufficient control over her voice to demand sharply, 'Well, what have you discovered?'

'Just that dear Theo has instructed his man of business to approach Colonel Halstead with a formal offer for his fine property which, I might add, the Colonel has accepted. So it very much appears as if we shall be having new neighbours in the not-too-distant future.'

Pique was instantly forgotten. 'Oh, Julian! You

don't possibly suppose that dear Theo might be contemplating matrimony to a certain lady of our acquaintance, do you?'

'I haven't the slightest idea,' he responded, resorting to that annoyingly superior tone she knew of old. 'In my experience conjecture is frequently inaccurate, and more often than not quite fruitless. Consequently I do not indulge in the practice. Furthermore, I make a point of not interfering in other people's personal concerns. If Theo wishes us to know his intentions where the delightful Miss Carstairs is concerned, he will apprise us in his own good time.'

'Well, upon my word!' The look she cast up at him managed to convey both astonishment and reproach. 'Who was it, may I ask, who induced Theo to pay a visit to Hampshire?'

He glanced down at her in surprise, the very picture of innocence. 'Merely a suggestion, my little love. I thought a further period in the country might benefit his health.'

It required great restraint, but she managed not to stamp her foot. 'Oh, I should know better than to bandy words with you!' she retorted, exasperation finally getting the better of her. 'My time would be better spent in organising some dancing for our younger guests, because it is quite obvious that you would never put yourself to the trouble of doing so.'

His shoulders shaking with silent laughter, he watched her glide across the salon, recalling quite vividly that, apart from the gorgeous hair, the first thing he had noticed were those striking eyes, shyly gazing up at him as he had sat astride his mount. Then he had been struck by the fluid way she had moved, as light on her feet as a professional dancer, graceful and sensuous.

'Her ladyship looks particularly lovely tonight, Julian,' a familiar voice unexpectedly remarked. 'Perhaps that is why you seem unable to keep your eyes off her. But allow me to remind you that it is unfashionable for a man of your rank to pay quite so much attention to his wife.'

Reluctantly he withdrew his gaze from the object of his admiration in time to catch a hard, calculating glint in the dark eyes of the woman now at his side.

He had noticed that same hostile gaze once before during the evening, when she had been glancing down the table at Dr Arnold. Melissa, he knew, had no very good opinion of doctors, always preferring to quack herself. Perhaps if she had called upon the services of a practitioner when her husband had first become ill, he might have recovered from the gastric complaint which had struck him quite without warning, sending him to his grave within a matter of days.

Since his visit to her house earlier in the week, Julian had been granted ample time to ponder long and hard over his relationship with his nearest neighbour, and had come to the conclusion that, although they had known each other for very many years, and he had always found her company both stimulating and enjoyable, he had never really looked upon her as a close friend.

None the less, he couldn't deny that, at one time, he had held her in high esteem for the way she had appeared to deal with life's cruel blows. Who would not feel a deal of sympathy towards a young woman who, denied the opportunity of forming an attachment with some eligible young gentleman, had felt obliged to marry a man old enough to be her own father in order to save the family home. Yet, during the past days, Julian had been forced to revise his opinion, and had begun to look upon past events in quite a different light.

Melissa, as far as he could recall, had never betrayed the least reluctance in marrying the rich nabob. Nevertheless, she had displayed no real sorrow at his sudden demise, either. Nor had she shown any degree of sadness when her young brother had found it necessary to remove himself from the family home after his disastrous liaison with his aristocratic neighbour's pretty young wife. In fact, Melissa had seemed blissfully content to reside at Wilburn Hall with only a handful of servants to bear her company. Which had led Julian to conclude that her dislike of Jennifer did not stem from the fact that she held her to blame for Geoffrey's departure.

One fact had, however, occurred to him during the past days, and one which now was causing him no little concern—on the two occasions Jennifer had met with some misfortune, Melissa had never been too far away. Coincidence, or something more sinister?

'Your appreciation is quite understandable, Julian,' she remarked, successfully drawing him out of his uncomfortable reflections. 'Yes, she does look particularly dazzling this evening. And those pearls! How very generous you are!'

He chose not to divulge that he had not purchased the fine necklace and matching earrings; nor that they didn't belong amongst the family jewels. He was mildly interested himself to know from where they had come, and was certain that if he chose to enquire he would undoubtedly have his curiosity satisfied.

'Yes, she certainly does look enchanting,' he agreed. 'It is possibly contentment, Melissa. She's very well pleased with the way your groom's young nephew has been taking care of her favourite mount.'

'I'm delighted to hear it,' she responded promptly, but Julian wasn't at all convinced that this was true. Jennifer's happiness, he felt sure, was of precious little interest to Melissa. Nor did he suppose for a moment that she had given a single thought during the past days to her groom's young nephew. He was fast coming to realise that there was a vast difference between what Melissa was thinking and what she said. The fact of the matter was, of course, he no longer trusted her. Consequently he did not hesitate to slip quietly away to enjoy more congenial company the instant her attention was claimed by Colonel Halstead's loquacious wife.

Although having been occupied in persuading one of the more mature ladies present to play a selection of music to enable dancing to take place, Jennifer had noted the little interlude between Julian and Melissa. She had noticed too that he had not seemed completely happy in the attractive widow's company, and could not help wondering whether she was to blame for this faint reserve she had easily detected in his demeanour.

She managed with little difficulty to thrust this guilty thought from her mind for the remainder of the enjoyable evening, but after she had bidden farewell to the last of their guests, and was making her way up to her room, her conscience began to prick her again, as she recalled that one minor flaw in what otherwise had been a delightful dinner-party.

Surely Julian did not suppose for a moment that

Melissa had really tried to poison his wife? Why, it was ludicrous in the extreme! she decided, taking off her jewellery as she made her way along the red-carpeted passageway to her bedchamber. What possible motive could Melissa have had to do such a malicious thing? If she had happened to be in love with Julian then, yes, there would have been some reason to it, but Jennifer felt certain in her own mind that this was not the case. Not once during recent months, or, indeed, in the distant past, had she detected even a flicker of a lovelorn expression on the widow's attractive features, nor any glint of desire in those deep-set, dark eyes.

The thought struck her most forcibly, and she paused for a moment, fingers clasped about the door-knob, before entering her room. How she wished she could say the same about herself!

Depositing her jewellery on the dressing-table, she wasted no time in slipping out of the silk gown, about which she had received numerous compliments during the evening. She had instructed Rose not to wait up in order to attend her. Which was possibly just as well in the circumstances, Jennifer reflected, for she had much to think about, and was in no mood for indulging in idle chatter.

After donning one of her modest nightgowns, she seated herself before the dressing-table mirror, her mind automatically returning to the main concern besetting her of late.

Melissa, of course, might possibly be extremely adept at concealing her feelings; she, on the other hand, was not; and she could no longer ignore the fact that she was finding it daily more difficult to keep her ever-increasing regard for Wroxam from showing.

More disturbing still was the fact that she was finding it difficult to conceal what she had always known to be true—that deep down she had never stopped loving him, though she had tried often enough to convince herself that it was quite otherwise.

She shook her head, unable to forbear a smile at her own foolishness. Oh, yes, she had been immensely foolish in trying to convince herself, times without number over the years, that she had married an unfeeling, arrogant aristocrat who cared for no one and nothing, save the proud name he bore. How wrong she had been! The truth of the matter was that she had never really known her husband; had never supposed for a moment that hidden behind that cool and dignified manner was a gracious and charming man who had proved to be an exceptional father. Most surprising of all, he was proving to be the very best of companions, a true friend.

But was friendship enough? She was not so guileless as to suppose that Julian was indifferent to her. She had glimpsed that certain look in his eyes, a look which betrayed clearly enough that he would be more than happy to resume full marital relations, and it was very much to his credit that he had never once demanded his rights as her husband. And, if the truth were known, she was finding it increasingly difficult to ignore her body's reaction whenever Julian was near; daily much harder to suppress the longing to be held in those strong arms, to feel those surprisingly gentle hands caressing her so tenderly, so expertly, just as they had done years before.

She must face the fact that a purely platonic relationship was not what she wanted any more. But what choice did she have? Her past infidelity would always come between them. True, it might be forgotten for a time, but it would always return, a constant torment, an ever-present threat to any future happiness, and she could not bear to be rejected, abandoned for a second time.

A light scratch on the door put an end to these heartbreaking reflections, for the time being at least. Assuming it must be Rose who, against instructions, had come to assist her, she did not bother to turn her head when the door opened. 'And what do you suppose you are doing here?'

'I am merely here to return an item belonging to you, my dear,' a deep voice laced with amusement drawled.

Surprised, but not unduly disturbed by his unexpected appearance, Jennifer didn't even attempt to reach for her robe, and merely held out her hand for the pearl earring he held between finger and thumb. 'Thank you, Julian. I wouldn't have liked to lose that. It has great sentimental value, you see—the pearls were my mother's.' She saw those expressive brows rise in surprise, and could not resist the temptation to tease him a little. 'As were the emeralds you saw me wearing during the Season. And were not, as you possibly supposed, from some ardent admirer.'

She had the satisfaction of glimpsing an expression of mild contrition. 'They had been safely kept by the family lawyer. My mother was an immensely sensible woman. She no doubt feared that Papa might sell them after her death in order to pay gaming debts. She also left me a considerable sum of money which I knew absolutely nothing about until my return to this country, and which came in very useful. A visit to the capital is not cheap, as well you know.'

'Indeed it is not,' he agreed, before recalling something that had occurred to him earlier. 'But why are you not wearing the family jewels?' He was not slow to note the distinctly guarded expression flit over the delicate features, before she rose from the stool to put on her robe at last.

'I've never been one to sport a dazzling array of gauds, Julian.'

One dark brow rose mockingly. 'And now may I be permitted to know the real reason?'

He moved slowly towards her, coming to stand so close that she had little difficulty in detecting the faint aroma of the brandy he always consumed before retiring for the night. She was painfully aware too of her body's instant response to his nearness.

'I have no right to wear them,' she managed to respond, before warm fingers were placed beneath her chin and she was forced to meet a gaze which had grown suddenly intense, and which betrayed clearly enough that he knew precisely what was passing through her mind.

'It would not, I trust, prove an unpleasant duty for you to rectify the matter, Jenny,' he murmured, his own voice little more than a husky whisper now. 'You know…you must know it is what I desire too.'

Oh, yes, she did know. And it was madness! She had to stop this before it went any further, before they allowed mutual desire to override common sense. She watched his gaze lower to focus on the ties of her modest nightgown. Her lips parted, but the refusal her mind was urging her to make lacked the conviction even to rise in her throat. It hardly mattered, however, for it was already too late, and she knew it.

Sweeping her up into his arms, Julian carried her

across to the bed, his lips fully occupied in alternately kissing and murmuring all the endearments he had for weeks longed to utter, while his hands expertly peeled away the final layers of clothing for the unfettered contact his passion demanded.

He felt her tremble, or perhaps it was himself, as he began at last to reacquaint himself with every inch of skin on that innocent girl he had instructed in the gentle art of lovemaking so many years ago. She had proved an apt pupil, and he swiftly realised that his gentle teachings had not been forgotten. When she began to caress him in return, hesitantly at first, and then with tender expertise, he could contain his need no longer, and was forced to pay a high price for the self-control he had exerted over himself during the past months. The consummation of their reunion was over far too quickly as far as he was concerned, but he contented himself, as he pulled her into the crook of his arm and began to stroke the mass of hair cascading over his chest, with the knowledge that they were once again husband and wife, and nothing and no one would ever come between them again.

He supposed he must have dozed, but something disturbed him, and he opened his eyes to discover himself quite alone in the bed. Panic welled until he saw her, naked and silhouetted against the window, that beautiful hair tumbling down in a V-shaped mass, covering almost every inch of the slender, straight back.

'Jenny?' he murmured, and thought for a moment that she had not heard, but then she said,

'I'm sorry, Julian. Did I disturb you?'

Grasping the coverlet, he rose from the bed, and

wrapped it about them both as he pulled her back against his chest, and slid his arms about the narrow waist, holding her gently captive. 'What were you thinking about?'

He waited in vain for a response. 'No regrets, I trust?' Again only silence, and he rested his cheek against her head. 'Come, Jenny, you wanted that to happen as much as I did.'

She didn't attempt to deny it. 'I cannot help wondering if it was the most sensible thing, though, Julian,' she admitted at last, and felt his body shaking with silent, tender laughter.

'Sense has little to do with it, my darling. When two people are in love, they show it in many different ways. And you do love me, don't you, Jenny?'

'I've never stopped loving you, Julian, though I tried often enough over the years to convince myself it was quite otherwise. I loved you from the first moment I set eyes on you.'

'I wish to God I could say the same!' His protracted and heartfelt sigh ruffled the fine strands of her hair. 'I merely felt that in you, innocent and unspoilt, I had found the ideal person to mould into my Marchioness… Perhaps it was in part a guilty conscience which deterred me from taking steps to end our marriage,' he continued after a moment's thought. 'I honestly don't know. But I do know that from the first moment I saw you again, a divorce was the very last thing I wanted. And when I made it impossible for you to leave here without my consent, it wasn't out of a sense of pique, or a desire for revenge, but because at some point, for the first time in my life, I'd fallen deeply in love…deeply in love with my own wife.'

He clearly detected what sounded like a suppressed sob. 'But how can you, Julian, after what I did?'

'Simply because when at last I acknowledged the depths of my own feelings, the past was of little consequence. Our marriage begins now, Jenny. It is our future happiness that's important to me, not past mistakes. They're forgiven and forgotten.'

'I wish to heaven my mind was so adaptable, Julian,' she responded, in a voice hardened by self-reproach. 'If I had been in love with Geoffrey, I could have understood. But I was never in love with him, which makes what I did unforgivable. And that is why I cannot forget.'

She felt the arms about her tighten, before she was swept up in them for a second time and carried back to the bed. 'Then, dammit, I'll make you forget if it takes the rest of my life!' he vowed, and attained the satisfaction of knowing, as he made love to her again, extracting those sweetly soft moans of pleasure, that her mind for the time being at least was not dwelling on the past.

Chapter Fifteen

The servants were immediately aware of the different atmosphere in the ancestral mansion, and as the weeks passed the happiness which pervaded the house showed no signs of diminishing.

On a bright, crisp morning in autumn, as he was crossing the hall, Slocombe caught sight of his mistress descending the stairs, and was suddenly reminded of that day when she had unexpectedly turned up on the doorstep of the house in Berkeley Square. He had thought then that things would never be quite the same again. And how delighted he was to have been proved right!

'Good morning, my lady. And a fine morning it is too for a ride, if you do not mind my saying.'

'I do not object in the least, Slocombe. It doesn't seem five minutes since we were enjoying all that lovely summer weather, and yet here we are already in the middle of October. The weeks simply fly by!' Jennifer glanced in the direction of her husband's inner sanctum. 'Is his lordship in his library by any chance? There is something I particularly wished to tell him.'

'He is indeed, my lady, and quite alone, I believe.'

Julian, seated behind his desk, raised his head as the door opened, that certain smile, frequently seen nowadays softening the grey eyes, coming effortlessly to his lips when he saw who had entered. 'No need to enquire how you intend to occupy your time this morning, madam wife,' he remarked, after casting an approving glance over the new bottle-green habit.

He held out his hands, and she needed no further prompting to plump herself down on his lap. 'Yes, I'm riding into town. There are a few bits and pieces I need to buy.'

A rueful smile tugged at her lips as a vivid memory returned. 'Of course, had I chosen to save all the ribbons on those old gowns I discovered hanging in the wardrobes on the day I returned here, I would have had trimmings enough for a dozen bonnets, and would have no need now to purchase new ones.'

She regarded him in silence for a moment. 'Why did you keep all my old dresses, Julian? Why did you issue orders that nothing in my room was to be touched?'

It was his turn to smile a trifle ruefully this time. 'It's difficult to explain. It was in part a guilty conscience, I suppose—not knowing what had become of you. And perhaps deep down I secretly hoped that one day you would return. In my mind it had always been your room. Certainly no other female ever crossed my path whom I would have wished to place there.'

He kissed her gently, before returning his thoughts to more mundane matters. 'Now, have you sufficient funds about you to cover your purchases?' he asked, and she could not help but smile.

She had needed to accustom herself to many things during the past weeks, not least of which was sharing her bed with her husband again. Not that she objected at all! One thing, however, she could not quite get used to again and that was being given pin-money, enough to buy most anything she wished.

'Of course I have. You spoil me, Julian. Really you do! Not that I'm complaining, you understand.' She glanced at the letter lying open on the desk, and recognised the handwriting at once. 'Oh, another letter from Theo. Does he mention when he's coming to visit us?'

'He intends to arrive tomorrow, and will be with us for two weeks, or thereabouts. He's wishing to oversee the changes he's making to the Grange. From his letter it would appear he's hiring an army of workmen to make alterations. He's in something of a hurry to get the place in order before the wedding, you see.'

Like an excited child, she couldn't suppress a little squeal of delight. 'He's asked her?'

'He most certainly has, and Miss Carstairs, being an immensely sensible female, didn't hesitate in accepting. Further-more, she sees no earthly reason why they should wait, and wishes to be married as soon as the house is ready. Also, she is hoping to persuade us to allow them to hold the wedding breakfast here at Wroxam Park, where she and Theo first became really acquainted. A sensible woman with a romantic streak, it would appear.'

'How lovely! I'll look forward to it.' Her sudden frown hardly substantiated this, however. 'I just hope they don't delay too long, otherwise I shall be unable to wear my new blue gown and matching pelisse.'

'Why won't you?' Julian enquired, betraying a faint interest.

'Because I shan't be able to squeeze into the outfit, that's why.' Watching a look of dawning wonder take possession of those beloved, aristocratic features, she couldn't resist a spot of harmless teasing. 'I cannot imagine why you're looking so surprised. It has been nothing—er—else since our reconciliation.'

'Any complaints?' His mouth curled into a wickedly provocative grin. 'When will the baby arrive?'

'Late spring. I thought we might tell Charles together later that it won't be too long before he has a baby brother or sister.'

Again he shook his head in disbelief. 'I am reputed to be a man of experience, and yet I really had no idea.'

This admission made her chuckle. 'No, you didn't the first time round, as I remember. History certainly has a habit of repeating itself.'

'Not if I have any say in the matter!' he countered with mock severity. 'I intend to take every care of you this time. And for a start, madam wife, there will be no more horse-riding for you. I'll exercise Oriel from now on.'

For a moment it looked as if she might argue, but then she reluctantly agreed. 'But you must promise to take good care of my baby.'

'I certainly shall,' the tender smile flickered again, 'providing you promise to take care of mine.' He released his hold. 'Now, off you go and change out of that habit. I'll take you into town in the curricle. I need to see one or two people.'

They arrived in the local market town later that morning. Julian left his curricle in the care of an ostler at the Fox and Goose, and arranged to meet Jennifer back at the inn later.

Since her return to Wroxam Park she had made a point of patronising the local shops. Consequently she was known by most all the local merchants, and her custom was much appreciated. Mrs Goodbody, the proprietress of the haberdashery, was always pleased to see her, for the Marchioness never entered the premises without buying something.

While waiting for her purchases to be made up into a parcel, Jennifer began to browse through an old edition of the *Lady's Journal*. The sudden tinkling of the shop bell announced the arrival of another customer, but she did not trouble to see who had entered, until she heard her given name spoken in a hoarse whisper. Then she turned, the colour draining from her face when she finally recognised the slender gentleman standing near the door.

'Geoffrey?' She could hardly believe the change in him. He looked so thin and drawn, his complexion the colour of parchment, that it was difficult to believe that he was not yet eight-and-twenty, for he bore the appearance of a man well into middle age. 'I—I didn't realise you were planning to return from Italy. I saw your sister only last week, when we dined at a neighbour's house, and she never mentioned anything.'

'Melissa doesn't know I'm here.' He took off his hat, revealing a head of hair that was more grey than golden now. 'I'm putting up at the inn here in town.'

'The inn?' Jennifer echoed, panic rising now that she had recovered from the shock of seeing him so vastly changed. Her eyes flew to the window. If Julian were to discover them together... Why, oh why must Geoffrey decide to return now—now when everything in her life was perfect?

'I was wondering how I could manage to see you. I thought of sending a note to the house, but I've been saved the trouble,' he informed her, little realising that he was the very last person in the world she ever wished to see again. 'I was on my way to pay a call on Dr Arnold, and I saw you slip in here.'

He took a step towards her, and she would have backed away had not the counter stood directly behind her. 'I must speak with you, Jenny. There is something you must know.'

Jennifer detected Mrs Goodbody's footsteps. 'We cannot talk here, Geoffrey. Besides, Julian is in town, and I...' Her voice tailed off.

'You'd rather he didn't find us together,' he finished for her. 'Yes, I can understand that. Could we meet tomorrow? You could come to the inn. It's very important that I see you.'

'Very well, I'll come in the morning,' she hurriedly agreed.

So eager was she to be gone from the town that she didn't delay in returning to the inn, and almost collided with a customer as she entered the coffee-room. 'Was that not one of Melissa's employees?' she asked, joining his lordship at the table where he sat enjoying a tankard of the landlord's home-brewed ale.

'Yes, her steward. Cannot abide the fellow myself, but he seems efficient enough at his job.'

Julian regarded her in silence for a moment before offering to order her some refreshments which she politely declined. Thankfully he did not linger long in finishing his ale, but Jennifer was conscious all the time of those shrewd eyes peering at her over the rim of the pewter tankard.

As they went outside to collect the curricle, she could not resist darting a glance down the main street in the direction of the doctor's house. Fortunately there was no sign of Geoffrey, but she found she could not relax until they had left the town's limits behind them.

Then grave doubts and a guilty conscience began to plague her, forcing her to wonder anew what on earth had possessed her to agree to the meeting on the morrow. But then, she reminded herself, she hadn't been given much choice. She certainly didn't want him sending notes to the house or, worse still, turning up on the doorstep, though what in the world he could have to say to her after all these years that was so important she simply couldn't imagine. One thing was certain, however, she could not, would not, sneak off in the morning to meet him clandestinely.

'Julian, I have something to tell you,' she said hurriedly, before she could change her mind. 'I saw Geoffrey Wilburn in town this morning. He walked into Mrs Goodbody's premises whilst I was there.' There was no response. 'I hardly recognised him.'

'No, neither did I.'

Jennifer almost found herself gaping. 'You saw him too!'

'Yes, I was on the point of crossing the street in order to escort you back to the inn, when I noticed him entering the shop. So I decided to await you as arranged.' He glanced at her. 'Thank you for confiding in me, Jenny.'

'There's more, Julian,' she responded, secretly moved by the respect she could detect in his eyes.

'He asked me to meet him at the inn tomorrow. Seemingly, he's putting up there.'

He frowned at this. 'Why not at Wilburn Hall?'

'I don't know. I do know that he hasn't apprised Melissa of his return.'

A brief silence, then, 'And will you go?'

'In all honesty I cannot say that I particularly want to, but I rather think I must. There is something I wish to ask him.'

Again he took his eyes off the road to cast a fleeting glance at her. 'Then, of course, you must go.'

'Will you come with me, Julian?'

'No.' There was no mistaking the finality of that decision. 'I trust you, Jenny, trust you implicitly. I do not, however, trust Geoffrey Wilburn. So I will make only one stipulation before permitting you to keep that appointment... Don't be alone with him.'

'Of course, I will do as you ask, but I do not suppose for a moment that Geoffrey would ever deliberately do me harm.'

'He may have done so once before.' He watched the frown of puzzlement crease her brow. 'Has it never occurred to you to wonder why you cannot remember all that took place in that cottage all those years ago? Has it never occurred to you that you might not have willingly given yourself to him?'

It was patently obvious by her astonished expression that it had not. 'Geoffrey might have forced himself upon me, you mean? No, Julian, I don't believe that for a moment.'

'From what I remember of him it does, I agree, seem highly unlikely. None the less, I would ask you not to put yourself in a position whereby you cannot call for help should the need arise.'

'Very well, Julian. I shall do as you ask.'

Chapter Sixteen

The following morning Julian stood at his library window watching the light travelling carriage taking Jennifer to the town sweep up the driveway. He was plagued by misgivings, but hadn't allowed these to surface. Understandably, he was anything but happy about the appointment she was about to keep. To have refused, however, might have given her reason to suppose that his faith in her was not absolute; worse still, it would have denied her the opportunity of finally putting the past firmly behind her.

He was sure that bitter self-recrimination didn't plague her often these days. And God only knew he had tried his very best in recent weeks to assure her that he no longer held her in any way to blame for their long separation! Nevertheless, he had chanced upon her more than once, staring sightlessly out of a window, those lovely eyes shadowed with sadness and regrets. The poor darling didn't deserve to suffer these periods of torment, rare though they were nowadays, and if talking to Wilburn could help, then Julian had no intention of standing in her way.

These reflections were interrupted by Slocombe entering the room with a pile of correspondence collected from the receiving office earlier that morning. Normally Julian would have left the job of sorting through them to his efficient secretary, but decided this morning to deal with the correspondence himself. He had almost completed the task when he clearly detected the sound of a cheerful voice raised in the hall, and a few moments later the beaming countenance of his friend Mr Dent appeared round the door.

'Theo, my dear fellow! Come in, come in!' Julian rose from the desk to shake his visitor warmly by the hand. 'Didn't expect to see you this early in the day.'

'Put up at an inn this side of Devizes, and made an early start.'

Julian, having poured out two glasses of burgundy, handed one to his friend, before seating himself in the chair opposite by the hearth. 'May I be the first in this household to offer my heartfelt congratulations on your recent betrothal. Have you decided upon a date yet?'

'Providing the house is anywhere near in order, early next month, we hope. I'll have a clearer idea when I ride over tomorrow.' A faint look of uncertainty flickered over his homely features. 'I say, Julian, if you're not happy about us holding the festivities here, you only have to say so. It was Serena's idea, and you know what the ladies are like when they take these foolish romantic notions into their heads.'

'My dear Theo, we shall be delighted. We were unable to attend Patrick and Mary's wedding, mainly because it took place so swiftly after their return to Ireland, although we are determined to pay them a visit some time next year.'

Relief clearly showed. 'Well, thank you, Julian.

Neither Serena nor I wish for a large London affair—just the immediate family, and a few friends, you understand.'

'There will be no problem. We've plenty of room here. Jenny is very much looking forward to it, providing you do not delay in fixing a firm date.'

Theodore frankly laughed. 'In a hurry to see me leg-shackled, is she?'

'Possibly, but that's not the main reason. Like a typical female, she's more concerned with her attire.' A faintly proud smile softened the aristocratic features. 'You see, my dear Theo, you are not the only one to be congratulated. I am to become a father for a second time.'

It took a moment or two for Theodore to digest fully what he had just learned, then his plump features once again wore a delighted smile. 'By Jove! This is good news! My dear fellow, I couldn't be more pleased. So everything between you is fine?'

'Almost, but not quite. I'm very much hoping, however, that it will be before the end of this day.' His lordship's sigh, though faint, was clearly audible. 'Unlike myself, Jenny isn't quite able to put the past firmly behind her, so she's meeting with Geoffrey Wilburn this morning.'

Theodore was stunned, and it showed. 'Geoffrey Wilburn is back? And—and you're letting Jenny meet with him!'

'I have the utmost faith in her,' Julian announced, with a return of that haughty tone of old. 'Wilburn poses no threat, I assure you. He never did, except...'

Theodore was not slow to detect the faint look of concern, and cursed himself silently for his thoughtless remark. 'Of course you've no need to worry. Besides, Mrs Royston will be there, won't she?'

'No, Jennifer is meeting Wilburn in town.'

'Oh, I see...' As Theodore sampled the excellent wine something occurred to him. 'Well, I expect everything will still be fine. I thought I passed Mrs Royston's carriage on the road. She was heading in the direction of the town.'

It was evident from his lordship's sudden, darkly intense gaze that this intended reassurance hadn't had quite the desired effect. 'You passed Melissa's carriage? Are you positive Mrs Royston was the occupant?'

'I didn't get a good look,' Theodore freely admitted, wondering what was making his friend appear so very anxious all of a sudden, 'and the carriage was travelling at a cracking pace. But, yes, it certainly looked like her.' He gaped in astonishment as his lordship suddenly stalked across to the door. 'Devil take it, Wroxam! Now what are you about?'

'I've always considered Geoffrey a weak and ineffectual person. His sister, on the other hand, is a different matter entirely.' Then, calling for his hat and crop, Julian went out into the hall, Theodore at his heels. 'I'm riding into town. You're welcome to accompany me if you wish.'

'Of course, I'll come, if you think Jenny's in any kind of danger,' he answered, easily keeping up with his lordship's long-striding gait, as they went outside. 'Got anything suitable for me to ride?'

'You can take my grey.'

'Fine. He's certainly up to my weight. But what are you going to ride?'

'Jemmy! his lordship called the instant he reached

the yard. The boy came scurrying from the stable. 'Have my saddle put on Oriel at once!'

The moment Jennifer arrived at the inn she began to suffer her own misgivings when one of the tavern maids showed her up a flight of stairs and into a private parlour.

'Can I fetch you anything?' the maidservant asked, addressing Geoffrey, who had risen from the table, where he had been sitting for the past hour, absently watching the comings and goings in the street below through the open window.

He had observed the Wroxam carriage pull into the inn yard, and could see now that his one-time friend the Marchioness was looking anything but happy and relaxed to be here, and thought to remedy this.

'Would you care for some refreshment, Jenny—a glass of wine, perhaps?' He could not resist a wry smile at the prompt refusal. 'Well, yes, perhaps you're wise to refuse. Supping wine with a member of my family can be a somewhat hazardous undertaking.'

She frowned at this, but let it pass without comment, as she took the precaution of re-opening the door a fraction, after the serving maid, having withdrawn, had closed it behind her. 'I promised Julian I would be back in time for luncheon, so I would be obliged if you would come straight to the point of your request to see me.'

He stared at her in silence for a moment, his pale blue, lacklustre eyes adopting a faraway look. 'I cannot recall your being quite so forthright. You've changed, Jenny.'

And so have you, she thought, studying the lined, thin face which had lost every vestige of the youthful handsomeness she well remembered. A mere shadow of his former self, he looked so pale and weary that when he pulled out a chair, she felt obliged to take it, fearing that if she did not he would remain standing himself. He appeared not to possess the strength to do even that, let alone attempt some physical attack upon her. Surely Julian's concerns were without foundation?

'You and Wroxam are happy together, Jenny?' he enquired, after coughing into a handkerchief which bore those telltale red stains, making her realise just how ill he was.

'Yes, we're happy….very happy, Geoffrey.'

'I'm glad…truly. It makes my being here all the more worthwhile. As soon as I learned of your return, I felt I must return too to warn you.'

'Warn me…? Warn me about what?'

'Melissa.' He watched a look of utter bewilderment take possession of those exquisite features. 'You really have no idea, do you, Jenny? You look precisely as you did that afternoon when you woke up in the cottage.'

His unexpected rumble of laughter turned into a fit of coughing, and it was a few moments before he began speaking again. 'The wine I gave you that day was drugged—drugged by my beloved stepsister in order to bring about your ruin, and attain for her what she most craved in the world. But that was all I did, though God forgive me that was dishonourable enough. And if it's any consolation, not a day has passed since when I haven't been tormented for my weakness in agreeing to Melissa's dastardly plot.'

'But why, Geoffrey?' Jennifer was having the utmost difficulty in understanding what she was being told, and was beginning to doubt her own intuition. 'Does Melissa hate me so much? Is she truly in love with Julian?'

Fortunately this time when he gave way to mirth it didn't result in a further bout of coughing. 'Love is an emotion quite foreign to dearest Melissa. No, she doesn't love Wroxam, and never has in my opinion. But she has always dreamt of becoming his wife. Social position is what Melissa craves.' He shrugged his thin shoulders. 'Understandable enough when you consider the stigma she has lived with all her life. Most people, no doubt, have forgotten that the first Mrs Wilburn was merely the daughter of an apothecary. But Melissa has never forgotten.

'She resented my mother very much,' he went on, 'mainly because the second Mrs Wilburn was well born. That is why Melissa went to live with her aunt for so many years, and where she learned all she needed to know about the mixing of potions which would prove so useful to her in later years.'

'Dear God!' Jennifer muttered, suddenly realising what a lucky escape she had had on that day she had visited Wilburn Hall. If she had drunk all her wine, perhaps she wouldn't have been here now.

'Melissa had no choice but to marry Royston,' Geoffrey continued, and Jennifer listened intently. 'It was either that, or risk losing the family home in order to pay the debts Father had left. She knew at the time that there was no earthly chance of extracting a proposal of marriage from Wroxam. Being only a couple of years her senior, he was nowhere near ready for marriage. And my dear sister is nothing if not a realist. She also has a keen regard for appearances, and so bided her time before deciding widowhood would suit her very well.'

It was an effort, but Jennifer managed to suppress a gasp. 'Are you trying to tell me that Royston did not, in fact, die of natural causes?'

'Personally, I have never believed so, no. But obviously I cannot prove it.' His shrug betrayed a certain amount of indifference. 'She was still young, and Wroxam was only three and twenty. All she needed to do was wait a decent period, and then the man she was determined to snare as a husband might consider her for a wife, or at least she hoped. Time means absolutely nothing to Melissa. Only she miscalculated, and delayed a little too long in attempting to snare the Marquis. His lordship left Wroxam Park one spring morning, and returned a few weeks later, bringing with him his pretty young wife.'

Jennifer could only marvel at how credulous she had been. 'And from that moment your sister planned my downfall.'

For the first time he seemed reluctant to meet her gaze. 'Yes, with my help. She couldn't have made the attempt on her own, Jenny. But I'd like you to know that my friendship was genuine. Unfortunately my desire for independence was stronger. She offered me money to live in Italy if I helped her... And may God forgive me, I agreed!

'It was an easy matter to discover precisely when Julian had planned to return from London. In your innocence you disclosed all we needed to know. I invited you out riding. It was my intention to take you to the cottage, and when it came on to rain that afternoon I had my excuse. Then I poured you wine, and a second glass, carried you over to the bed, and waited for Melissa. I remained outside whilst she undressed you.' His lips were twisted by a bitter smile of self-disgust. 'I possessed that much decency at least. All I had to do then was wait for Melissa to return with Wroxam, and slip into the bed beside you.'

'And the gullible Marchioness's downfall was assured,' Jennifer murmured, at a loss to understand why she had never guessed the truth long since.

'Yes...except your subsequent disappearance was not foreseen by my cunning sister. She expected Julian to file for divorce. She knew it would take years, but she was prepared to wait, and as I've already mentioned time means nothing to Melissa. I, on the other hand, have very little left to me. That is why as soon as I'd learned of your return from some English visitors touring my adopted country, I came here to put you on your guard about Melissa. She'll never give up, Jenny. As long as she feels there's a chance that one day she'll be given the title which you now hold, she'll never give up.'

'How well you know me, my dear brother... But your warning comes a little late.'

So stunned was she by Melissa's unexpected appearance that it was as much as Jennifer could do to rise from her chair. She was vaguely aware that Geoffrey had risen too, but she didn't attempt to look at him, for her attention was captured by the malevolent gleam in the widow's dark eye, a look no less dangerous than the lethally formed piece of metal which she held clasped in her right hand.

Geoffrey edged a little further round the table. 'Jennifer knows everything. It's over, Melissa.'

'It is certainly over for you, dear brother,' was the

swift response. 'I do not take kindly to being betrayed.'

If the threat unnerved him at all, there was certainly no evidence of it in his voice. 'And what do you propose to do…kill us both?' He scoffed, determined to brazen it out, it seemed. 'You'll never get away with it.'

The contemptuous curl to the full lips grew more pronounced. 'Oh, I rather think I shall. Unlike you, dear brother, I've always been well respected in these parts. The tale I'll spin will be believed, and my steward will not be slow to verify my story. He'll confirm that I was ignorant of your return until he apprised me of the fact this very morning, and that I immediately left the house in a high state of agitation, afraid of what you might do. I'll merely inform the authorities that my brother, in a state of jealous rage, killed the woman he had always loved, when he learned of the reconciliation between her and her husband, and I arrived in time to see him put a period to his own existence. You see, dear brother, I think of everything. I took the precaution, before leaving the house, of collecting those duelling pistols you had years ago.'

Jennifer, who had noticed that Geoffrey had continued to edge his way towards her, watched Melissa raise the pistol in her hand, and take careful aim. Before she could even manage to scream out for help, there was a deafening report and Geoffrey, who had placed himself in the line of fire, slumped to the ground. The next moment the door was thrown wide, and Julian, miraculously appearing in the room, was prizing the second pistol from Melissa's hand.

It was an unequal struggle. Julian swiftly had the

weapon safely tucked away in his own pocket, and was glowering at Melissa, his eyes as cold and merciless as hers had been only moments before.

Unscrupulously ruthless Melissa might have been throughout her life, but she was certainly no fool. Julian's expression of loathing betrayed clearly that he had heard and seen enough to condemn her. For the first time her eyes were shadowed by fear, as she backed away from him, muttering incoherently. She cast one brief glance towards the open window. The room then echoed with a shout of hysterical laughter and, before Julian could reach her, she had thrown herself out of the window to land beneath the wheels of a passing dray.

Women's screams, mingling with the sounds of terrified horses, rose from the street below. Unlike Julian, who had darted across to the window, Jennifer concentrated on the figure lying on the floor and, kneeling, gently raised Geoffrey's head on her lap.

'Julian, quickly! Fetch the doctor,' she called, but Geoffrey, managing to raise his arm a little, arrested his lordship's progress across to the door.

'No,' he murmured. 'Melissa was right—it is too late for me, and it's better this way.'

Seeing the blood oozing from the wound in the thin chest, Julian knew at once that a doctor would be of no help. He had every reason to despise the man lying at his feet, and yet he experienced no enmity now. Geoffrey had more than made up for the great wrong he had inflicted by saving Jennifer's life.

'Wroxam, I never touched her,' the weakening voice was barely audible. 'I want you to know that. She has always been yours. I swear I never laid a finger on her that day.'

'I know,' Julian replied softly, and only hoped that his words had penetrated before he watched the life fade from the pale blue eyes.

Bending, he gently placed Geoffrey's head on the floor, before drawing Jennifer to her feet. She was, understandably, pale, but thankfully betrayed no other outward signs of distress. His one thought now was to remove her from the scene of the tragedy, and help was at hand in the form of Mr Dent who, having forced his way through the small group of inn servants gathered about the door, stepped into the room.

'Theo, take charge of things here while I take Jennifer downstairs.'

His lordship might have changed during the past months, but not to the extent that he could not command respect when he chose. One brief and very idiomatic sentence sent the servants scurrying about their business, and a brief consultation with the landlady ensured that his Marchioness would receive the utmost care and attention until his return.

After a further brief consultation with Theodore, he organised the removal of the bodies, and then returned to the person who remained his main concern, to discover her sitting in the landlady's private sitting room, looking remarkably composed in the circumstances, and willing to relate all that had taken place before his timely arrival at the inn.

'I should have known,' he said softly, after learning all. 'As soon as I believed you truly retained few memories of that afternoon, I certainly suspected something. My suspicions, however, were directed at the wrong person entirely. It was only after your accident a few weeks ago that I began to wonder whether Melissa's fell hand had not been behind all our misfortunes. That is why as soon as I discovered that she was heading here, I didn't hesitate to follow.'

He drew her gently to her feet. 'Come,' he coaxed. 'I shall need to return to town later, but in the meantime I intend to see you safely home.'

Shielding her from the tell-tale red stains on the road where Melissa had met her end, he guided her round to the inn yard where the carriage stood in readiness for them to leave. A familiar whinny reached their ears, and Julian ordered the ostler, who was doing his best to keep a firm hold on the reins, to release the troublesome black hunter, and Oriel came trotting over, greeting Jennifer in his usual inimitable fashion.

'So, you rode to my rescue on my baby.'

'Yes, and I thank God I did! Had I arrived a minute later, I would have been too late. And I think he knew. He brought me here like the wind, bless him.' Shaking his head in wonder, Julian stroked the sleek black neck. 'I have never had any rival for your affections, save one. And I don't object in the least to that.'

After securing Oriel to the back of the carriage himself, he caught hold of Jennifer's hand. 'Come, let us go home.'

Still very shaken though she was after the tragic events of the morning, Jennifer somehow managed a wan smile. 'There was a time when I would never have believed it possible that I would come to look upon Wroxam Park as home...but, yes, my love, take me home.'

* * * * *

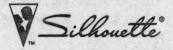

HARLEQUIN®
Presents®

The world's bestselling romance series...
The series that brings you your favorite authors,
month after month:

Helen Bianchin...Emma Darcy
Lynne Graham...Penny Jordan
Miranda Lee...Sandra Marton
Anne Mather...Carole Mortimer
Susan Napier...Michelle Reid

and many more uniquely talented authors!

Wealthy, powerful, gorgeous men...
Women who have feelings just like your own...
The stories you love, set in exotic, glamorous locations...

HARLEQUIN®
Presents®

Seduction and Passion Guaranteed!

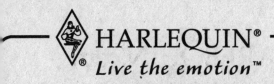

passionate powerful provocative love stories

Silhouette Desire delivers strong heroes, spirited heroines and compelling love stories.

Desire features your favorite authors, including

Annette Broadrick, Ann Major, Anne McAllister and Cait London.

Passionate, powerful and provocative romances *guaranteed!*

For superlative authors, sensual stories and sexy heroes, choose Silhouette Desire.

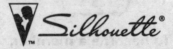

passionate powerful provocative love stories